FORGOTTEN STAR

COLIN WELDON

Copyright © 2020
Colin Weldon
Forgotten Star
All rights reserved.

No part of this publication may be reproduced, distributed, or transmitted in any form or by any means, including photocopying, recording, or other electronic or mechanical methods, without the prior written permission of the publisher, except in the case of brief quotations embodied in critical reviews and certain other non-commercial uses permitted by copyright law.

Colin Weldon

Printed in the United States of America
First Printing 2020
First Edition 2020

10 9 8 7 6 5 4 3 2 1

For Hayley and David
For all your hard work

Acknowledgements

A special thanks to Analieze Cervantes for all her editorial work. To Paige Lawson for her line edits. Thanks to Fiona Weldon and Conor Smyth for all their feedback. To Jules Charlton for pulling me through the trenches. To Renee for the constant support. To Will, Ben and Emma for being my teammates. To Paula for your kindness. A special thanks Vanessa O'Loughlin who continues to always fight in my corner. To Alex Barclay, who believed in me when I'd almost given up.

PROLOGUE

YEAR: 2729

The little girl watched the stars drift past the frozen glass as the escape pod listed gracefully through the nothingness. White wisps of cold breath escaped her mouth as she wrapped a blanket tighter around herself. She took a small bite of the last ration pack, making sure to leave enough for the evening meal, probably her last, before turning to the communications panel. She blew the tips of her fingers and stretched them out, hoping to circulate her cold blood so she could press the buttons.

'Hello? Is anyone there?' she said, teeth chattering, 'My name is Tamara, and I'm nine years old. I'm all alone out here and I need someone to help me. The food machine thing isn't working anymore, and the lights keep going on and off. The computer is telling me that the life support is low, and I don't know how to fix it. My mom is the one who always fixes things and I don't know what to do. I don't see any planets out there still. Can anyone hear me?'

She paused and looked out at the stars, her last shreds of hope leaving her now weakened muscles.

'Anyone.'

She looked slowly down towards the screen.

'Hello?' she said softly, 'The red light is flashing, and it says it's working OK. I've been transmitting all the time–every day for weeks. Why won't anyone talk to me? Is it because this is all my fault? I didn't mean to push the button. I really didn't.'

It was an accident, I promise. I just want to go home. I just want to see my mommy and daddy. I won't do it again. I promise.' She peered into the darkness. 'The stars haven't changed. I don't know where the Arcturus is. Did they really leave me behind? Something happened on the ship. It started shaking really bad. Mom told me I would be safe. That something bad was happening and to wait. It had something to do with the black ship. I saw it when I left the Arcturus. It was huge. I've never seen a ship that big–not even the LAL ships.'

She looked at the blinking light on the transmitter, as a tear ran down her cheek.

'I miss my mom and dad. If anyone can hear this, can you please tell them I'm sorry? This is all my fault. This pod is too small. My chest feels weird. I can't breathe properly and… I'm so . . . cold.'

She released the button, closed her eyes, and wept.

1.

22 Years Later

Captain Tamara Cartwright wiped the sweat from her face and pushed her hand through her now-soaking brown hair as she wrestled with the flight controls of her ship, The Massey Shaw. The comm system crackled to life as an angry male voice pierced through the flight deck.

'Disengage, Massey Shaw—that's an order!'

The heat in the cockpit was ferocious and the two-handled flight control stick was red hot. The metallic ARION device attached to her ear was starting to burn, but she couldn't remove it yet. It was projecting a heads-up display in her field of vision, giving her precise flight data from The Clorinda, the distressed freighter, which had taken a hit from a solar eruption, knocking out its engines and main deflector arrays.

'Get that asshole off my comms!' shouted Tam, as she tried to see through the blinding light of the red dwarf star they were now hurtling towards.

'Got it,' said Chuck.

Chuck Redmond, muscular and steely eyed, was her second-in-command. He tapped his code into the computer, isolating their frequency, blocking the incoming transmission from the ESDA cruiser, The Lassen, which was twenty minutes out—too far away to do anything about stopping the Clorinda from tumbling into the corona of the star. Another transmission crackled into the cockpit.

'Massey Shaw, this is the Clorinda' came the female voice. 'Hull temperature now red-lining. Engines are non-responsive. I don't think we're gonna—'

'Hold on, Clorinda,' said Tam. 'We're coming.'

She activated the comms system and connected to the engine room.

'Jacob–I need that extra ten percent, now!'

'Captain, you've already got it,' he replied.

Tam clenched her teeth as the flight controls began to shake.

'Then, get me another ten.'

'The only way to do that Captain—'

'Is shut down life support–I know!'

The logical side of her, the rational, clear-thinking side that effortlessly assessed the variables of every mission, was telling her this wasn't going to go her way. The distress call had come too late. They were too far out. The Clorinda would be the first ship she would lose on her watch. She'd lost people before but never an entire crew. A rage began brewing in her stomach. It wasn't good enough.

The other side of her saw something beyond the numbers. There were families on board that ship. The lights on the flight deck dimmed as life support powered down. She sensed Urhan's presence behind her, about to tell her what she already knew.

'Tamara,' he said, 'the risk to this vessel now outweighs the possibility of our reaching the Clorinda.'

His voice, deep and powerful, cut through the chaos with ease. Standing at two meters, he was an imposing figure, but to Tam, his real strength was in the gentle, meditative nature that reined in her reckless side.

'I'm a little busy right now Urhan,' she snapped.

Urhan was a member of the Lal–the first alien race that humans had ever encountered, the race that had saved them from the great plague two hundred years ago. His slender grey body shimmered in the lights of the flight deck. His skin, almost a translucent grey, looked like it belonged to some sort of deep-sea fish rather than a humanoid. The thin robes he wore around his slender frame draped all the way down to his ankles.

The Lal had gifted humanity with the STC molecule–a synthetic compound, which allowed for the space-time compression effect to finally open the door to the stars. She felt her palms start to burn as her options ran out.

'Captain,' said Chuck.

Tam didn't respond. Something absurd had popped into her mind; it was probably suicide. She turned to Urhan. He stared at her with his wide, glowing green eyes and blinked twice. Tam looked back at her console.

'Arion–please calculate the exact distance between this ship and the dorsal hull of the Clorinda. Calculate an STC jump allowing for the increase in mass of both ships'

'What?' Chuck asked.

Tam raised her right index finger, silencing him.

'An STC jump that close to the corona of a star could cause a disruption in the star's gravity well and create a singularity,' Chuck continued.

'Tam, I do not advise…' said Arion with his low gravelly voice. Tam imagined Arion sounding like her grandfather. He was a kind man with a soft but commanding tone, a byproduct of a lifetime in the military.

'Do it,' said Tam.

'You serious, Cap?' said Chuck.

Tam tapped her comm system.

'Jacob, get ready for an STC jump. This one's gonna be tricky. Extend the ventral docking clamps. We're gonna jump right onto the bottom of the Clorinda's hull, clamp on and STC out,' Tam said.

'You're gonna do what?' said Jacob.

Tam suddenly felt a hand on her shoulder.

'Tamara,' said Urhan, 'any use of the STC molecule that causes galactic damage or destruction is strictly prohibited. You know this. My oath, as guardian of the molecule, will not allow it.'

Tam gritted her teeth and whipped her head around to face him.

'They're going to die, Urhan. Your people can do what they like with me when this is over, but you either help me now or get the hell off my flight deck.'

'You require my access to activate the molecule,' said Urhan. 'And removing me from the flight deck won't do you any favours.'

She looked at Chuck.

He smiled at her.

'Where you go, I go,' he said. He turned to Urhan. 'Give her the code, you big Oak tree,' said Chuck.

Tam turned to look at Urhan. 'Please Urhan, I can save them.'

Urhan paused, his pale grey skin shimmering in the light.

Tam touched a hand to his arm, 'Let me save them.'

'Very well,' said Urhan, reaching down to where the STC cylinder was secured between the two flight chairs. He pressed his long fingers against the panel. It beeped and displayed several characters in the LAL language. Inside the clear polymer tube, a bright blue crystalline pinpoint of light waited, suspended in midair. Tam smiled at him.

'Arion,' said Tam, 'have you got those calculations locked in?'

'Yes, Tam,' replied Arion, 'you have 13.24 seconds to lock onto the Clorinda and activate the second STC jump, that includes the six-seconds it takes to activate the molecule. The Clorinda's hull is beginning to buckle.'

Tam felt her chest tighten. 'Got it.'

'Arion giving you bad news?' Chuck asked.

Tam ignored him.

'On my mark, Chuck, you'll have less than five-seconds to grab them.' She turned to him. 'Do a good job.'

Chuck placed his hand on the cylinder and nodded. Tam took a quick breath.

'Do it,' She said.

Chuck pressed down hard, sliding the cylinder all the way into the main STC drive conduit. The ship shuddered as the molecule released its energy. A-high-pitched sound reverberated through the hull as the space around the ship effectively ceased to exist, separating it, for the briefest of moments, from the universal laws of physics. The burning light from the star blinked into darkness. A millisecond later, a blinding light flooded the flight deck.

The long cylindrical hull of The Clorinda was now directly beneath the ship. Tam's grip slid, momentarily, from the flight controls. Arion's voice sounded in her ear.

'Three-seconds in.'

From the corner of her eye, Tam saw Urhan open the STC cylinder and reload it with another molecule.

The Clorinda was twelve meters away.

'Six-seconds in.'

Red warning lights fired in sequence across the console.

'We've got a breach!' Chuck shouted, over the noise of the alarms.

The flight controls vibrated in Tam's clenched grip, the impact powering through her entire body. The ship struck The Clorinda with great force and was shunted forward against the console. She screamed as her right wrist cracked, then gasped for air as her harness cut into her shoulders before slamming her back hard against the seat.

Chuck gripped the grappler controls hard, never taking his eyes off the target.

'Nine-seconds in.'

Tam heard a crunching sound.

'Got them!' shouted Chuck.

The temperature gauge read 72 degrees.

'Twelve-seconds in.'

Ignoring the pain shooting up her arm, Tam reached over to the STC cylinder and tried to insert it. It wouldn't move.

'Urhan—the code!' she shouted.

He was slumped on the deck beside her, Urhan raised his arm pressed his hand down on the control panel. It flashed, then slid open. Tam heard something erupt from deep within the bowels of the ship and wondered if the engine core had just given out on them. The blinding light from the star blipped out of existence and the ship was plunged into darkness.

Tam's eyes began to readjust to the endless star field of the galactic core. Chuck's gaze was fixed on the instrumentation panel. His body slumped, he turned to her. They stared at each other, red-faced, drenched in sweat, heaving for breath.

'We got her,' said Chuck. 'I've got faint life signs.'

Tam closed her eyes. She felt a line of sweat run down the side of her face.

'Well, that was crazy,' Chuck grinned.

He pointed to the atmospheric readouts of the flight deck.

Tam nodded and clicked her inter ship comm system again.

'Jacob, get life support back up.'

'On it,' said Jacob.

A few seconds passed as the lights in the cockpit flickered on, and the air began to circulate again.

Tam turned to Urhan. 'You all right?'

He gave her one of his cold looks before gently nodding.

She started to rise from her flight seat when a blast of white light filled the front windows.

'Oh, shit,' said Chuck, looking at the console.

Tam already knew what had happened.

'The star's collapsing,' said Urhan, his tone flat.

Tam looked back at Chuck.

'We're far enough away for now,' said Chuck, 'but we need to get out of here in the next . . .' He looked at his readings, 'Seventeen minutes.'

Tam felt a knot form in her stomach.

'We need to get those people off the Clorinda,' she said.

Chuck glanced down at Tam's wrist, the flesh tight and swollen, her hand the same. 'You're in no position to go anywhere, Captain,' he said turning to Urhan, 'Advise med-bay that the Captain is en-route.'

Tam knew he was right–an injured rescue party would only delay them.

Chuck turned to her. 'I'll suit up.'

She nodded. With her left hand, she began extending the umbilicus towards the Clorinda's airlock. She looked out at the forward windows. The stars' exploding energy streamed out in a chaotic but almost beautiful plume of unimaginable energy.

While there were no planets in the habitable zone surrounding the collapsing stellar material, four worlds had orbited it, and she couldn't help but wonder what a few billion years could have yielded, what future life she had just rendered an impossibility.

The computer console began to chirp.

'We've got company,' Chuck said.

Tam leaned over to see the signal data. It was the Lassen, coming in hard and fast on their port bow.

'Shit,' said Tam.

If it had been any other ship in the fleet but the Lassen, she wouldn't have given a damn. But it was Oscar's ship and there would be hell to pay.

She could see the Admiral's face now, looking down at her with his disappointed eyes. Another dressing down, another reprimand, another court martial and maybe now a death sentence.

She wondered if she would ever Captain another ship again.

2.

ESDA Research Station
In orbit around Saturn

Ona Mendel pressed her hands against her temples and clenched her jaw as the unwanted voices burst into her mind.

'I'm not going to kill you.'

'I know,'

'How are you feeling today?'

'They're afraid of you,'

'The code is six, three, seven, seven, nine,'

'Our time together is coming to an end,'

'Eighty meters down the corridor, then second door on your right, the one with the yellow stripe,'

'I don't understand,'

'Run Ona!'

She let out growl as she tried to drown them out and squeezed her eyes shut. They continued.

'So many possibilities,'

'She'll protect you,'

'I still had so many questions,'

'I can't go with you,'

'Are you hungry?'

'Sunset,'

'Your journey is your own, perhaps it's we who follow you,'

'Don't look back!'

Ona rose from the fabricated grass and looked to the blue-sky overhead. She stared directly into the holographic sun and screamed.

'Stop it!'

Tears fell and the voices abruptly stopped. She fell to her knees, exhausted, and placed her hands on the grass. She dug her fingernails into the soil and began taking long controlled breaths. She pushed her short brown hair away from her face. She looked to the tall Bigtooth Aspen tree that sat just across the riverbanks. She'd wondered how many destinies she'd changed; how many lives had been created and destroyed because of her.

She watched the sun glisten off the surface of the water as she stood, taking one last glance at the tree she'd tried to hang herself from. It was pointless to even consider such an action now, not when they were watching her every movement. The snapping of a twig startled her. She turned quickly to see the man standing at the top of a mound. He smiled and waved at her. His thick white beard and round cheeks revealing the only warm human contact she'd practically ever known. She smiled back. He'd obviously just seen her have another episode and come straight in.

'Hello Ona, how are you feeling today?' he said, 'beautiful sunset huh?'

Doctor Eoin Tatum's silver hair, which seemed to blend in perfectly with the colour of his beard, had been Ona's only human contact since she was nine years old. She'd sometimes wondered whether or not he was the only person left alive in the galaxy. He was a kind man, for a jailer. His long white coat fluttered in the calm breeze as he approached. His face always seemed to glow a crimson red and his large shoulders had provided a comforting place to rest her head whenever she needed a good cry. His smile showed concern and she wondered how long he'd been watching her. She remained sitting as he sat on the gras beside her. She thought very carefully about what to say to him.

'Hello Eoin,' she said.

He glanced around briefly at the beautiful woodland vista that was spread out for kilometers in all directions.

'Are you all right? Are you hungry?'

Ona shook her head feeling a chill come over her at the familiarity of the question.

'I don't think I've ever been all right,' she admitted.

'Depends on how you think about it,' he said.

Ona tilted her head towards him, waiting for him to say something familiar, something already predestined.

'It's never going to stop is it?' she finally said.

'Truthfully, Ona, I don't know. I think the only person who is able to tell anyone that, is you.'

He paused.

'Anything dangerous or frightening today?' he asked.

'I don't know,' she replied, careful not to alert or change anything.

'Would you tell me if there was?' he said, meeting her eyes.

She shrugged her shoulders. He took a deep breath.

'I know how hard this has been for you,' he said, placing a hand on her shoulder.

The warmth of his gesture sent another tear down her cheek. He released his hand and reached inside his jacket pocket removing something and handing to her. It was a small box wrapped in coloured paper.

'Happy birthday,' he said.

She looked at him curiously.

'Yes, it's your birthday, you didn't know I was going to say that?'

She shook her head taking the small box.

'Twenty today,' he said.

She ran her fingers over the texture of the paper before slowly opening it. Contained within the wrapping was a small wooden box with a decorative gold latch. She clicked it open. Neatly placed on the velvet interior was a small bracelet with a heart locket attached to it. She removed it and looked at the filigree work etched over its surface.

'Open it,' said Eoin.

She ran her fingernail through the indent and the locket popped open. She looked at the two images inside, both familiar to her. Her mother and her father. Seeing their faces was like a warm blanket had just been spread across her body.

'Here, let me,' said Eoin, taking the bracelet and attaching it gently around her right wrist.

A wave of anger flowed through her as she looked at the beautiful piece of jewelry.

'When can I leave this place?' she demanded.

He took a breath and leaned backwards, resting his hands on the grass.

'I would try and explain it, and maybe I already have, you already know what I'm going to say anyway so, in a strange way, I am left with whether to tell you again or not. But that doesn't matter either way, does it? Not unless you decide to change things. There are so many possibilities. You know, sometimes I come in here to talk to you knowing that my fate has already been played out in your mind. It's an unsettling feeling. You already know why they won't let you leave.'

Ona didn't respond.

'They're afraid of you,' he continued.

A small chill ran up her spine.

'Don't think I don't understand how you're feeling Ona, I know,'

Without thinking, Ona responded.

'If I am so dangerous why don't they just kill me and be done with it?' she said.

'I'm not going to kill you, and I'm not going to let anyone else try,' Eoin said, 'you remember when you first came to this station?'

Ona nodded.

'So many stars,' she said.

'Yes, that's true,' Eoin said.

'These ones seem different,' she said, 'I know they're not real, it's a prison.'

'They are different, everything is, everything has changed, and it's time you saw the real world,' he said, looking back at the river.

He moved closer to her and tapped the data pad in his jacket. Ona heard a soft bleeping noise.

'Listen to me very carefully,' Eoin said.

Ona frowned.

'Something is about to happen here. I don't want you to be afraid,' Eoin said.

Ona tilted her head.

'They can't hear us, just listen to me. About a year ago, I began to realize what they were doing, what HE was doing, and it was something I could not be a part of anymore. You need to hear me now. Perhaps, you already know what I am about to say but can't quite put it into context?' he asked.

She didn't answer.

'Well, this is one occasion where I am going to have to repeat myself, it's too important. There's about to be a loud noise, but don't be afraid. When I say, I want you to get to the open door that's about to show itself right over there. I want you to go as fast as you can, eighty meters down that corridor then take the second door on your right, the one with the yellow stripe. The code is six, three, seven, seven, nine. Repeat the code to me.'

'What are you...'

'Repeat the code,' Eoin said

'Six, three, seven, seven, nine,' Ona said.

Eoin's face was turning red.

'Get into the pod and strap yourself in, the computer's already been programmed to read your bio-signs and will launch in time to escape,' he said.

'Escape?' Ona said.

'Our time together is coming to an end Ona.'

'Why?'

'I can't go with you,' Eoin said, 'I need to make sure that you make it away safely before it happens.'

'Before what happens?' Ona said, her face frowning in confusion.

Eoin ignored her and continued.

'You're going to meet someone; her name is Tamara Cartwright. She'll protect you. Trust her as you have trusted me. She will find you, so don't you be worrying,' he smiled at her, 'your journey is your own, perhaps it is we who follow you. I still have so many questions.'

Ona was about to respond when a deafening boom, followed by a blinding white light erupted into her previously serene world. Ona screamed and placed her hands over her eyes. She felt Eoin's hand on her back as her environment began flickering out of existence. The stream melted away into a mist of photons, followed by the trees and the sky, revealing a cold grey wall coated in endless speckles of neatly arranged lights. The grass beneath her shifted to a cold hard surface. From somewhere off in the distance she heard a siren as she looked up to meet Eoin's eyes.

'Don't be scared, get up let's go right now,' he said, leaping up and taking Ona with him.

Her heart was now bursting from her chest as the only place she'd ever known winked out of existence.

'What is this place?' she shouted.

'There's no time, come with me,' Eoin said.

The explosion had left a gouge in the newly formed light encrusted wall they were both now running towards. Sparks rained down from beyond as they reached the hole where Eoin stopped, still clutching her arm. He carefully peered around the jagged edged corner. He pulled back as part of an electrical circuit burst outwards towards them. He shielded Ona's face with his hand, before looking out into the room that lay beyond.

'Come on!' he urged.

Ona had very little time to protest. She recoiled instantly at the sight of a body on the ground. It was a man, dressed in black overalls. His severed right arm was laying a few feet away in a pool of blood. She could feel her body go cold.

'Don't look at it, move!' Eoin said, stepping around the corpse.

The ground shook suddenly. She heard another booming noise, coming from somewhere beneath her. They reached a doorway and Eoin placed his eye over a small yellow box. It immediately slid open to scenes of chaos beyond. She saw various people running around the corridors, some shouting, then she saw him, a tall man dressed in the same overalls as the dead person they had just stepped over. He was pointing a weapon at them. He had large eyes, a pronounced jaw, and muscular shoulders.

'Don't move,' said the man.

Eoin put his hands in the air.

'There's been an explosion, we have to get her off this level, can't you see that?' Eoin responded.

'Move or I'll shoot you Doctor Tatum,' said the man taking a step towards them.

Eoin didn't move.

'Listen to me, it's too dangerous to…'

Eoin suddenly lunged towards the guard with aggression and speed, grabbing the weapon. Ona saw a flash of green light impact Eoin in his abdomen. He recoiled, but somehow found enough strength to hit the guard with such force, it knocked him out cold. Eoin then collapsed onto the ground. Ona froze. Time slowed. Her hands trembled and she felt light her chest would explode. She saw Eoin slowly role onto his side, a large gaping wound in his midsection. There was a strange pungent smell of something rotten as she gazed down in horror. A trickle of blood escaped from the side of his mouth as he looked at her, his eyes wide. He was afraid. His mouth moved ever so slightly. Without a moment's hesitation, she dived to the ground. She heard a strange gurgle in the back of his throat as he tried to mouth something. Tears were now in free flow down Ona's cheeks as she placed her hands on his bloodied chest and leaned forward.

'I don't understand,' she said through quivering lips.

He took a long shaky breath.

'Run Ona,' he growled as his mouth filled further with blood, 'don't look back!'

His eyes listed upwards and his body went limp. Ona felt another large vibration, this one seemed to come from right underneath her feet. The lights flickered as she saw thick black smoke emerge from the end of the corridor. She paused for just a moment to take one last glance at the man who had raised her. She got up and followed his last request. She began to run. Somewhere from behind her she heard shouting. Someone telling her to stop. A flash of an energy weapon streaked by her ears and hit the wall beside her. She covered her face but didn't look back. Her legs were now carrying her fast. She saw the door with the yellow stripe. She glanced behind her, the corridor, now filled with smoke, created strange silhouetted shadows. Another bright flash of green energy grazed her arm. She felt a sharp pain but ignored it. She began to cough as she felt for the access pad. She entered the code and the door slid open. She dove inside, this time narrowly missing another energy blast. The door closed quickly behind her as she saw what was inside.

There were two recessed seats facing each other at the front of the cabin and a large curved window at the front above a console station.

'Please secure harness' said a soft computer voice.

Ona heard scratching sounds coming from the hatch. She climbed into one of the seats as a shoulder harness zipped automatically over both her arms. She began to feel weak as the adrenaline began wearing off. She glanced around at the various control panels and lights which ran from wall to wall.

'Launching' said the computer voice.

She felt a tug as she was thrust sideways. The momentary increase in gees subsided as the large forward-facing windows lit up with stars. She saw the rings of Saturn sparkling around the giant orange world. She watched the small pieces of rock and ice as they danced in unison. The escape pod turned abruptly, and she saw the space station. It looked small now, like a miniature spinning top gently turning, yet glowing a pure white light as the sun's rays reflected off its smooth exterior. A few seconds later a bright light forced her to cover her eyes as a fireball engulfed the orbiting structure. The large spinning top, now a collection of rapidly expanding debris, drifted outwards in all directions. The escape pod maneuvered again and headed away from her destroyed home, somewhere unknown towards the stars. She looked to the centre flight control system and saw a cylindrical transparent tube in its centre. It was glowing blue.

Stand by for STC, said the computer voice.

Ona had no idea what that meant. She felt a strange sense of nausea followed by an all too familiar sensation. She looked out the window and saw the stars twist and distort and then blink out of existence.

3

ESDA Central Command Base
The Moon

Fleet admiral Rubin Edge leaned against the large window of his office and stared past the lunar landscape at the stars above. He glanced briefly down at the ore processing station to the South and watched as another lander from Earth docked gracefully beside it. He reached up and rubbed his right temple, the pain of a migraine beginning to wake from its welcome slumber. He looked up again at the point of light he'd been staring at, Saturn. His eyes glanced over at the broken glass on the floor at the far end of his office. A reminder of the communication he'd just received from an ESDA forward-monitoring base on Europa. Rubin Edge was famed for his calm but imposing physical presence, earning him the nickname 'the Tank'—a nickname he had not in any way tried to dissuade, as it conjured up images of the old ground warfare vehicles used hundreds of years in the past. There was, of course, nobody around to see his outburst; the holo-communiqué had disconnected only seconds before. It was the betrayal that had overwhelmed him in the moment—Eoin Tatum had blown up the station. It was a reminder to him that no matter how long the friendship, or how loyal the man, nobody could be completely trusted. Edge had known betrayal and lies, had spent his life working through the political garbage that had been put in place on the twenty-three colonial planets. Three of which had erupted in civil war because of one simple truth of human existence. No matter what the LAL thought of human potential, that craving for war couldn't or wouldn't evolve, despite the romantic notions of some, we were what we were. And now she was gone. The only possible defense against the darkness that lay on the galactic horizon. A darkness only few had seen and only one had lived to tell the tale.

The chime to his door rang. He was about to leave it unanswered, allowing himself more time to get control of his anger, but time was a factor here. He turned to his desk and released the locking mechanism. The large metal doors at the end of the long rectangular room slid open, and in walked commander Matthew Norr, Edge's liaison officer and head of all base operations. Norr cut a stocky figure at five foot ten, a fourth-generation military man whose uniform was practically a second skin to him. He was serious and efficient, and while up until this morning Edge would have considered him to be loyal to the death, he was finding himself looking at Norr with suspicion that the man hadn't necessarily earned. The dark-haired soldier approached Edge with a well-practiced stride, coming to a stop a meter or so in front of his desk to salute him. Pleasantries were not something Edge exchanged with anyone, least of all those under his command.

'What have you got for me, Commander?' Edge said, rounding the table and taking a seat.

He began running through the report of the incident, which was already open on the inset screen.

'Well, you're not going to like it, sir, but there is nothing in Dr. Tatum's communiqués or logs to or from the base in the last ten years that the algorithms can pick out to explain why he did what he did,' Norr said.

Edge curled his fingers into a fist before tapping on his console, bringing up the last images of the security feed. He froze the image of Tatum lying on the floor, the girl crouched over his body.

'As you know, sir, the Arc Royal and Sirius have been dispatched to try to track the pod. We found several security access requests to the ejected pod over the last three months, eight in total, to be exact. As you know, it was Dr. Tatum who helped design many of the propulsion and engine specifications that are now installed in the newer fleet designs,' Norr said.

Edge glanced up at Norr, who cleared his throat.

'None of our tracking stations were able to get an exact fix on the course plotted by the escape pod, and the normal particle traces left when the engine is burned were not present, nor was its beacon activated. Whatever modifications were made to it, sir, he'd rendered it undetectable,' Norr said.

Edge felt his temples begin to burn.

'I see,' he said calmly. 'Anything else?'

'The explosion on the station was a result of two primary charges. We're analyzing their composition now. One was placed in the observation room outside the simulation area where the girl was being kept. This one was detonated first. The secondary charge was placed on the main reactor core itself. This was detonated nine minutes later,' Norr said.

Edge's anger suddenly subsided and was replaced by a strange sensation of sadness and regret. He hadn't expected to feel that way, but there was something in that last image. He looked down at the feed again, then into the face of the man who he had once considered a friend. He looked to the young girl and wondered what she had done to him, what she had said that had twisted and confused his mind.

'Sir, if she's headed for one of the colonies, or even back to Earth . . .' Norr said.

'What else?' Edge said.

Norr was about to respond when there was a ping from Edge's desk. He raised his hand, indicating for Norr to hold on, before tapping the control panel on the desk. 'Edge,' he growled.

'Sir, we have an incoming transmission from the Lal home world, encoded for your eyes only,' came the female voice.

Edge looked up at Norr, who needed no further instruction. He simply nodded, turned on his heels, and left the office.

'Put it through,' he finally said.

Thousands of tiny pinpoints of light emerged from the centre of his control panel and began swirling together to form what appeared to be a solid surface hovering above the table. The floating screen flickered to life as the large green eyes of the Lal leader peered coldly out from its surface.

'Premier Diren,' Edge said.

For over a hundred years, Diren had overseen the progress of Earth's vast expanse into the unknown. He had been a god to Edge as a child, and even now, having visited LAL himself over two dozen times, having met hundreds of the LAL and overseen their placement on ESDA ships with the guardians of the STC molecule, the sight of Diren still gave Edge an involuntary shiver up his spine.

There had always been something about the LAL, something that Edge couldn't quite put his finger on that had kept him up at night. He had always trusted his intuition up until an hour ago. Now he wasn't sure about anything.

'Admiral Edge,' said Diren, bowing his head ever so slowly.

Diren reciprocated by bending his own, making sure to take twice as much time to complete the standard Lal greeting which was custom when speaking to someone of greater importance.

'How may I be of service?' Edge replied.

'There has been an unfortunate incident in the Roturan sector involving one of your rescue ships,' Diren replied.

Edge felt his stomach tighten. *Don't be her,* he thought to himself.

'An incident?' Edge said.

'It would seem the ship utilized the STC molecule on the edge of a star's corona. The resulting space-time distortion has caused the star to collapse,' Diren said.

Edge lowered his head. It was one of three unbreakable conditions the Lal had placed as doctrine for the use of the molecule—conditions that had severe consequences. The tension in the room began to rise. The floating head with his piercing eyes glared down at Edge.

Please don't be her, Edge thought. 'I must say that this is a shock,' he finally said.

'As you know, Admiral, any damage caused to the natural flow of the galaxy is strictly prohibited. We consider the destruction of a star to be the gravest violation of our agreement to allow humans to utilize our technology.'

Edge felt a bead of sweat begin to form on his forehead. He suddenly remembered the penalty for misuse of the STC molecule: the complete withdrawal of all molecules from the human race. It would be devastating, not only leaving the colonies stranded and alone scattered across the stars, but also essentially ending space travel and leaving them completely defenseless against alien aggressors. He suddenly raised both his hands.

'Stop,' he said.

Diren tilted his head at the gesture.

'Just hold on. Let me investigate and hold whoever it was accountable for their actions,' Edge said. 'The ESDA has held our end of the bargain. We would not have intentionally done anything to end our agreement. The circumstances must have been out of our control.'

'The ship in question has been identified as the *Massey Shaw*,' replied Diren.

Edge felt his jaw lock up. His eyes narrowed.

'I believe the captain is a member of your own family?' replied Diren.

'She is,' Edge said.

'I wish to speak to you in person,' Diren said, 'I want you to rendezvous with me on Arana, there are some,' Diren paused, 'progressions we wish to make.'

Edge felt a chill run through his body.

'I will have to clear that with the President, we have had an incident within our solar system which requires my immediate attention,' Edge said.

'I am aware of that Admiral, I will relay our request immediately,' said Diren.

'I understand Premier,' Edge replied, knowing full well this wasn't a request.

The image suddenly vanished as the light molecules that made up the Lal premier dissipated into thin air. This time Edge couldn't control it: he raised both his arms and slammed them, close fisted, onto the desk, causing it to crack.

He slammed his hand onto the comm panel.

'Yes, Admiral,' came the response.

'Prep my shuttle for launch,' he growled.

4

The Taurus
ESDA Science Vessel
Current assignment: Planetary and Environmental assessment
Planet G234/223445
54 light-years from Earth

Amita Puri pressed her eyes firmly into the microscope and stared at the latest microbial analysis from the soil samples taken from the northern continent.

Please don't be true, she thought to herself.

'The Captain isn't going to like this,' said Victor Pollard, stood next to her.

'The Captain doesn't like anything,' replied Amita, watching the interaction of the tiny organisms.

'That's not true.'

'Oh?'

'You should have seen him down the mess last week beating the snot out of Ensign Hammond on the chessboard.'

'Yeah, did you see him smile?'

'Well, no, but he had that glint in his eye,' Victor said.

Amita raised her head and stared up at the screen. Her heart sank.

'Where the hell did that radiation come from?' she said, 'what depth was this taken from?'

'Seventy-five meters,' said Victor.

'You sure the pod wasn't contaminated when it was coming back to the ship?' Amita asked.

Victor scowled at her.

'I'm not saying you screwed up before you get all pouty at me,' she said quickly.

'The seals were checked six times before I brought it back, the shield was intact,' Victor said.

Amita slid her chair over to the circular table in the center of the room and brought up a holographic representation of the planet. She pulled a strand of hair away from her light brown cheeks and tucked it behind her ear. She caught him looking at her in that adorable way she'd only started picking up on recently. His awkward crush was endearing. She liked Victor's soft way and respected his mind even more. She knew he was building up to it and was taking a little bit of relish in seeing him pluck up the courage to do something about it.

The hologram formed above the table. Amita poured over the various data readings indicating surface temperatures, soil PH's, atmospheric compositions, weather, rotation, gravitational fields, life form clusters and other readings that they had gathered over the last month or so.

'Solar flare?' Amita said, checking the Ozone layer readings.

'Maybe, a few hundred years ago,' Victor said.

'Could be just an isolated event.'

Victor shook his head and pointed back to the screen. 'It's not just on this continent; it's planet-wide.'

Amita felt her hopes for the beautiful world fade away in an instant.

'No,' she said.

She placed her hands on the table and bowed her head.

'We can't grow anything,' Victor said softly.

'Well, not for a hundred thousand years or so,' Amita said, 'you're right, the Captain isn't going to like this.'

The pair stared out at the green pearl below.

'It was so beautiful,' she said.

Victor looked down at her and smiled, 'plenty of fish in the sea.'

She looked up at him and smiled back. The look lingered. Amita's pulse quickened. His green eyes gazed into hers as he stepped closer to her. She leaned into him when a klaxon suddenly sounded in the room. Red strip lighting flashed on all the monitors breaking the moment.

'All hands, this is the Captain, general quarters, this is not a drill, all crew to defensive stations, I repeat this is not a drill.'

Victor and Amita looked at each other before moving to the window.

'You see anything?' Victor asked.

Amita shook her head and moved over to the holographic display of the planet and accessed the ship's sensors. She saw that the bridge was already using them, doing a full scan of the star system but focusing in on one particular point about seventy-five thousand kilometers towards the planets closest moon. She felt Victor behind her right shoulder as she sent the data to the main diagnostic screen at the rear of the lab. She felt a light vibration on the deck as the ship fired up its engines. The screen switched suddenly to an outside view of the ship, matching the telemetry information being fed to the view screens on the bridge. Amita felt her blood turn cold.

'What is that?' Victor said.

The image showed something massive. It measured almost twelve times the mass of the Taurus and was approaching fast. It had a strangely designed hull, flat on both sides with a semi-cylindrical top and bottom. The stars were blinking out from behind it like an expanding solar eclipse. Amita tapped into the other sensor information and began running it through the computers ship identification. While the Lal had hundreds of variations of their cruiser, battle, and transport vessels, she was already certain on what they were looking at.

'Is that a Ghost ship?' Victor said.

Amita didn't answer.

'What do we do?' Victor said.

Amita followed the ship closely as it approached with the confidence of a giant sea fairing predator.

'Maybe it's something else,' he said, 'what's the Captain doing? Shouldn't he be jumping us out of here?'

'Standard contact protocol,' Amita explained, 'in the event of an encounter with an unknown spacefaring race, contact must be attempted.'

'I know that, but he'd also have full access to classified Ghost ship encounter logs, so surely we should be getting the hell out of here by now, no? So, maybe it's something new?'

Amita couldn't fault the logic, but the Captain wasn't one to tuck tail and run without at least getting as much information as he could. The alien ship turned suddenly, exposing its port side, which was smooth, reflecting light off the nearby sun like a mirror.

'I don't see a propulsion system,' Victor said.

He was right. There didn't appear to be any openings at all, as its aft hull came into view. It grew larger in the screen.

Victor tapped the console, enlarging the aft section of the hull. 'How the hell is it moving?'

'Whatever it is, it doesn't look friendly,' Amita said.

Victor looked at her.

'Not exactly a scientific viewpoint,' said Victor.

Victor turned to the screen again.

'Sensors can't get a reading on it,' he said, looking at the readings.

'What the…' Amita said, moving closer to the screen.

She watched as the holes began to open across the surface of the ship. Some sort of gas or liquid began pouring out.

'Can we get a reading on that?' Victor asked.

Amita was about to try and access the sensor readings when the screen went completely blank. 'What?'

The power in the lab suddenly shut off, all consoles and displays going dark. She looked at Victor.

'Look!' he said, pointing out of the window.

Amita turned to see the planet veering off to one side.

'We're moving off,' Victor said, 'why did they shut down the power?'

The lights in the lab suddenly shifted from white to yellow, denoting the emergency power had just kicked in.

'He's diverting all power to the defensive systems,' Amita said, 'He's spinning up the STC drive,'

'Maybe we should get out of here,' he said.

Amita shook her head.

'No, this is the safest place we can be right now.'

Amita was suddenly thrown sideways into the storage shelving on the wall. Victor was thrown into chemical storage locker next to it. They crashed to the ground as glass rained down on their heads. Amita felt warm liquid seep down her cheek. She tried to get her breath back as she looked to Victor, he lay on the ground, unmoved.

'Victor,' she croaked, through a strained lungful of air.

Her hand hurt. She looked down to see a large cut across her palm. The room around her blurred as a wave of nausea swept through her. She pressed her hands against the floor and looked to Victor again, placing a hand on his shoulder.

'Victor,' she said, more assertively and his body moved. He moaned as she turned him onto his back. His eyes slowly flickered open.

'Wake up,' she said, looking over him to see if he'd been injured.

Blood trickled down the side of his head. He swallowed and let out a light moan.

'What's happening?'

'Can you stand?'

He nodded, placing his hand on his forehead as they stood. 'You're bleeding.'

'It's nothing. I think we have to get out of here,' Amita said.

'Hang on,' Victor said, turning behind him and opening a wall-mounted med-kit.

He removed a dermal regenerator and quickly activated the beam next to Amita's head wound. Several seconds later he cut the beam off, removing his hand. Amita nodded her thanks as they both moved to the large window and peered out. The ship seemed to be listing out of control.

'We're drifting,' Amita said, reaching to the comm panel on the wall.

'Dr. Puri to the bridge,' she said.

No Response.

'Puri to bridge.'

'Comm systems are working, Amita. They're receiving, just not responding,' Victor said.

Amita moved to the door of the lab and tried to activate it. It didn't budge.

'Hang on,' he said, 'shouldn't we stay here? This room is airtight, and we don't know what the situation is going on out there, where do you want to go?'

'To the bridge,' Amita said, 'they may need our help Victor.'

'All hands abandon….'

Amita froze. What sounded like the Captain's voice, but somehow different, as if he were struggling to breathe, came bellowing out of the comm system. There was a deep grit to his tone as if it were his last words. Amita activated the comm system again.

'Captain?' she said.

No response.

'Bridge, come in,' she said.

Amita tried to think.

What the hell was going on?

'Okay we have to get out of here,' she said, moving to the door, 'listen to me, whatever is out there, whatever happens, you get to the pod, and you don't look back.'

'Where the hell are you going?' Victor said.

Amita gave him a reassuring look.

'I'll be right behind you, Cap says we gotta go, then we gotta go,' she said.

Victor took a breath. 'We're about to disappear, aren't we?'

'Not if I have anything to do about it,' she replied, 'remember that underground cave system on the southern continent?'

He nodded.

'We won't get anywhere in escape pods if that's a Ghost ship. We go full tilt to the planet surface and deep into that cave system, maybe we can hide it out,' she said.

Victor was about to respond when they heard a faint scream from outside the lab doors. It sounded like it was coming from another section of the ship, like a ghostly haunting tone floating from its underbelly.

'Hurry,' Amita urged.

Amita released the door locking mechanism.

'Okay, okay on the count of the three, ready?' she said.

Amita looked into his soft face, seeing him give her a smile, and there was something about his look that she couldn't help herself. She reached her hand around his face and kissed his cheek before letting go. There was no time to reciprocate. Victor just smiled and turned back to the door. In one swift motion, it slid apart with a jolt. She peered around the empty corridor lit by the same emergency lighting as the lab.

'Come on,' she said, taking his hand.

They moved quickly out of the lab and down the corridor.

'Where is everyone?' Victor said.

Amita didn't know but said, 'Probably in the pods.' They continued to move swiftly towards the escape pod access hatches. Amita peered into one of the other labs. It was empty.

With emergency lighting now the only thing guiding Victor and Amita, it was hard to see. They made their way steadily down the dimly lit corridor.

'They couldn't have all gotten off so quickly,' said Amita.

'Wait,' Victor said.

She turned her head and saw him stop dead in his tracks.

'What's that?' he whispered.

Amita turned to try and see what he was looking at. She strained her eyes. Something was moving in the darkness at the end of the corridor. It looked like a shadow at first, creeping its way across the walls towards them. She didn't move, thinking that perhaps it was some of the crew members making their way towards the pods. As it grew closer, she saw that it was something different. She took a slight step backwards. It wasn't a shadow. It looked like a cloud, like the same substance that was billowing out of the alien vessel. It was filling the space ahead of them and moving faster now. She turned to Victor.

'Run!' she shouted to him.

Victor didn't hesitate. He turned on his heels. Amita followed fast, something snapped onto her leg, holding her in place. Amita screamed as she looked down to see part of the strange substance wrapped around her ankle. She looked up to Victor.

'Go!' she told him.

He wasn't far enough away for her not to see the sudden terror in his eyes as a large tendril of smoke or gas or whatever it was shot out from behind Amita and enveloped his whole body. She heard him give one more muffled scream before his face disappeared into the cloud. Amita couldn't move. She felt cold as the strange thing began to engulf her entire body. Her chest contracted, the air being squeezed from her lungs as the corridor and world around her faded into cold darkness.

5

Tam sat on the bed as Doctor Silvia Augustine placed the last of the healing wraps around her wrist. She felt a tightness as they adjusted themselves and compressed. She glanced at the bio beds behind her to the young girl being treated for radiation burns. They had taken the most critical to the med bay on the Massey Shaw and already transferred the remainder to the Lassen. The girl, she must have been eleven or twelve, lay unconscious on the bed. She would require a few weeks in a regeneration chamber, but for now, she was stabilized. Sitting next to her, her mother. A tired-looking woman who'd taken the trip in the hopes of finding a new life on one of the outer colonies. She smiled at Tam, who returned her gesture with a simple nod before looking back at Augustine.

'Give it twenty-four hours then come back, and I'll take them off,' said Augustine, looking into her eyes.

Tam turned her head away and stared across the med bay at the display panel on the wall, not focusing on anything in particular, just preparing to hear the lecture she was about to get.

'I didn't say anything,' Augustine said.

Tam glanced back at her and smiled.

'I didn't say you did.'

'But,' Augustine started, looking back at Tam's wrist, 'if I was to say something.'

'Doc, I really don't want you to.'

'Well, tough,' Augustine said, 'that was a stupid thing to do Captain,' she said, looking to the girl on the bio bed, 'balsy?... Yes, but it was incredibly stupid.'

'They don't seem to think so,' Tam said.

'Was that really about them?' Augustine said.

Tam furrowed her brow. Augustine raised her hands already anticipating her response.

'I'm only saying,' Augustine said.

'Well, don't doctor,' Tam said.

Augustine took a breath and focused back on Tam's wrist. There was a tense moment between the two.

'What did Urhan do?' Augustine said.

'He's bound by law to report it to the Lal home-world,' Tam replied.

'He wouldn't,' Augustine said.

'He already did,' Tam said.

Augustine stopped.

'That son of a bitch.'

'I didn't want him suffering the consequences of my decision. It was my call,' Tam said.

'They'll put you to death,' Augustine suddenly said.

'I'm well aware of that, Doctor,' Tam said.

'You could run,' Augustine said.

'I'm not running from anyone,' Tam said, 'I made a call that saved lives, if I have to, I'll make it again, not like that's ever going to happen.'

Augustine sighed and shook her head.

'Well, Chuck won't stand for that, if you think he's going to let you hand yourself over to our babysitters you've another thing coming,' Augustine said, running another medical instrument over Tam's head.

'Have you spoken to him?' Augustine asked.

'Who?'

Augustine looked at her and raised an eyebrow. Tam huffed.

'No,' Tam said.

'He's gonna throw you in his brig.'

'Captain Deangelo will have to shoot me before I allow him to do that.'

She smiled. 'That would be some turn of events.'

Tam returned her smile. 'It would indeed,' she said, 'can I go?'

Augustine nodded. Tam hopped off the bed and placed a hand on Augustine's shoulder.

'Thanks,' she said.

'We've got your back. You know that, right?' Augustine said, 'and Tam,' she said, smiling, 'Well played.'

Tam smiled and moved to the exit, taking one more glance at the girl on the bed before making her way into the corridors.

Urhan's Quarters

Tam tapped the pad next to the entrance and waited for a response, which came swiftly. She heard the locking mechanism release and placed her hand on the door, sliding it open. White light streamed out from inside. Tam shielded her eyes, so they could adjust before stepping inside. Urhan's privacy was something he'd insisted on. She was the only person authorized to enter his quarters, something she hadn't done in months. Urhan was standing in the middle of a brightly lit cylinder of energy, his re-gen machine. His arms raised upwards, as if basking in it. The walls of his quarters were white, coated with a property from the Lal home-world. It was designed to absorb and reflect the energy being emitted by the re-gen. Tam felt the heat from the device on her face and hands. She felt energized by it. The device was said to have astonishing healing properties, while some were declaring it a sort of fountain of youth for the human skin. While the energy itself was considered to be unsafe long-term use by humans, it had, like most forbidden LAL technology, never really been put to the test. She stood, feeling a sense of euphoria sweep over her body. She looked down at her injured wrist and moved her fingers. There was no pain.

She waited, hoping Urhan would allow her several minutes basking in the energy. She closed her eyes. It was like taking a warm shower and exactly what she needed. After only a few seconds more, the light shut off completely, the energy filtering through her skin dropping back to normal levels. Tam could understand how this could be addictive to some as the euphoric feeling lingered in her blood.

'You could have let me have that Urhan,' she said, watching as he stepped off the slightly raised circular platform.

'Your body is not accustomed to it,' Urhan said, stepping towards her and folding his hands behind his long back.

Tam began to feel light-headed and moved over to a small chair. She sat down and leaned her elbows on her knees.

'You see,' Urhan said.

'At least you've no modesty,' Tam said, rolling her eyes.

Urhan's naked body was something that Tam had never really gotten used to. It had a smooth muscular surface and no visible sexual organs. Their gender was determined only by the coded genetic material beneath the palms of their hands, which was transferred from one to another. The females of the species then gestated their young on a flexible skin sack located on their backs.

'Your species is unique in that respect,' Urhan buttoned up his robbed attire, 'how are you?'

'Take a guess,' she said.

'I had no choice.'

'Yeah, well don't tell the crew that, I told them I ordered you to inform the Lal home-world,' Tam said, 'you could have at least waited a day or two.'

'Tamara...'

'Don't,' she said, raising her hand to stop him.

'I informed the high command it was an act of bravery to save the lives of the transport ship.'

'And?'

'They wanted to know our exact location so that you could be picked up by a Lal ship.'

'A location you gave them?' she asked.

Urhan looked away.

'Urhan?' she pressed.

'The communications systems were cut off mid transmission, probably from the effects of the supernova,' Urhan said.

Tam straightened her back and smiled at him. Deception was not something that the Lal understood. It served no purpose within their societal structures, or so she had been led to believe. They had self-appointed themselves as guardians of the human race. It was a frustration for humanity but at the same time a gateway to the stars. She turned her attention back to the curious thing that Urhan had just done.

'You did that on purpose?' she said, blankly.

'Did what exactly?' Urhan said, tilting his head and looking her with those glowing green eyes.

'You cut off the communications before giving our location,' she said, folding her arms.

'I have no idea what you are talking about Captain,' he said, turning away from her and moving over to his equipment locker and removing Tam's Arion unit.

'What are you doing with that?'

'I was upgrading its response software. I detected a lag of several nanoseconds,' he explained, handing it back to her.

'Several nanoseconds?' she said, widening her eyes.

'I do not like imperfections.'

'Arion won't like that you said that.'

'His audible transceivers are deactivated, so he will never know,' said Urhan.

Tam laughed, 'Oh Urhan, you do have a sense of humor.'

'I was merely stating a fact.'

She lifted the Arion unit and placed her hand on Urhan's shoulder. He flinched. Tam didn't remove her arm.

'Relax,' she said.

Urhan's eyes relaxed as he accepted the touch.

'It's meant to be taken as a thank you, you didn't have to do that,' Tam said.

She removed her hand from his arm.

'Have you spoken to him?' said Urhan.

Tam sighed, 'Why is everyone so obsessed over whether or not I've spoken to Captain Deangelo?'

'Given the past coupling, I would assume that the two of you would have a pair-bonding not uncommon to human sexual relations. You tend to bond uniquely once you've exchanged bodily fluids, regardless of whether or not you have managed to reproduce or not,' said Urhan, 'although that does not always appear to be the case with you.'

'Excuse me?'

'You seem unable to form lasting sexual pair bonding with human males.'

Tam laughed, 'what the hell would you know about it?'

'Mere observation.'

'Thanks' for that, I don't quite know what to do with that information but… thanks,' she paused, 'do me a favor, see if Jacob needs a hand, I want to know what shape my ship is in. Also, how many STC molecules do we have left onboard?'

'Twenty-seven,' Urhan said.

There was a beeping noise as the ship-wide comm system activated.

'Captain, please contact the flight deck,' came Chuck's voice.

Tam stood and walked to the comm panel next to the door to Urhan's quarters.

'Go, Chuck,' she said.

'Captain Deangelo would like to see you on the Lassen,' he said.

'Understood. Chuck get the ship ready to fly, transport the remaining survivors onto the Lassen,' she replied.

'Yes, ma'am, what do I do if…?'

'I'll be back Chuck, just get her ready.'

Tam heard him grumble something.

'Maybe I should go with you,' he said.

'Chuck,' she said.

'Okay, okay but if he locks you up, I'm coming to get you.'

Tam smiled before deactivating the comm system. She turned to Urhan.

'I did not intend any offense by suggesting that you are unable to…' Urhan said.

'Urhan,' she said

'Yes?' he said.

'Shut up,' Tam smiled at him before exiting.

6

The Lassen

Tam waited at the airlock hatch after walking calmly through the umbilicus connecting both ships. The hatch rolled aside. She was greeted by two security personnel, both over six foot tall, and almost as wide. They glared down at her.

Coward, she thought.

She smiled at them and extended her wrists.

'Well, go ahead, clamp me in irons if you're gonna do it,' she said.

The one on the left, who had a tight crew cut and one of the thickest jaw lines she had ever seen, wasn't amused.

'Captain would like to see you on the bridge,' said Jaw Line.

Tam nodded, lowering her hands.

'He figured it would take two of you?' she said.

They both frowned.

'Interesting,' she said, raising her eyebrows, 'well, lead on gentlemen, I'll be on my best behavior. I promise.'

They turned and began leading her through the corridors of the Lassen. At almost five times the mass of the Massey Shaw, the Lassen was an impressive ship and a bustle of activity. It was a cruise class vessel. The second generation of the one she had been on as a child. The internal layouts hadn't changed much. The corridors were an eerie reminder of a childhood memory. But she pushed the darkness from the forefront of her mind. The vividness of the screams, the images of that last look she had gotten before making the mistake that had cost her everything.

She kept her eyes forward as she passed one of the escape pod access doors. She glanced through, seeing the ghostly face of a little girl returning her look. They reached the elevator, the two security guards standing aside to let her enter first. The ride was filled with an awkward tension. The door eventually slid open and Tam stepped onto the expansive layout of the bridge. A far cry from the small cockpit set up her own ship, this had at least ten crew members staffing an array of consoles laid out in a circular configuration with the Captain's chair at the centre. The crew turned and stared at her, as she was led across the bridge to another door, which Jaw Line activated with his hand. After a few silent seconds, it slid open and Tam saw Captain Oscar Deangelo standing next to the full-length window beside his desk.

She gritted her teeth and entered the room, leaving the two guards outside as the door slid shut behind her. Deangelo turned slowly and smiled at her. His thick black hair and sallow skin a product of his Spanish mother, his light blue eyes from his Irish father. She suddenly remembered how handsome he was. It had been almost a year since they'd seen each other. A year since she'd pulled her own STC jump as far away from him as possible. The last night they'd spent together flashed through her mind. She pushed it aside quickly. His office was almost identical to that of her fathers and she suddenly felt an overwhelming urge to get out of it. She was angry to have been summoned like this. The pair regarded each other.

'Security guards? Really?' she snapped.

Deangelo lowered his head and sighed.

'What did you think I was going to do,' said Tam, 'steal something?'

He flicked his eyes up at her and gave her a cold stare.

'No, that's not something I thought you'd do,' he said, leaning against the table.

'What do you want Oscar?'

'It's Captain,' he said, 'and what I want isn't important. You disobeyed an order and put the entire fleet into a shit storm.'

She regarded his tone. There was a bite in it that she was sure wasn't entirely the result of her simply disobeying an order.

'Okay, so what does brass want to do with me?' she said.

There was a chirping noise from his console.

'We're about to find out,' he said, touching the control panel.

She felt her pulse quicken.

'You're joking me,' she said.

He turned the screen around. Admiral Edge glared back. She felt her jaw clench. It was an ambush. There was a long pause before he spoke.

'Tamara,' he finally said.

Tam nodded, 'Admiral.'

'I wanted to make sure you didn't think I was taking this action frivolously, nor taking it without speaking to you myself. I felt I owed you that much.'

'And what action is that Admiral?'

'You're to be taken into custody for violation on two counts of disobeying an order and violation of code 1, the wilful and prohibited use of the STC molecule in proximity of a stellar object.'

She thought she heard something akin to satisfaction in his tone and restrained every muscle in her body to control herself.

'Well, what so you have to say for yourself?' he pressed.

She regarded Deangelo.

'With all due respect,' she paused, 'sir, The Massey Shaw is given discretion when human lives are at stake.'

She saw Edge's face go red and thought back to the arguments they'd had. The fury at his lack of action to help her find her father, his brother.

'With all due respect,' he said with a growl, 'the Massey Shaw is not the centre of the universe and, by disregarding the only damn rule that the LAL have in place to safeguard interstellar travel, you've put our entire way of life at risk.'

'The LAL can't possibly think that they'll remove FTL from us over this for god's sake!' Tam said exasperated.

'That isn't your call, Tam!'

Tam stepped towards the screen, all semblance of control leaving her, old arguments and family wounds writhing to the surface.

'It's Captain!' she said, her insubordinate tone in of itself warranting her dismissal. She didn't care. She hated him. It was the only true thing left in her.

It was Deangelo that put a stop to it.

'If I may interject?' Deangelo rose his hand.

Tam glared at the screen. Edge glared back.

'Admiral, perhaps the LAL would be open to a dialogue given the extenuating circumstances,' he said.

'Captain Deangelo, place Captain Cartwright in the brig and order the Massey to accompany you to Thiral,' he said, 'Edge out!'

Tam was about to respond when the screen went blank. She glared up at Deangelo before turning her back and pacing to the end of the room.

'That's some family you've got there,' he said.

She felt a break in the tension and turned to him. She couldn't help but laugh. He gave her a warm smile. And a strange sadness fell over, of guilt and regret of not being able to see the bigger picture.

'See all the trouble I saved you from?' she said taking a seat.

The memory of her slipping out in the middle of the night still fresh in her mind. He took a deep breath.

'You could have said goodbye,' he said, still smiling.

'We're not doing this.'

'It wasn't that bad, was it?'

'Oscar, there's only two things I can attach to/'

'Let me guess,' he said, 'your ship and crew.'

'My ship and crew are one of them.'

'And the other?'

'Something no one else can compete with,' she replied.

He looked away, 'as you well know, you don't get to our positions without knowing how to navigate risk.'

'Next you're going to tell me that danger is your middle name,' she said.

He smiled. There was a momentary pause. She couldn't keep it in any longer.

'I'm sorry,' she said.

'For what?'

'Everything.'

'You're sorry for saving those people's lives?'

'No,' she said.

'It's just choice.'

'Yes, it is,' she admitted, 'and now you have to make yours.'

His face dropped, 'some are out of our control.'

'Yes, they are,' she replied, standing up and moving to the door.

She activated it. Jaw Line was standing there, waiting. She turned back to Deangelo, who nodded at the guard.

'See ya round Captain,' she said, as the guards escorted her out.

7

IGO PRIME

The crimson hues from the setting red sun cast their warm glow over the tower that lay at the heart of IGO Prime's largest planetary city, Sadum. Located between the peaks of two colossal mountains, it stood as reminder of the old hate that now extended far beyond the boundaries of the eleven worlds that spun slowly around the giant red star. For over a million years, they had lived within the boundaries of their star system, isolating themselves from all else.

The tower stretched upwards as high as the tallest peak of the two Sadum Mountains. It was truly a glorious site to behold. The IGO Royals had maintained that they had been called after the divine creator who had implanted their blood into the very foundations of every piece of matter as the very first race, heralding from another universe to seed this one. He would be able to see Royal's glistening light shortly as the suns light faded.

Crick looked up at the setting of the red ball of light as it sank beneath the two peaks. To say that he looked would be inaccurate, as the IGO had no eyes per-say. The intensity and size of the IGO twin stars had given rise to an array of adaptable and highly sensitive light absorbing cells which spread all over their long, ink black exteriors. These cells fed information about their surroundings in infrared and ultraviolet spectrums. His body, sitting atop three retractable legs was more alike a cuttlefish than any other creature. He redirected his gaze from the setting suns and deactivated the grey pod he had been traveling on. He stepped off in one fluid motion and moved smoothly across the polished diamond coated surface of the grand entrance. He emitted a long echolocation sound from the pair of air sacks located in his mid-section, announcing his arrival. The thousands of onlookers froze in unison, each bending a tendril-like leg in respect. He emitted a secondary sound, this one slightly higher pitched, acknowledging their signs of respect as movement resumed. As he approached the entrance to the main hall, he looked behind him, not needing to move his head, merely shifting the concentration of his light detecting cells. He peered back towards the valley of Sadum, lined either side with exposed geodes of rock, which had been created after the millennia long bombardment during the dark times. While the valley had become the gravesite to millions of his kind, he was instantly touched by how beautiful the crystal structures protruding from the rock face were… Beams of yellow, orange, purple and blue split off in all directions, piercing as high as the thin layer of cloud that now hung over the valley. In the distance, at the end of the long river that coiled its way through, he could sense a storm was coming, a dark cloud contrasting the colours from the light. It was truly one of the sights that had made IGO Prime the most beautiful place in the entire galaxy. A far more precious jewel than anything he had seen on a thousand worlds inhabited by lower life forms. He moved his attention back towards the tower, peering up to take in the splendour of its construction. In a moment, he would be at its summit, the highest point on IGO Prime.

~ ~ ~

Matter recombined as every cell in Protector Crick's body was reassembled in the command centre of the tower. A series of barrelling noises greeted his presence as legs bended in respect. He reciprocated by emitting a series of clicking sounds.

'Continue,' he said with clicks.

Red light oozed through the large windows of the main command centre, which spanned a half a kilometre in diameter. Crick glided over to one of the windows and peered out, taking in the last few seconds of light as the day was replaced with the vision of the heavens above. He waited as the stars revealed themselves. To the North, IGO Royal began to appear, its glistening rings cut through the sky like dazzling blades of golden ice. He looked back towards the central command centre, hundreds of IGO peered out waiting for the chime, which followed shortly after. This was the moment that Crick had hated the most. The global pause while IGO Royal was saluted. Part of the agreement made millennia ago to assuage a conflict their ancestors had nearly lost. Three chimes sounded from the central column. In unison, they kneeled on all their legs, emitting sounds that were identical and in unison, matching the chime that was now being felt around the planet. Crick, of course, joined them. The IGO then chanted another series of clicks.

The King, The Queen, The IGO!

They then stood, as did Crick, and resumed their tasks.

Crick again looked at the shining planet above before gazing past it to the West, to a small point of light in the sky, to IGO War. The real power. He turned and began moving steadily towards the large processing orb. He was met by Kumu, a relatively new addition to the protectorate who had been indoctrinated into the honoured circle. Kumu had the sole responsibility for monitoring all logistical communications to and from IGO War. A stripe of yellow bioluminescence lit up across his front as he greeted Crick, who reciprocated. It was a characteristic amongst all IGO, with three distinctive and separate colours for each line of the species. Yellow for IGO Primers, white for members of the Royal blood and blue for members of the IGO War lineage. It had been the only visible difference between the species and impossible to change despite some down the ages trying to do so. Once you were born into a particular genome, that was your path for life, and nothing could change it. After the greeting had ended, Crick took a small step towards Kumu and began to speak.

'Is there news from Royal?' said Crick.

'Nothing, we have been waiting fifteen suns and still they do not speak,' said Kumu.

Crick turned his sensory cells and glanced once again at the ring of light above.

'They are receiving yes?' he said, turning his attention back to Kumu.

'Yes, of that we are certain. This is not usual during the birthing,' Kumu said, 'how would you like us to proceed?'

'We will give them time Kumu, they do this for one reason alone, to make us wait. What news on IGO War?' Crick said.

'Outer system shield has been reestablished after the latest ship returns, two hundred thousand in all this day,' said Kumu.

'Good, what resistance?' said Crick.

'Some from a race discovered in the Lita star system, strong physical makeup, their vessels equipped with weapons more powerful than expected. We have dissected them to be brought back for closer inspection,' Kumu said.

'They were able to inflict damage on our ships?' Crick said.

'Of course not, it was just something to make a note of Protector, it merely took a few more seconds than usual for collection,' Kumu said, he continued, 'more bipeds from the Cita's and Rolla star systems.'

Crick waited.

'How many in the harvest?' Crick asked.

'Two million,' said Kumu, 'I know you asked for more, and I realize that number is half of what IGO war had forecast, another fleet is due to arrive after five suns, I expect that they will have enough to meet our quota.'

'Perhaps that is why the Royal have chosen to not contact us,' Crick said.

'Perhaps,' Kumu said, 'I do not believe there has been any contact between Royal and War Protector, if there had, I would have been made aware.'

'How's the system defence report?'

'As always, perfect.'

'Nothing is ever perfect Kumu, you would be reminded of that. Where is the report from the latest test?'

'It has not been completed as of yet,' Kumu said.

Crick extended his frame by a few inches and moved towards Kumu. 'Why not?'

'Protector, with forgiveness, War has been processing the latest collections,' Kumu said.

'You are telling me the grid was reactivated without it being tested?' Crick said.

Kumu was silent, 'I will transmit it now Protector, you have a test done immediately.'

In one snap motion, Crick formed a long razor-sharp tendril and thrust it into Kumu's upper body. Kumu emitted a screeching noise that drew the attention of the others in the control room. Crick retracted his newly formed arm, pulling Kumu towards him, who was still writing in agony. He then extended another tendril and thrust it into the stricken Kumu.

Crick then pulled both of his arms apart, severing Kumu's torso in half, allowing both parts to crumple onto the polished floor.

He retracted his arms until they disappeared once more into his body mass. He glanced up at the nearest IGO.

'Replace him,' he said.

'Of course,' replied the IGO.

'Dispose of this,' Crick said, as he walked to the central interplanetary display grid being shown high above the floor of the tower command hall.

The data flowed freely across the open space in a web of connected spherical balls, each tied to one another by silk like fibres. Crick observed the data before focusing his energy at one point. He aligned his thoughts to it and reached up with an extended arm. A cluster of little spheres changed colour from blue to orange as he plucked it from the air. It descended towards him and hovered in front of his body. He formed fingers at the base of his arm and activated it. The little sphere expanded into a series of alien symbols. It was the latest test of the IGO system shield performed a day earlier. He examined the information from the network of sentinels orbiting the star system and found no errors. He then sealed the data file and returned it to the network cloud high above the floor. He opened another one. The collector reports from IGO War. The little data sphere opened, this time giving a live visual feed into the processing plants on the northern continent of IGO War. He watched as hundreds of ships hovered above the processing plant. Beams of blue light emanated from their underbellies. Inside the light he saw the thousands of containment pods as they floated down towards the surface. He reminded himself to pull the logs from the collectors and study them intently. He wanted to know how far the life forms had come. They were growing too quickly, too fast, and still they didn't have enough. Every sunrise brought the infestation closer, pulling the galaxy too near to their home worlds and still, wasn't enough.

That would change soon.

8

The Lassen Brig

The reinforced glass door sealed tightly as Jaw Line entered his access code, locking Tam in the brig. He winked at her as he moved back.

'I wouldn't do that again if I were you,' she growled.

Jaw Line gave her a smug grin and walked away. Tam took a moment to imagine her knuckles striking the ample target of his face. The moment was soon lost as she turned to investigate her new surroundings. Her anger was swept away when she saw the locking mechanism. She was trapped. The brig was no bigger than five meters square with a small shelf bed at its rear, and a wash basin beside it. A waste unit was tucked in the opposite corner. Her heart rate quickened as she tried to fight what she knew was coming next. She tried to remember the last time Augustine had given her meds. Had she skipped a dose?

'Take it easy,' she whispered to herself, voice shaky.

Acute claustrophobia had unique triggers. Working in deep space didn't help, but at least on her ship, she could slip on an EVA suit and escape into the largest open space there was. The infinite bounds of the universe were only a bulkhead away.

Her heart started to pound, the smooth white walls seemingly drawing closer. She reached into her pocket and removed the Arion device. She activated it and waited as its legs extended and it crawled up her arm and around her ear.

'Hello, Captain,' came the calm voice, 'you appear to be in some difficulty.'

'Yes, Arion, well spotted.'

She took a few deep breaths and began pacing slowly, counting each step. It was just a room. The walls weren't closing in on her. She was safe. It was a locked room with no escape. Her chest tightened.

'I can't breathe,' she said, desperately trying to suck in what air she could.

'Tam, please sit,' said Arion.

Tam ignored him. She could feel her hands pressing against the cold glass of a memory. The coffin she'd been in alone, grieving as a child as she drifted through space, buried alive. Her hands began to shake. Sweat broke out across her forehead. She paused, extending a hand, and leaning against the bed frame.

'Tam, sit!' said Arion, this time amplifying his voice, so that it sounded like a clap of thunder. The effect was potent. Tam clapped her hands over her ears.

'Okay, Okay!' she said, angry, but thankful.

She lowered herself to the floor, and sat, cross-legged. She closed her eyes and began to take deep slow breaths.

'Arion,' she said, softly, 'Access my personal file database and play log entries for Lieutenant Ann Cartwright.'

'Which ones would you like me to access?'

'Any of them,' Tam said.

'One moment,' Arion said.

An image screen opened in the centre of her vision. The face of the woman smiling back had an almost instantaneous effect–those soft hazel eyes and maple-coloured hair, always tied back, revealed a beauty and kindness that sent a wave of calm through her.

'Play the file,' she said.

She lay back on the floor and watched as her mother spoke.

'Personal Log Lieutenant Ann Cartwright,' said her mother.

Tam noticed the dark circles under eyes.

'Another all nighter,' said Ann, rubbing her eyes, 'We caught a glimpse of some gravitational wave fronts coming in from that damn black hole we've been studying for the last month and you know how I get when we discover something new from a black hole.'

Tam tilted her head slightly, feeling her blood pressure return to normal.

'You should hear the sounds these things make,' her mother continued, reaching for something off screen, eventually bringing her hand up with what looked like a speaker. 'Check this out,' she said, activating it and holding it up beside her head.

The speaker began emitting strange noises. Tam watched the side of her mother's mouth part in that crooked little smile she so often gave, full of mischief, like she always knew a little secret that nobody else did. Ann turned her head and shut off the speaker as if hearing something from behind her. She turned back to the screen.

'I think I just woke up the little dot,' said her mother, staying silent for a second to see if she could hear anything else.

'Maybe not,' she said.

She looked back up to the screen. She lowered her voice.

'Tam, if you ever get to see this. You're asleep in the room next door right now, you're four years old and you'll look back on this time of your life and have lots of questions. Like why your mother was practically a ghost.'

A sadness formed in her eyes.

'I'm sorry about that little dot,' she said, 'I really am. This is a strange life your father and I chose for you out here amongst the stars. I guess most people would have done the normal thing and gotten a little house on Arana or Thiral or somewhere like that, but believe it or not, not many kids get to see the things you're about to. Maybe you'll grow up to resent it, the hours we work or the lack of green fields for you to play in. Your grandparents weren't happy about it, that's for sure. I guess it was selfishness on my part, but I wanted you with me. I mean, look at this…'

She placed her hands on the camera that was recording her, and lifted it up, bringing it over to the window in her quarters. Tam felt warm, at ease, forgetting where she was entirely, her captivity and close quarters feeling a million light years away. She watched as the screen showed the star field outside the windows in the quarters where she spent the first years of her life.

'We're drifting amongst the stars, you and I,' said her mother, taking the camera away from the window and placing it back to face her once again.

'Your dad and I wonder what you'll be when you grow up. He thinks you'll end up as a starship captain because you keep sneaking on the bridge whenever you get a chance. You seem to love that more than you do coming down to my lab. I don't know if being a scientist is going to be your thing, you're bored whenever you're with me for the day. You've such an adventurous spirit and such a kind heart that he's probably right. I think you're more like him than you are me. I love to see it, but there are times when it makes me sad.'

Tam felt her eyes water.

'I see the way you look at him,' tears brimmed her mother's eyes, 'I see the sparkle in your eye and it makes me wonder whether I was the mother you wanted. Nobody really knows how to be, but if you ever have children. You need to know that we make it up as we go along.'

Her mother's voice was shaky.

'It's hard when I have to become the bad guy, which is what I seem to be turning into these days. The look in your eye you give me when you've done something wrong once I'm in front of you, breaks my heart because it's the same way I used to look at my mother every time she used to walk into a room.'

She looked away.

'Are we all just destined to turn into our mothers? It's probably why I took you away from a traditional upbringing. I thought that maybe if I gave you an unconventional life, I could spare you all that. Maybe I made it worse.'

She shook her head.

'Sometimes I think you hate me. Or… you will.'

Tam felt a tear roll down her cheek.

'Well, if you ever see this,' said her mother, 'if anything ever happens to me, I want you to know that my work, my endless hours looking at chemical compounds and molecules and space dust, that… you were more important, you always were and that…' She paused and turned her head.

Tam waited for the moment she loved the most about this particular log entry. In the video, she saw herself come into the room—four years old, holding a teddy, rubbing her eyes.

'Hey, Little Dot,' said her mother. 'I am so sorry—did I wake you?'

Tam watched her little self, nod sleepily as she moved towards her mother, crawled onto her lap, and place her head on her mother's chest, wrapping her small arms around her waist and instantly falling back asleep. She watched her mother kiss her gently and pull a loose strand of hair over her little ears. She looked at the camera and smiled, raising her left hand, and pointing to her.

'Look how cute you are,' she said, whispering to the camera and hugging Tam as she swayed her side to side.

'We'll figure it out, you and me,' said her mother, 'goodnight, Little Dot. End log,' she said, as the screen went blank.

Tears streamed down Tam's face, as she closed her eyes and felt herself drift off.

9

Office of the Combined Earth President
Shanghai
06:00

Edge sat patiently across from the large oak desk while President Arav Puri looked over the data pad in his hand. Puri was a large man at six foot six, and just as wide. He was charismatic and sharp, a former surgeon from a poor family. He'd broken the bonds of an unremarkable lineage and cut an impressive career. His eyes drifted to the flickering light of a candle that was placed next to the digital photograph of Puri's wife and daughter. He noted the unmistakable look of a man who hadn't slept. Puri was a spiritual man. A calm and reasoned man and one of the few Presidents that Edge had encountered who seemed to grasp the importance of order. That wasn't to say that he trusted him. Edge trusted no one. He allowed himself the moment to gaze out at the stunning views of the sun coming over the city. The warm hues of Earth's sun reflecting off the busy hovering transports the few in military precision through the skyscrapers.

The air felt different here, unprocessed, cleaner somehow.

'Do you miss the mother land Admiral?' said Puri suddenly, catching Edge off guard.

'Pardon me?'

'I know that look,' said Puri, 'a recognition of the beauty of that which we chose to leave behind when we stretch to the stars.'

'I hadn't noticed Mr. President,' replied Edge.

'Of course,' Puri said, his smile wavering into sadness.

He stood from the desk and moved over to the window, a ray of light casting a warm glow across his sallow skin.

'It looks like we have both lost things of great importance, perhaps today is the beginning of the end of our way of life in the darkness?'

'I am confident that we can navigate this situation' Edge said.

Puri kept his gaze towards the city.

'My wife awoke late in the night screaming,' Puri said.

'Sir?' Edge said, becoming slightly uncomfortable.

'I had to give her a sedative,' Puri admitted, 'she said the same two words over and over.'

Edge waited.

'The dark,' Puri said, turning to face him.

The way he said it sent a chill up Edge's spin.

'There is a bond between a mother and a child that transcends through space and time,' Puri said, retaking his seat.

'The dark has taken our little girl,' Puri said.

'Yes, sir, I can't understand what that must mean,' Edge said.

Puri tilted his head.

'Can't you?' Puri said.

Edge was becoming uncomfortable. Puri leaned back in his large leather chair.

'I apologize Admiral, let's get back to business,' he said taking a breath, 'you've lost Ona Mendel, your niece has destroyed a star, and The Taurus crew were encountered with a Ghost vessel with all crew missing. Does that about sum up our day here?' Puri said in flat tone.

'That about sums it up Mr. President,' said Edge, shifting in his seat.

'And it's only 6 a.m.,' Puri said.

'Sir, I did not mean to downplay the severity or stress that this is causing you, but I must try and formulate our response to this,' said Edge.

Puri opened his hand, inviting a response.

'Captain Cartwright will stand trial on the LAL home world for what she has done, it may buy us negotiation time with Diren,' Edge said.

'And Abraham offers up his son Issac to god,' said Puri.

'Sir?' Edge said.

'It is your niece is it not?'

'She knew the risks.'

'As did Amita, but that does not negate the sacrifice we ask of our own to survive, does it?' Puri said.

'No, sir,' Edge said.

'I would hope not, Admiral, for if we lose our compassion, we lose our souls,' Puri said.

Edge suddenly wanted to get out of there.

'We must find a way to neutralize this threat posed from the Ghosts, or at the very least make contact to find out what they want from our species,' Puri continued.

'I am working on that Mr. President,' Edge said.

Puri's face changed. His eyes widened and that sense of serenity appeared to empty.

'Work faster,' Puri said, with something that very closely resembled a threat in his tone.

Edge straightened his shoulders.

'Did you discover the cause of the destruction of the station?' asked Puri.

Edge clenched his jaw, looking Puri in the eye.

'It appears to have been a malfunction in the central core, our engineers are working on getting the full data.'

'A malfunction?'

'Yes, sir.'

Puri looked to the flickering candle.

'I'll admit that I am not entirely comfortable with Premier Diren requesting an audience with you on Arana, despite my best attempts, he seems to only want to speak to you.'

Puri paused.

'Any reason why you think that is?'

'Perhaps because it involves a member of my family, he wishes to what my response will be,' Edge said, 'I'll be traveling on the Orion within the hour.'

'Find me answers Admiral,' Puri said, 'before the LAL decided to pull all our plugs.'

Edge stood.

'And Admiral,' Puri said, softly.

Edge turned.

'Try and save my daughter from the Dark.'

10

Amita Puri tried to open her eyes but couldn't. She gagged at a noxious smell unlike anything she'd ever experienced. She couldn't move a muscle, every inch of her body compacted. Her lips and nose were sealed yet, somehow, she was still able to breath. She was buried alive, in a void of nothingness. Somewhere off in the distance, she heard something akin to whale-song followed by a series of clicking noises.

She had been on a ship. Of that she was certain. Had there been an accident? Was she in a coma? She remembered Victor's face, the look of desperation and then nothing. The clicking noises now seemed closer, as if they were right next to her head. Terror descended all around her. She felt her muscles tense, a cold shiver running all the way down her back. Something was close to her, some… THINGS were close. The clicking intensified in speed and pitch to a level that now began to hurt her ears. She tried to scream but nothing came out. The clicking stopped. She heard the whale-song again, not so distant now. It repeated itself, growing closer. A single click to her left was reciprocated by a single click to her right. She saw her father's face, seeing her off as she boarded the shuttle to leave Earth. She saw his proud smile, felt his large arms embrace her and nearly squeeze the life out of her. She remembered her mother's plea to stay on Earth with them. Her warnings about the dangers of the unknown, about the responsibility of being an only child should anything happen to her. She said sorry in her mind, sorry for the reason she would never see her again, to tell her she'd made a mistake, and that she was right. She wanted to hug her so badly one last time before the darkness took her permanently.

She then began to feel lightheaded, fuzzy. She heard the whale-song, now a booming emanation of ever-increasing high-pitched calls. She thought it sounded quite beautiful. She felt something touch her arm. Something long, like a snake, sliding up and down her arm as she felt lighter and lighter. The strange sounds and fear were replaced by a wonderful sense of calm and serenity as she surrendered herself to the moment, a moment she believed was the end. She said sorry one last time and begged for forgiveness as another void opened up and swallowed her whole.

11

Tam's eyes opened. A white light glared down at her from above. She rested her hand over them before turning to look at the glass wall of her prison.

'How are you feeling Tam?' came Arion's calm voice in her mind.

'I'll live,' she said.

'Of course, you will. While you were asleep, I accessed several neurotransmitters in an attempt to increase your levels of Serotonin,' Arion said.

'You got me high?'

'Not quite, Tam. A mild increase has had a satisfactory regulatory effect within your nervous system, it will only be temporary.'

'Well, I'll take it,' she said.

She sat up and swung her legs over the side of the bed. She stood up and moved over to the transparent wall.

She pressed her face against it and saw that the corridor outside was empty.

'There is something you should be aware of,' Arion said.

'What's that?' Tam asked, keeping her eyes on the transparent wall.

'I've been receiving instructions from the interlink on board the Massey Shaw.'

Tam frowned, 'What?'

'A set of schematics to this cell and deck were uploaded a few moments ago from the aft computer section in engineering on board the Massey,' Arion explained.

Tam stayed silent wondering what the hell Chuck was up to.

'That's all?' she said.

'Currently, I am compiling the information as we speak, one moment,' Arion said.

They were up to something.

'I've received a new set of instructions Tam.'

'What's going on Arion?' she said, whispering as quietly as she could to avoid the auditory sensors in the cell from picking it up.

'Interesting,' Arion said.

'What is? Dammit Arion, what are they doing?'

'Stand by.'

Tam grumbled to herself and stepped away from the glass. Her mouth was feeling dry, so she went to the back of the cell and poured herself a glass of water. She gulped it down, tilting her head back while taking a fleeting glance at the small camera in the corner. She looked over at the small shower unit and thought about how much she needed one. It had been twenty-seven hours since her last and she was starting to feel it. And smell it.

'What's going on Arion?' she said, growing impatient as the seconds tick by.

'I'm feeding you through Chuck's proposal now Tam,' Arion said.

Tam began seeing images and text flow across her vision.

'Chuck, are you out of your damn…' She started.

Soon after she sighed.

'Can you get a message to the Massey?' she whispered.

'Negative, the carrier wave is unidirectional into my core processor, I do not have the facility to transmit along the same carrier wave without being detected from the Lassen sensors,' Arion replied.

'Perfect,' Tam said.

~ ~ ~

An hour passed as Tam kept watch, while Arion took care of his end of the plan. She kept her eyes firmly peering outside the glass. After a few moments, she felt Arion crawl up her leg, up the small of her back and then onto shoulder and neck as he reattached himself to her ear.

'Done,' he said, as his auditory output inserted itself into her right ear.

'Okay,' said Tam, feeling her pulse quicken slightly.

She heard a door sliding open and waited, surprised it had taken this long. After a few moments, Jaw Line appeared in front of the glass. She smiled at him.

'What's up sweetie?' she teased.

Jaw Line scowled at her as he activated the locking mechanism and stepped inside. He held his arm out.

'Give it to me,' he growled at her.

'Give what to you?' she said, taking a step towards him.

She could see his agitation growing with every word she spoke.

'Your Arion unit in your ear, hand it over to me, now,' he demanded.

Tam raised her hands up in the air.

'Okay tiger, take it easy, you'll blow a blood vessel in that large head of yours,' she said.

Jaw Line gave her a piercing glare, she had to restrain herself again from knocking his block off.

'You heard the man, Arion, off you go,' she said.

'See you shortly,' Arion replied.

Tam nodded as Arion detached from her ear and made his way down her arm to her open outstretched palm. His legs folded into his body as his compacted himself into a small disk and powered down. Tam handed the unit to Jaw Line.

'Don't break it,' she said.

Jaw Line didn't answer, he snatched the Arion unit from her hand and disappeared out of the cell. She heard the locking mechanism and suddenly lost her joviality. She once again began to feel the walls of her enclosure threaten to fall in on top of her. Arion's presence, it would seem, was the only thing holding it at bay.

'Not now,' she said, clenching her hands into two fists.

She heard footsteps again, breaking her concentration and stopped in mid stride. Jaw Line and Chuck appeared in the front of the glass. She met Chuck's gaze as he gave her a wink. She didn't reciprocate.

'Captain,' he said, nodding.

She nodded back and looked at Jaw Line.

'Five minutes,' Jaw Line said, looking at Chuck

Chuck gave him a salute with two fingers pressed against his forehead. Jaw Line, with a downturned mouth, turned and moved away.

'I'm guessing this is a bad time to say I told you so,' said Chuck.

Tam crossed her arms.

'Report,' she said.

'Oh, the usual,' he replied, 'we're in a shit storm sandwich and living on the edge.'

'Wouldn't have it any other way.'

Chuck looked down at his data bracelet. Tam stepped towards the glass.

'The good news is that Urhan is currently in your flight chair,' Chuck said.

'I honestly never thought he'd fit,' she replied, 'let's hope he can fly stick.'

'Let's hope he doesn't have a change of heart and lock us out of the ship entirely.'

'He wouldn't do that,' Tam said, 'he's too afraid of what you would do to him.'

'You willing to bet your life on that?'

'We're about to find out, aren't we?'

'Yes, Ma'am.'

Tam looked into his eyes. She was about to tell him to walk away. He was too quick for her.

'No,' he said

'This is my deal,' she said firmly.

'No offense, but while you're behind this glass; I'm in command.'

'I can blow the alarm on this right now.'

Chuck glared at her.

'And leave me alone with Jacob and lurch?' Chuck said, 'I'm genuinely hurt.'

Tam smiled.

'Now, if you don't mind, time is short,' Chuck said, tapping his wrist comms and raising it up to his mouth.

'Now!' he said.

The deck shook suddenly underfoot. Tam pressed her hand against the glass window as she heard a male voice shout, followed by the sound of a heavy thud. Chuck looked down the corridor as the Arion unit came scampering up at speed.

'Hurry,' Chuck said to the little device, as it made its way up his leg and body to his outstretched arm.

He held it in his palm as the Arion unit interfaced with the locking mechanism on the door, after a few seconds the lock released. While Tam's adrenaline was beginning to make its way around her body, she felt a huge sense of relief at the sound of the door sliding open. She quickly left the cell, taking the Arion unit in her hand and placing it on her ear.

'Thank you, Arion,' she said, as she followed Chuck down the corridor to the main entrance to the brig.

'Always a pleasure,' said Arion.

They approached the unconscious bodies of the two security guards, Jaw Line being one of them. She kneeled beside him and took his pulse gun; Chuck did the same with the other guard as the pair stood at the entrance to the door.

'We've got about five minutes before they figure out where the electrical discharge came from,' Chuck said, checking the charge levels of his pulse gun. Tam did the same before the pair placed the weapons in their rear belts.

'Lead the way Captain,' she said with a grin.

Chuck smiled and activated the door before the pair made their way into the main hallways of the ship. Red lights flashed along the walls as they made their way at speed towards the main elevator. Tam kept her eyes forward, their ESDA uniforms at least blending into the chaos. They reached the elevator and waited. The doors opened and they got in. Chuck hit the airlock deck and the lift took off.

'Well, that wasn't so bad,' Chuck said.

After a few seconds, the doors opened. They were greeted almost instantly by the glaring eyes of more security guards. There were four of them guarding the entrance to the airlock, they all turned and instantly raised their weapons.

'Stop!' one of them shouted.

'Arion, weapons hot!' Tam said.

Arion instantly complied, detaching two of his legs from the side of Tam's face. They combined as one, the nanotech fusing and reforming into the barrel of a small, but powerful pulse gun.

A targeting array activated in Tam's vision. Chuck raised his weapon and instantly opened fire. Arion followed suit, autonomously sending bursts of electrical energy towards the welcoming party. Tam struck one with a clean shot, sending him into a crumpled heap on the ground, unconscious but alive. Arion's weapons had a lethality to them, but Tam had never thought to ask him to activate it. The last thing she needed was another death sentence for murdering an officer of the ESDA. She saw a bright flash of light whiz past and strike Chuck on the left leg, dropping him to his knees.

'Chuck!' she shouted.

Chuck looked up at her and nodded, standing on his good leg.

'To hell with this,' Tam snarled, ducking down and taking a breath, 'Arion, I need you take them out, you got it?'

She heard a surge of power come from the side of her head.

'Five-seconds,' he said.

She waited. The oncoming fire continued. She heard a clicking sound.

'Ready,' Arion said.

She rolled out of cover, turning her head, and looking at the guards. She saw Arion overlay crosshairs on all four men and felt the heat of the four shots as they let loose, hitting all targets, and dropping them like a sack of bricks. She rushed over to Chuck and grabbed him under the arm.

'Can you walk?' she asked.

'No choice, get moving,' Chuck set through gritted teeth.

He put his arm around her shoulder, Tam taking most of his weight as the pair scrambled to the airlock door.

~ ~ ~

Tam slammed her hand on the activation release for the flight deck and rushed inside. Urhan was sitting in the flight chair awkwardly. Chuck hobbled in after her.

'Get out of my seat,' she ordered Urhan, 'help Chuck and get Augustine up here to give him something.'

Urhan complied quickly and swung his large legs over the central flight control system and STC chamber. Tam shuffled past him and jumped into her seat.

'I'm fine,' Chuck groaned, as Urhan linked his arms under his, 'just get me to the chair.'

'You do not appear to be…'

'Urhan!' Chuck growled.

Urhan nodded, taking him over to the seat next to Tam.

'You spin up the cutter?' Chuck said, as he slid into his seat, releasing an agonizing yelp.

'As requested, it's fully charged,' Urhan said, before clicking the comm system, 'doctor to the flight deck, medical emergency.'

'Blowing the umbilicus,' Tam said, looking to Chuck, 'you up for this?'

'It was my damn idea,' he replied.

Tam looked up through the main windows, seeing the Lassen's grappler firmly attached to the hull of the Massey's mid-section. She swung the main cutting beam to bear on the arm of the grappler and took a breath. The Massey had no weapons to speak of, but the cutter packed a serious punch. It was needed for slicing through hulls and penetrating deep into rock for complex rescue operations. She looked to Chuck.

'There's no going back if we do this.' she said.

The comm system chirped. They both looked at the screen at the same time. Captain Deangelo's face glared at them.

'What do you think you're doing Tam?' he demanded.

She looked at Chuck who gave her a mischievous smile, then back to Deangelo.

'Sorry, Captain, it's not you, it's me,' she said, deactivating the transmission.

She aimed the cutter and fired two powerful short-range bursts. The grappler arm disintegrated, and the Massey swung free.

She let go of the control for the cutting beam and grabbed her flight controls, throttling up to full power.

'Urhan,' Chuck said, pointing to the locked and loaded STC chamber.

'Not yet, we're still too close,' Tam said, clicking the comms system, 'Jacob…'

'I know, I know, you'll have a boost in a few seconds, I'm working on it,' he said.

The flight deck door opened, and Augustine entered. Tam saw her reflection in the mirror but kept her eyes forward.

'Doc, Chuck's taken one in the leg, field dressing please,' Tam said.

Augustine didn't reply. She simply moved to Chuck as the ship rocked suddenly to one side. A flash of light skimming past the window.

'That son of a bitch,' Tam growled, a rage boiling inside her.

She flicked on the comm system again and hailed the Lassen. Deangelo's face appeared. She glared at him.

'Did you just shoot at me?' she said angrily,

There was a definite look of guilt in his eyes, well hidden by his practiced stern and arrogant face.

'I told you not to do this Tam, you're leaving me with very little options here. Come back and we can figure this out, don't involve your crew,' Deangelo said.

'You just took a god damn shot at my ship!' Tam said.

'For god's sake, Captain, what am I supposed to do?'

'You're gonna pay for that!' Tam said, knocking off the transmission.

She gripped the flight controls tightly.

'Hold on!' she said, as she dropped down the power to the engines and pulled up hard, hitting the top aft thrusters causing the Massey to flip over 180 degrees. The gees of the manoeuvre hit hard. Augustine was thrown to the ground.

'Sorry!' Tam said to her, 'Chuck, can you get a lock on her forward cannons?'

'Roger that,' he said taking the cutting beam controls in his hand. Augustine righted herself and pressed something onto his leg.

'Thanks doc,' Chuck said.

The Lassen came into full view in the forward-facing windows. Tam aimed the Massey's bow directly at her and throttled back up to full power. She flicked the comms on.

'Engine room, I need an after burn in fifteen-seconds,' she said.

'You'll have it,' Jacob confirmed.

She turned to Chuck. 'You'll have one shot.'

'It's all I need,' he replied with a confident grin.

'Urhan,' she said, 'stand by STC.'

Urhan placed his hand on the chamber as the Lassen grew larger in the screen. Another two shots from its forward cannons streaked by the main windows. The flight deck shook.

'He's not messing around,' Chuck said.

Tam frowned. Deangelo was involved in the civil war on Proxima, a decorated and highly competent commander. If he wanted her blown out of the sky, she would be molecules by now.

She held her collision course for another eight-seconds before nudging the nose down skimming under her bow.

'Now!' she said to Chuck.

He activated the beam. Red pulsing light exploded out from the cutting beam, striking its target as the Massey, which outmatched the Lassen's manoeuvrability with ease, passed underneath.

'Got him,' Chuck said, 'cannon disabled.

Tam flung her flight controls hard right and looked to the atom-breaking thruster power levels. They were at 106%. 'Good man,' she said, softly.

She hit the boosters, used for both atmospheric gray-escape velocity and landing procedures. Tam was squeezed into the back of her seat. The Massey's distance from the Lassen increased exponentially. 'Urhan, hit it!' she said.

Urhan complied, sliding the STC molecule into his containment chamber. The stars distorted, the universe expanded and collapsed as the Massey blinked away into the space between spaces.

12

Ona pressed her fingertips to the window and leaned her forehead up against the glass. The strange distortion effect had given way to a star field unlike anything she'd ever seen before. They were everywhere. She turned her head in all directions, listening to the soft chirping sounds of the computer systems coming from inside the escape pod. She had seen the stars at night, the ones created for her in her holographic prison, but they hadn't been anything like this before.

She rubbed her eyes again, wiping away the last remnants of tears. He was gone. She had misjudged him, his intentions, his will, and his attachment to her. She was free, free to float amongst the stars, alone, for what was left of her life. She didn't know how to work the controls of this ship, she didn't know how to fly it, what direction to go in, who to try to call for help. Perhaps his last gift to her was to let her drift through the cosmos where the voices couldn't get her. She turned back to the computer console and spoke. 'Play the message again,' she sat on the floor.

She heard a beep as the computer recognized her instruction and began to play the recording.

'Ona, I don't know if I'm with you, but the odds are that I'm probably not. I am so sorry about that, I truly am… but this can work, it will work. They wanted to take your young life away and I've lived mine, seems like a fair trade in my book. If I've gotten my calculations correct you should be thirteen light years from Earth near a remote star system with a class B planet, deemed too hostile for human colonization. You'll be safe here.'

There was a pause on the recording.

'Ona, you've been living on a space station your whole life, orbiting Saturn's moon Titan. I'm guessing you've figured that out by now. I wish we could have had more time, but they wanted to take you away from me, to another facility back on Earth and I just couldn't have that. Your father, Ona, was an STC molecular scientist. I don't know how much you remember about the experiment. You weren't supposed to be there that day. Ona, you've got something inside you that's very, very important. It must be protected, at all costs. You cannot allow anyone near you, especially the LAL. If they find out, who knows what they'll do,'

He paused.

'I can't pretend to know what a burden that's been thrust upon your shoulders. You didn't deserve it. I put you in this position and I know you can never forgive me for it but we're here now, and we need to get you out of this mess. The Captain of the ship I sent the signal to, her name is Tamara Cartwright. You can trust her. She won't know who I am, but I knew her parents. She knows what it's like to be alone and will take care of you, I know it in my heart.

'All the data I've learned about you is encrypted on the bracelet I gave you. Give it to Tam. Don't let yourself be taken by the LAL; they've kept the secret of the molecule for themselves for a reason. They want to keep us within their control, for what reason I do not know, but there is something they are not telling us.

'Ona there's something else you need to know. During all our time together, I did manage to learn one thing. Your transportation, every time you left the facility to go god knows where in the universe, there was a spike in your heart rate and frontal cortex activity that would suggest an emotional response.

'You have the power within you, don't let them take that away from you. If they won't listen, if they attack you, run. Do you hear me? Run to the edges of the universe, and don't come back.'

13

Massey Shaw Simulator Room

Tam tapped her crampon gently into the ice sheet, making a small groove before gripping her right foot tightly into the surface of the frozen waterfall. She tested the foothold lightly before trying her full bodyweight. It held as she looked up towards a relatively smooth area and brought her ice axe up to bare. She tapped the ice, releasing small shards that fell next to her cheek. Her next swing was smooth, relaxed, and powerful as the blade sunk its teeth deep within the crevice. She pulled down, making sure it was secure before looking at her belt. She took a moment to take in the hundred-meter drop to the frozen lake below before turning her head and looking south towards the Ippinar Mountain range that carried out towards the Arana horizon. The cold air brushed against her cheek as she flexed her arms. She took a breath and relaxed into the pain. She looked across to the great ocean that lay to the South. She saw the unmistakable humps of a school of Arana Blue. Whales that would dwarf the largest of the Earth's largest mammal.

She focused back on the climb. She closed her eyes for a second and allowed the feeling of the openness to flow through her, the memories of the panic induced from being inside the enclosed spaces faded.

She opened her eyes again and pushed her body upwards, when she suddenly heard something. She stopped and listened. It sounded again. The deep low reverberation of a subsurface crack somewhere beneath. She held her position and examined the surface of the ice. She couldn't see anything. She looked below and saw the top of someone's head.

'What the—?' she cut off.

The face looked up and smiled at her, waving his own axe. It was Jacob.

'What the hell are you doing?' Tam shouted.

'Thought you might like some company,' Jacob shouted from below.

Tam scowled at him. She wanted to be alone. Needed it, and he was stomping all over her ice sheet and peace like a dumb ox.

'Are you crazy? You know this ice sheet can't take the two of us,' Tam said.

'I come in peace, you looked like you needed a friend,' Jacob shouted up. He continued to try and lodge his ice axe into a section of the waterfall. Tam watched his confused face as he hacked away at it, growing more and more frustrated. Her frustration faded with the look on his face and she couldn't help but smile at his efforts.

'Oh, for the love of…' Tam said, letting out a sigh, as another deep cracking sound filled her ears.

She linked her rope through the safety harness and waited, wondering how long they both had until this whole thing gave way. After several minutes, Jacob's face appeared just below her. He looked up at Tam and gave her victorious thumbs up.

'I know you're angry, I can tell, I have a way with people,' Jacob said.

'What did I tell you about this? I climb alone, always—always alone. You could have gone to the gym!'

'Yeah, well, not today,' Jacob said, giving her a look, she'd seen from him before. The look that had led to a mistake. One she shouldn't have let happen between her and a member of her crew. Despite the eccentric way he had with machines, and his boyish comic defence mechanisms. Beneath it lay a pain that Tam connected with. She'd hurt him, she hurt everyone, she knew that much. Despite the assumption he would transfer off, he stayed, accepted it, worked through it, and did his job. But more than that, he became a loyal friend.

A splitting crack interrupted the moment as the ice beneath them vibrated. Tam looked down at her feet to see a large split in the ice traveling at speed between the two of them.

'Oh shit!' said Jacob.

Tam's reflexes kicked into motion as she looked up and immediately released her feet, pulling the ice axe out of its holding and allowing her body to free-fall. She then slammed her axe in the ice just above where the crack had formed. It scraped along the surface before finally boring a small hole deep enough to stop her descent. She felt her shoulder jerk as it took the full brunt of his body weight. The ice below her began to move, breaking away from the main solid as she quickly released a line of rope from her belt and dropped it down to Jacob.

'Hook on!' she shouted

Jacob quickly attached one his hooks to the end of Tam's as the ice finally gave way. Tam felt the full combined weight of the two as the shelf sheered away, leaving Jacob dangling in mid-air. She heard another crack, this time coming from above. She felt her arm begin to burn, the lactic acid building up steadily.

'You gotta let me go,' Jacob said, in a melodramatic voice.

'You're so annoying!' Tam said, through now gritted teeth.

Jacob reached inside his pocket and brought something out. It was a knife.

'I gotta cut the cord, you're too important to the mission to lose,' Jacob said, now in full character.

Tam was not amused, her arm now starting really hurt.

'Well?'

'Well, what?' Tam said.

'You're supposed to say, don't do it man, I got you, or something,' Jacob said.

Tam remained silent.

'I'm gonna do it, I'm really gonna do it,' Jacob said.

Tam smiled at him.

'I'm waiting,' she said, as the crack above her head now widened.

'Tell my wife I love her,' Jacob said, as he brought the knife to the edge of the rope.

'You don't have a wife, or a girlfriend or a cat,' Tam said.

'That's cold,' Jacob said, feigning being hurt, 'farewell,'

He cut the cord and began to fall

'Oh, for Christ sake,' Tam said, watching as Jacob fell a few meters before vanishing from sight.

She looked up, glancing at her beautiful ruined afternoon one last time before the ice gave way above her. Her body followed suit, falling through the cold air. She tried to enjoy the view one last time before the simulation vanished and was replaced by the white walls of the simulation room. The gravitational effects of the fall lessoned as the simulation readjusted to the normality, allowing her body to land on the floor of the room with a soft thud. Jacob stood by the doorway, hands on his hips.

'Okay that was fun, you can't say that wasn't fun,' he said.

Tam got up and began rolling up her climbing rope.

'You killed us,' she said.

'Ah come on, another half hour of that and you would have been bored out of you tree,' Jacob said, rolling his eyes, 'admit it.'

Tam smiled at him.

'See,' he said.

'How's my ship?' she asked.

'Well, let's see,' Jacob said, taking off his climbing gloves, 'I don't exactly know what caused the overload on deck two. I think that last pot-shot your ex-boyfriend took at us got a little closer than we think. The bastard may have nicked the outer hull.'

Tam glared at him.

'Sorry,' he said, holding his hands up.

'Continue,' she grumbled.

'I need to do a visual on it, that's job number 127 on today's roster. The hull stress from that suicide run you did, rescuing the Clorinda is what's got me more worried,' he said, turning to her, 'hell of a job you did on that Cap by the way, to hell with what the LAL say. You did the right thing.'

Tam smiled at him. He gave her a caring smile back

'What kind of stresses are we looking at on the repaired sections?' she said.

Jacob looked at the screens.

'Fifty-one percent on the aft, I'll get her up to spec. I'm reinforcing with an electrical polymer but I didn't have the chance to charge it fully before shit hit the fan. I need at least twelve hours before we attempt another jump or else you risk a permanent hole in the side of the ship.'

'Noted. I don't think we'll be going anywhere for a while yet, but I know Deangelo, he's persistent and even more so when his ego has been bruised,' Tam said.

'Is that right?' Jacob said, looking a little hurt.

Tam sighed, 'thank you, by the way.'

'For what?'

'For always giving me that extra ten percent,' she said.

'Jacob always has another ten percent,' he said, in a corny seductive tone.

Tam began walking towards the exit, 'Meh.'

She opened the door to leave. Jacob followed.

'Meh? What do you mean, meh?'

His voice began to fade as she made her way through the corridor.

'Captain?' he shouted, 'what do you mean by meh?'

14

Tam entered her quarters and sealed the door shut. She closed her eyes and let out a sigh before unzipping her jumpsuit, allowing it to crumple in the middle of the floor before she untied her boots and headed straight for the shower. She placed her hands on the glass container and let the warmth of the water seep through to her bones. She felt the steam around her face as she let her mind drift to the choice she'd made and how to fix it. She'd never been a criminal before.

She felt lost. She activated the interface on the wall and brought up her mother's old log entries. She stopped at one named: Science Log, Ann C, Oct 3, 2729'

She pressed play and leaned her head against wall, closing her eyes.

'Science log, Lieutenant Ann Cartwright, Oct 3, 2729 Earth standard' came the voice.

'Bioremediation of sample sixteen continues to be progressing as anticipated, however, the sample is still reproducing too quickly, which would explain the lack of efficiency against the human immune response on the colony on Proxima two. We will remain here at the nebula for a further two weeks collecting samples of the primordial elements for more testing and after that we'll…'

'Hi mom' came Tam's young voice, 'what's this?'

'Tamara put that down,' said Ann.

'Why there's nothing in it'

Tam smiled listening to her brash little tone.

'Just because you cannot see anything, it doesn't mean it's not there. I told you to do something, now do it,' said Ann.

'No!'

Tam's smile broadened.

'Excuse me?' Ann said.

'No, you said you would be only an hour and I've been waiting for you to come and play with me all day and it's so boring in here and I'm hungry,' said young Tam.

'Tamara Edge, you put that down right now and come over here.'

There was a moment of silence on the recording as Tam tried to remember what sort of face she was pulling at that exact moment. She remembered placing the container on the table and furiously crossing her arms, before gently taking one step towards her mother. A minor capitulation to her mother's demands, enough to save a face.

Tam smiled at her reflection in the shower as she tried to mimic how her younger self would be behaving. The face-off continued for several more seconds. She remembered her younger self breaking, taking another step. Her mother, holding her ground and glaring down at her from her nearly six feet in height, was like a towering goddess. Her long brown hair tied back and framed her soft face. She remembered those large hazel eyes and while she knew she was now furious with her, there was a playfulness in the glare. The game now changed from one of stubbornness to something more light-hearted. She remembered her mother taking a small step towards her, her frown softening slightly and a lightly dimpled grin beginning to form. It was a look that could melt a heart and Tam remembered responding to it with her own side grin, mimicking her. It was at that point that her mother rushed down to meet her, sweeping her off her feet and holding her aloft, swinging her around as the tension melted away into the last happy memory she ever had. She heard giggling on the recording. The voices sounded distant now, as if a few meters away from the microphone as she heard her mother say the last wholesome words to her.

'You love me' she said, tickling her.

'Maybe!' young Tam giggled

Tam turned her head suddenly

'Stop playback,' she said, not wanting to hear what happened next.

The images of which were now burned into her heart for the rest of her life. A nightmare she couldn't wake from. Knew every sound, every alarm, every scream, and every order shouted. She didn't want to hear it again, not tonight at least.

She shut off the shower and stepped out, wrapping herself in a towel as her comm system bleeped.

She raised her head to the heavens and let out a sigh before hitting it.

'Cartwright,' she said.

'Captain, I have what looks like an ESDA escape pod distress beacon,' said Chuck.

Tam frowned.

'Out here?'

'Yes, Ma'am you better come up and take a look; it's coded specifically to match our communications encryption keys,' he said.

Tam looked at her reflection in the mirror. Her younger self stared back.

'On my way.'

15

Tam opened the door to the cockpit and moved inside, she nodded to Urhan and Chuck.

Then she flung herself into her flight chair and glanced at Chuck's leg.

'It's fine, doc sowed it right up, be a bit stiff for a while,' he said, noticing her gaze.

'You should rest,' Tam said.

'Not my first rodeo Cap, try breaking your back, this is nothing, trust me,' Chuck said.

'I stand corrected,' Tam replied, 'what's happening?'

'There appears to a signal tethered directly to the Massey Shaw communications sub routines,' Urhan said.

'That's odd,' Tam said, accessing the information on her computer.

'Very, it's definitely an ESDA coding however it requires command authorization to activate the transmission.'

Tam looked at Chuck.

'You're eyes only,' Chuck said, 'could be a virus sent by the ESDA to shut us down and get a location on us.'

Tam looked back at Urhan.

'I assure you Tamara, I have not intervened,' Urhan said.

'You better not have,' Chuck growled under his breath.

Tam glared at him.

Urhan remained with his long arms behind his back. Tam turned her attention back to the signal.

'Urhan, any way we can determine whether this thing in infected or not?' Tam said.

Urhan took a step forward and leaned closer over her shoulder. He peered at the computer console.

'Not without activating it,' he said.

'Surely you guys have fancy tech to get behind it no?' Chuck said.

Urhan glanced at him coldly.

'Technology is still bound by the laws of mathematics Mr. Redmond,' Urhan said.

'Okay then,' Chuck said with a shrug.

Tam regarded the flashing message requesting command code access and thought about it for a minute.

'They can't knock out our STC drive, its isolated on its own circuit and once we still have that we can just jump the hell out of here if it's a locator beacon. Even if they manage to shut down our flight controls, they can't stop us from moving,' she said.

'You are correct Tamara,' Urhan said.

'Screw it,' she sighed, entering her command codes.

There was a momentary flicker on the screen, then a face appeared, a face she had never seen before. It was man with a white beard and a coat that made him look like a lab technician.

'Hello Captain Cartwright,' said the man on the screen.

'Who the hell is that?' Chuck stared at the screen with a confused expression.

'Shhh!' said Tam.

'We've never actually met but I feel like I've known you my whole life,' said the man, 'my name is Doctor Eoin Tatum, I was a friend of your fathers and your uncle Rubin.'

Tam felt a knot in her stomach.

'We actually met once, a very long time ago, when you briefly lived with your uncle, but you were too young to remember.'

Tam felt herself grip the sides of her chair.

'I am not a good man, not someone you would have wanted to know nor someone with whom you should hold a high regard. I am, however, someone for whom you should listen to. My career was purely a scientific one and dedicated to unlocking the secrets of the STC molecule.'

'It was something that I believed the human race couldn't be bound to anymore, as did your uncle. We have been tethered for too long and we needed to stand on our own. So, for twenty-seven years, I disappeared, deep within the confines of our laboratory orbiting Saturn. We were close. Very close to unlocking its structure when there was an accident. An accident that gave rise to something unexpected, dangerous than anyone could have imagined, but also even more wondrous.'

Tatum paused.

'What the hell is he talking about?' said Chuck.

Tam ignored him, now gripped by every word.

'You might ask why I have contacted you and you alone given the circumstances? Well, in all likelihood, I am dead. But the accident is not. While your father was an honourable man, a decorated man who befell the strange fate that many of our ships have succumb to over the years, your Uncle, did not share his exploratory and righteous virtues.'

'No shit,' Tam muttered under her breath, rolling her eyes.

'Like all those bestowed with great power, the bounds of right and wrong become merged into a strange dichotomy. Where the mind becomes lost into the freedoms that it provides.'

Tam clenched her teeth.

'Two brothers, on such different paths,' he said, pausing again.

Tam shook her head, now feeling confused. Tatum looked away from the camera before returning his gaze, this time with a steely intent.

'There is young girl, on an escape pod, the locater beacon codes are embedded in this transmission,' he said with grit in his tone, 'I want you to pick her up.'

He paused.

'It is perhaps no mere accident that her fate is not dissimilar to yours.'

Tam began to feel tightness in her chest as the memory of being cocooned came flooding back. She felt small beads of sweat begin to form on her forehead.

'You have dedicated your life to the rescue of those in dire need. This is the direst need you are likely to face. Her name is Ona Mendel. She has been in my care since her father's death over fifteen years ago. She is the most closely guarded secret in human history, and I am sorry, but she is now your responsibility. I know of no-one else that I can trust. I know this to be true because of your record and I believe that you are indeed your fathers' daughter.'

He took a breath.

'She is running out of time Tamara; I have installed a dampening field on her escape pod so there is nobody else coming to her rescue. Only you have access to her location. Only you can save her.'

'Your uncle, the man who assigned me to this project, to Ona, never told me his real intent. I was to observe only. I cannot tell you, for fear that this transmission is somehow intercepted, how special this girl is Tamara but listen to me very carefully.'

Tam leaned towards the image.

'You cannot let her fall back into ESDA hands. You need to find a man called Biron Desaltas. He's on Thiral. The last I knew; he was living in the valleys on the northern continent. He'll take Ona from there. Get her to Thiral Tam, undetected. I know you can do this simple favour and in return I've encoded something in this message that may help you in the search I know you've spent your life pursuing.'

Tam's chest tightened once more.

'Something that may provide some answers to your own great loss. Perhaps a closure that so many have lived without.'

Tatum paused.

'The last log entries of the Arcturus. The ones not encoded into your own pod when you jettisoned from the ship. The classified entries and last data collected before your parents disappeared.'

Tam's mouth gaped open.

'Be gentle with her, Tamara, approach her with care. Protect her as you would your very own.'

The image suddenly cut out and the screen went black before switching back to the peaks and troughs of an incoming signal.

'The computer has a set of coordinates,' Chuck said, as he activated the navigational decoding software and began pinpointing the location.

Tam remained silent. She wasn't sure what to say. She began combing through the rest of the data received in the signal and sure enough, she found the file named ARCLOG. She didn't activate it.

'What are we doing here Cap?' Chuck said.

'Give me a minute,' Tam said, clearing the lump in her throat.

She looked down at her hands and noticed that they started shaking.

'Where is it?' she said softly.

Chuck took a breath.

'Two light years,' he said.

She looked behind to Urhan, 'you said, we have twenty-seven left?'

'Twenty-Seven molecules, that is correct Tamara,' Urhan confirmed.

She looked at Chuck. 'Load one up,' and grabbed the flight controls.

16

Arana

3.4 Light Years from the LAL Home World

The shuttlecraft was sleek in design, arrow shaped with reflective edges that gave it an almost imperceptible camouflaged effect as it descended quietly towards the landing pad. Edge placed his hands behind his back. He turned to Norr, who'd accompanied him on the Orion, and checked that his uniform and shoes were pristine. He wasn't entirely sure why. Norr was always turned out to perfection and at this particular juncture he didn't really give a shit what Diren thought of them, but old habits.

They were both standing on the rooftop of the New Colonial Nations building in the heart of the Arana forest. The temperatures on this world, which rotated about its star every thirty-one hours, was fairly temperate, if a little humid for his liking. The air was clean and the sky rich with crystal clear blue and violet hues. Humans were now in their fiftieth year on this newly claimed planet. Edge had an affinity to the world and in particular to a type of horse like mammal that the LAL called the Hux. Claimed by many who had settled there to be untameable. They were roughly 20% larger than Earth's biggest Shire horse and at least twice as powerful. Edge believed them to be magnificent creatures and had taken a particular interest in trying to do exactly that. Although he had yet to be successful.

He watched as the LAL shuttle extended its landing struts and cleared his throat as he waited for Premier Diren to emerge. As the door to the alien craft slid open, a small ramp descended onto the landing pad. Edge watched as a line of robed LAL began exiting. A procession of at least twenty in single file made their way towards them.

Diren's entourage circled Edge and Norr, a common practice when greeting the higher echelons of the LAL. A perfect shield to protect their supreme ruler in case of attack.

While there had never been a conflict between humans and the LAL, there had been some fringe factions that had at least threatened Diren. There were still factions who believed the LAL's motives were less than transparent, Edge being one of them. He'd always sensed that behind the calm austere of superiority that radiated through the pale skins of their saviours lay a thin guarded layer of distrust.

The tall, lean form of Premier Diren descended from the landing platform. He was considerably taller than most of the LAL Edge had ever known, and broader too. While the societal structures of much of their home world still remained somewhat of a mystery, their leadership caste was always physically larger than the STC Guardians and those of the science and other members who lived on Arana and the other human colonies.

It hadn't been the leadership caste who had made first contact with Earth all those years ago when it had been on the brink of extinction but members of the explorer caste, who were similar in shape and size to the STC Guardians. Diren stood at over seven feet and his muscular shoulders swayed in perfect unison with his long bare legs and arms. He wore a long open white robe that split in two just below where a naval should have been but wasn't. The protective circle of guardians split, stepping backwards to allow Diren to enter the protective circle. Diren stepped through the gap and approached Edge, whose neck began to crane upwards to make eye contact. Diren paused a few feet in front and peered down, it was almost impossible to tell at the best of times what was going on inside such an emotionless face. Edge placed his hand on his chest and bowed his head.

'Premier Diren,' he said.

Diren reciprocated with his long right arm.

'It does us good,' Diren said.

'It does indeed,' Edge said, raising his head, 'how was your journey?'

'The same as others,' Diren said.

'Welcome back to Arana, your presence honours us,' Edge said, trying his best adhere to at least some sort of diplomatic protocol.

Diren looked at Norr.

'I would like to speak privately Admiral,' he said.

Edge looked at Norr and gave him a stiff nod.

'Of course, if you will accompany me inside, we can have some privacy,' Edge said.

Edge motioned towards the set of glass doors that led inside a large circular rooftop observation deck which spanned around the building. Diren motioned to his security detail to wait for him, Edge did the same with Norr, who placed his hands behind his back and assumed a formal stance.

A pair of sliding doors opened, Edge gestured for Diren to enter and followed behind, sealing the transparent door behind him.

In the centre of the room lay a round wooden table carved from one of the local trees, whose wood was a bright crimson contrasted by pure white growth rings.

'May I get you something to drink?' Edge said, moving over to a drink's cabinet.

Diren tilted his head at the request.

'I know, you don't drink anything, it was merely a pleasantry as I felt like wetting my whistle,' Edge said, as he opened a bottle of Bourbon.

He poured himself a glass, not really caring if Diren joined him or not.

'Strange the habit of humans to consume liquids that inhibit their higher brain functions,' Diren said.

'I find many other things in the universe to be far stranger,' Edge replied, taking a sip, 'So, how would you like to handle the…'

'Where is the girl?'

Edge looked up at Diren, his luminescent eyes glaring down at him. A deathly silence descended into the room. Edge raised the glass to his mouth once more. He moved to the table and pulled out one of the chairs, taking a seat. He looked up at Diren.

'Have a seat,' he said.

If the game was up, Edge was going to control the outcome, it was the only way. He wasn't going to be bullied by the LAL anymore. It was perhaps only a matter of time before they found out anyway. Diren didn't move.

'Premier Diren, I really don't want to have to stare up at you all day, it gives me a strain in my neck and I'm not in the mood for silly games, so either take a seat, or get back on your shuttle and get the hell out of here.'

Diren's face was expressionless. There was a curious flicker in his eyes as all decorum and diplomatic formality was ejected from the situation. Much to Edge's surprise, Diren complied. He slid back one of the seats and gently lowered his large frame into it.

'What do you know?' Edge said.

'Everything,' Diren said, 'we know everything.'

'Enlighten me,' Edge said.

'Admiral, humanities attempt at harnessing our molecule and learning its secrets is something we've permitted as your technology is a thousand years away from even scratching the surface of its construction. We allow it because it gives a semblance of purpose. You humans like to think you're in control of your own destinies, when, in fact, that control is an illusion. Without it, your species seems to digress into a state of panic and conflict. The fight for reason and purpose is something we do not share with your species. We merely are.'

'Premier I'm not a philosopher,' Edge said.

'No, you are not, you are an instrument,' Diren said.

Edge smiled.

'An instrument?'

'A function and consequence of your societal structure that needs to believe you have all the answers. You are children,' Diren said.

Edge clenched his jaw.

'If you think so little of us, why did you save our race from extinction?' Edge demanded.

'Because we see much further than you,' Diren said, 'a purpose for you that is far greater than you can possibly imagine.'

'Then why not let us free?'

'You are not our prisoners,' Diren said.

'Aren't we?' Edge said, 'you're spoon feeding us, after all.'

'I do not understand.'

'What about the girl?' Edge sighed.

'That is a situation we cannot allow,' Diren said.

'So, this isn't about the star,' Edge said.

'We're beyond that now,' Diren said, 'she must be held accountable, but what you have done is far more severe.'

'We didn't do anything,' Edge said.

'You have merged a molecule with a human host,' Diren said.

'It was an accident, we don't know how it happened,' Edge said.

'Where is the girl?' Diren said.

'I don't know.'

Diren leaned back.

'That is unfortunate,' Diren said, removing something from inside his robe.

Edge straightened his shoulders as Diren placed a small silver disk on the table.

'Your hand please,' Diren instructed.

'Excuse me?'

'Place your hand on this please.'

Edge peered out of the glass windows to Norr.

'Close windows,' Diren said.

The glass surrounding the room frosted instantly, blocking out the outside world. Edge's instinct told him there was an immediate threat. He began to reach for his side arm when Diren lunged out, grabbing his wrist tightly.

Diren stood, lifting Edge out of the seat, and raising his entire body a few feet off the ground. Edge let out a painful growl as he dangled from Diren's powerful grip.

'What are you doing?' Edge snarled at the emotionless eyes, which now looked somewhat predatory.

Diren reached to the table and took the disk. He turned Edge around and slammed it onto his neck.

Edge felt a shockwave of pain explode in his head. He tried to scream but nothing came out. He felt something penetrate his skin. A thousand boiling needles made their way into the base of his skull, his shoulders, his back, his arms. It felt like a boiling liquid was filling up his entire body.

He had completely misjudged this. He was being assassinated, in cold blood.

The pain stopped. His mind felt heavy. Strange images began forming within. Languages he'd never heard before but now understood, his own sense of self began seeping away. His thoughts were being pushed downwards, somewhere dark. His vision changed. He could see more of everything. He felt light. Voices began filling his mind. Occupying every thought. His arm moved involuntarily upwards. Diren released his body back to the ground. He turned to face Diren. Calm now, controlled by something else. His thoughts were gone. Inhabited by something else. A thing that was now walking beside Diren towards the exit. He wasn't entirely dead or alive.

This new thing he had become walked out into the sunlight towards the others. He looked to the Norr thing and spoke.

'Contact the Lassen,' the new Edge said, 'I want to board her immediately.'

The Norr thing nodded as Diren's thoughts merged with his.

'They will come to you,' said Diren's voice.

The new Edge replied in his mind.

'I understand,' it said.

17

Tam glanced out of the window of her quarters and watched the bright colours of the STC distortion effects. The blue and green hues streaked past as they twisted and melded into the pocket of space-time the Massey Shaw was passing between. She turned back to the open file directory and sat on the small stool in front of the screen. She looked at the descriptor and paused, wondering whether now was the time to actually do this or not. She stared at the blinking file name 'Captains log' and pressed it. She leaned back as her pulse quickened. Within a few seconds of the files being accessed, the image of her father, Martin Edge, appeared. She immediately felt the sinking in her chest at the sight of the silver streaks in his hair. He was forty-three when she'd last seen him but had looked much older. The pressure of being in command of a cruiser had added ten years to him and he looked tired. He'd always looked tired, but those charismatic and focused blue eyes never let on that fact. His face was clean-shaven and thick hair swept neatly to one side. She remembered his soft but firm voice as the memories of him tucking her into bed seeped through her mind. She tried, mostly in view to ignore them as she listened.

'Captain's log, Arcturus, November 2, 2729,' he said.

Tam made a note of the date. It was nine days before the incident.

'We're now fifteen days into the exploration of the nebula. All ship operations are nominal. STC drive is operating within normal parameters and engineering reports that the problem with our aft thruster control units have now been repaired. I've put in a request to replace the driver coil assembly on the affected systems when we put into Arana for our next overhaul but have placed it as nonessential. Medical reports nothing out of the ordinary. A few cases of flu, one of the engineering staff sustained third degree burns while opening an electrical conduit but is expected to make a full recovery.'

Tam watched as he leaned back from the camera.

'For the record, I don't like keeping my crew in the dark; I wanted that noted on my log. My first officer is questioning the reasons behind this so-called exploration.'

Tam moved closer to the screen.

'We've been pushing the long-distance sensors now pretty hard and we've found nothing so far,' he said, looking away again.

Tam focused hard.

'The region of space we've been sending pulses out to still appears to be completely empty. I still don't fully understand why we can't just jump out there to see what the fuss is about. All this prodding just makes it feel like a fishing expedition without any bait. There isn't a single habitable star system within fifty light years of our position and this nebula story isn't gonna fly for much longer. I'm going to recommend to command that they just let me take the Arcturus direct to source. If there's anything out there that poses any threat that at least we'll know it.'

He paused again.

'My only concern is, regrettably, a personal one. I shouldn't have brought them along.'

Tam felt a pang in her stomach as the screen went black. There was a genuine look of regret in her father's eyes. She recognised it as fear.

'What the hell were you doing there, Dad?' she whispered to herself.

She flicked through the logs again to the next one. His face appeared again.

'Captain's log, Arcturus, November 6, 2729,' he said, appearing again, this time his face had the unmistakable look of a man who hadn't slept the night before, a five O'clock shadow graced his cheeks.

'Long range sensors picked up something at 05:23 this morning,' he said, this time with a sharp tone in his voice, 'readings are indeterminate at this time and imaging scanners aren't able to get a lock on whatever the object is. At first, we saw it was just a rogue comet, but its trajectory is on a direct course to intercept. I've change course three times in the last hour and each time the object has altered to match. H'reck just left my ready room with an odd request. Our LAL guardian has never interfered with mission parameters before and rarely comes to the bridge. He asked me to jump the ship away from these coordinates. I pressed him on it, but he wouldn't be specific. H'reck knows something that he's not telling me. I've never known him to approach me about mission specifics as that's not their way. The guardians have never, to my knowledge attempted to interfere with ship operations.'

Tam placed her hand on her mouth, already knowing what choice her father was about to make.

'I'm not going anywhere until I find out what that thing is, we didn't come all this way just to sit on our hands.'

Tam shook her head.

'Get out of there,' she whispered to the past, gritting her teeth to the point of pain.

'Whatever it is, it's under intelligent control. I'll have the STC drive on standby, but we need to get a reading on it. If this is what we think it is,' he paused again, 'then we need to see it.'

He paused again, looking away from the screen before looking back. Tam felt a connection she wasn't expecting. It was as if he was looking directly at her. She placed her hand on the monitor and couldn't help it anymore. Her eyes watered up.

'Dad,' she said, as a smile seemed appear on his face.

The screen went black. Tam lowered her gaze.

'What did you do?' she said, wiping her face and peering back at her own reflection in the screen.

The bleeping sound of the comm panel took her out of the moment. She pressed the answer button.

'Go,' she said.

'Cap we're almost there,' Chuck said.

Tam took a breath.

'On my way,' she said, disconnecting the call and looking once again to list of file names.

There was more to look at, so much more.

Flight Deck

Tam shook off the slight feeling of disorientation as the stars reappeared though the forward-facing windows.

'Report,' she said, staring out at the star field.

'Calculating,' Chuck said, 'we're right were we're supposed to be.'

There was a light humming sound as the SCT chamber, now empty, automatically withdrew itself from the main injection casing.

'Do a full scan,' Tam instructed.

'Already on it,' Chuck said, as he looked at the monitors, 'Got something.'

Tam placed her hands on the flight controls and activated the ships manoeuvring thrusters.

'Send it to me,' she said.

Chuck relayed the data to Tam's flight panel as she gripped both joysticks in her hands and followed the flight path indicated. She turned on the forward-facing lights of the ship with the flick of a switch and focused her eyes.

'There,' Chuck said, pointing out the window.

Tam saw Urhan take a step forward and lean down to look, she immediately saw what Chuck was pointing at as the powerful lights shed their glow onto the small craft. It was an ESDA escape pod all right, listing lazily in the dark with both its forward and aft beacons blinking red every few seconds. She fired the forward thrusters to slow their approach as she matched the rotation and attitude of the craft.

She watched the sensors carefully on her screen and locked her automatic docking beacon on the pod, letting the computer do the rest of the work. The Massey made contact with the pod and activated the airlock umbilicus.

'We're locked in,' Chuck said.

'You have the con,' she said, leaping out of her chair.

'You don't want me to come with you?'

'Stay here,' Tam said, 'you too Urhan, load up the chamber and any sign of trouble get us the hell out of here.'

She moved past Urhan and hit one of the comm panels on the wall

'Doctor Augustine, meet me at the main airlock immediately,' she said.

'On my way,' replied Augustine.

Air Lock

Tam approached the main airlock door; Augustine was already there waiting as the med bay was on the same deck.

'What do we have?' Augustine asked as she entered.

Tam peered through the window to the sealed pod hatch before looking back at her.

'Not sure yet, possibly one occupant. I don't know what sort of physical condition she's in but be prepared for anything,' Tam said.

'Understood,' Augustine said, checking the contents of her med kit before giving Tam the nod.

She activated the airlock pressurization and made sure the seal integrity was solid before opening the door and stepping through. Augustine followed closely behind. It was only a few steps to reach the hatch of the pod. As they approached, Tam pressed her face up against the circular porthole of the craft and peered inside. A thin layer of ice covered the glass making it hard to see. She looked back at Augustine.

'Ready?' she said.

Augustine nodded.

Tam then reached over and gripped the rod-shaped manual release, she then turned it counterclockwise before pulling it out completely. The door hissed before popping outwards. She pulled it back and pushed it to one side, peering into the pod. It seemed empty. She stepped inside slowly. The air felt cold. She stopped suddenly as she saw movement out of the corner of her eye under the main flight control centre at the front of the craft. She peered down and saw two small feet.

'Hello?' she said softly.

She saw Augustine move forward and raised her hand to stop her. She leaned forward before slowly kneeling and peering under the main panel. She saw long dark hair covering the face of a girl who had her arms wrapped tightly around her knees.

'Ona?' Tam whispered.

She didn't respond. Tam lowered the tone of her voice to a whisper.

'Ona, it's ok, my name is Tamara Cartwright, I'm here to help you, I'm a friend of Eoin Tatum, he sent me to find you,' she said.

Tam saw the girl tilt her head to the side and saw an eye look towards her. She didn't look scared, far from it, there was something akin to recognition in her eyes.

'Are you hurt?' Tam said.

She saw Ona shake her head slowly.

'Are you sure?'

Ona nodded her head as she looked up at Augustine.

'This is Doctor Augustine, she just wants to make sure that you're okay, you're in no danger I can promise you that. Are you hungry?'

Ona shook her head slowly.

'Okay, I'm going to take a step towards you would that be all right?'

Ona nodded. Tam remained low and began her approach.

'Not nice to be stuck out here all by yourself is it?' Tam said, 'trust me, I know all about it.'

Ona shook her head. Tam approached and sat down on the floor next to her, never taking her eyes off her.

'I like your hair,' she complimented.

Ona raised her head slightly, revealing more of her face. She had soft sallow skin and was pretty but the dark circles under her eyes told Tam she hadn't slept in a long time.

'Sorry if the noise scared you,' Tam said, 'that was just my ship locking on. She's called the Massey Shaw, she's a rescue ship.'

Ona glanced upwards towards the forward-facing windows of the pod.

'Can you see her?'

Ona looked back down and nodded.

'She's a beauty, isn't she?'

Ona shrugged.

'Well, I guess you can't see much of her from here, I can show you around, if you like?' Tam said.

'You will,' Ona replied.

Tam tilted her head at the odd response.

'Is it okay if the doc just runs a quick scan?'

Ona shook her head.

'No?' Tam said.

Ona shook her head again.

'That's okay, we can do that later if you feel like it. Listen you have nothing to worry about,' Tam said, 'Ona, you're going to have to trust me,' she said, extending her hand, 'can you do that?'

Ona looked at Augustine before turning back to Tam and slowly nodding. She extended her hand and took Tam's who lightly grasped it.

'Come on,' Tam said, gently standing.

The trio then made their way out of the escape pod and back through the air lock.

18

Massey Shaw
Med Bay

'You're shivering. Are you cold?' said Augustine to Ona as she stood next to the bio bed.

Ona shook her head and looked up at Tam who was standing next to her, close enough to let her know she was protected.

'We'll get you some fresh clothes,' Augustine said, nodding to a nurse to get something else for Ona to wear.

'Would you mind if I just run this scanner around you Ona? It won't hurt a bit,' Augustine said.

Ona nodded.

'Okay then,' Augustine said.

'Everything is going to be fine Ona, we're just making sure you didn't get sick while you were in the pod that's all,' Tam reassured her.

The doors to the med bay opened and Chuck walked in. Ona looked at his large frame and took a step back, eyes widening in fear. Tam motioned to Chuck to stay where he was.

'Ona that's a friend of mine, his name is Chuck, he's the one who found you. You don't have to be scared of him,' Tam said.

Ona took a sidestep towards Tam, resting her shoulder next to hers. Tam nodded to Chuck to approach. He smiled at Ona.

'Welcome aboard, I'm Chuck, oh wait she already told you that… right,' he said, smiling.

One looked blankly at him.

'Tough crowd,' he said, looking at Tam.

'Report,' Tam said.

'All systems on the pod were all optimal, what do you want to do with it?'

Tam thought about it.

'Shut her down, all systems, uncouple the Massey and destroy it,' she finally said.

Chuck nodded and turned to leave.

'Chuck, before you do, download anything from the onboard computer, there might be some information we need,' Tam said, hoping there was something on her parent's disappearance.

'Understood Cap, nice to meet you Ona, maybe I'll see you later,' he said, before turning and leaving the med bay.

Tam turned back to Augustine who was looking at her scanner and frowned. She looked up at Tam and flicked her eyes to the right.

'Ona would it be okay if you waited here for a minute?' Tam asked.

Ona nodded and sat on the edge of the bio bed while Tam and Augustine went into her office. Tam gently slid the door behind her.

'Well?' she asked

Augustine pulled her hair out of her headband and tied it back up.

'Well, this is odd,' Augustine said, moving the data from her hand scanner to the main screen on the wall. A host of biometric data appeared.

'She's physically fine, there's no question about that. She's a little underweight but within norms, heart rate, blood pressure, and reflexes all fine,' Augustine said.

'Okay, so she's normal… what's the story then?'

'It's her blood,' said Augustine.

'What about it?'

'Oxygenation is normal, haemoglobin, platelets all fine…'

'Doc…'

'Her red blood cells are emitting some sort of radiation.'

Tam unfolded her arms.

'Don't worry, it doesn't seem to be effecting the surrounding area, I've checked three times,' Augustine said.

'I don't understand. What sort of radiation?'

'Well, here's the weird thing,' Augustine looked up at the data. 'Look at this,' she manipulated the display with her hand and brought up an image.

Tam looked at the readings, 'Okay?' she rose an eyebrow.

Molecular biology wasn't her strong suit.

'Where have you seen this waveform before?'

Tam took a step towards the screen.

'That's…'

'The decay signature you get whenever we purge the STC waste into space every time we use it,' Augustine replied.

'That's impossible,' Tam took a closer look.

There was no doubt.

'Yes, it is,' Augustine said, 'yet there it is. Who is this girl?' Augustine wondered.

'Is she in any danger?' Tam said.

'Probably,' Augustine said, 'quite frankly, I don't understand how she's not dead already. What we know is that any human contact with any part of this element is fatal. I recommend we quarantine her fully. I think Urhan should look at this. I don't know how long that material will stay in her system and if there's even a slight chance that some of it gets loose on this ship then it's lights out for all of us,' Augustine said.

Tam nodded firmly. 'Right, where do you want her?'

'The radiation lab on deck two is the only place with enough shielding to give us a chance if something goes wrong,' Augustine said, 'I'll put a bed and supplies in immediately.'

'It's your call, Doc,' Tam said, 'have it set up and I'll bring her down.'

Tam slid the door open to the med bay when she was suddenly hit by a blast of air that nearly knocked her off her feet. The sounds of glass bottles and instruments crashing and falling on the ground filled her ears. It was like something had suddenly exploded. A strange snapping sound followed as she covered her eyes and then everything went quiet. She turned to look inside the med bay. It was a mess. A nurse was laying on the ground next to the wall. She felt a pair of hands under her armpits as Augustine pulled her up on her feet.

'Are you all right?' she asked.

Tam nodded and looked around the room for Ona, she was nowhere to be seen.

19

IGO WAR

Protector Crick materialized on the main docking bay and looked upwards at the collector ships as they descended through the artificial ionosphere of IGO WAR. He was met by Raz, The Keeper of War and general of all the harvested.

The planet, a construction that he himself and his progenitors had designed and overseen thousands of cycles ago, was truly a sight to behold. A sharpened blade that had cut through the universe with deadly and unstoppable lethality. While the Royal's had sat within their golden planetary palaces, it had been Prime and War that had granted them this sublime existence.

Crick watched as the centurion ships came low over the silver horizon. He enjoyed watching them approach. New blood, alien aggressor blood within their bowels, so arrogant in their own self-beliefs, so bold as to try and extend their pitiful reach into a galaxy that was theirs. The hulls of the centurions glistened from the bright lights of endless processing plant facilities that stretched as far as the IGO vision could see. Thousands of shining cylinders that breached the surface of IGO War to the underground conversion areas.

Raz approached and spoke.

'Protector, what news of the sowing from Royal?' Raz said.

'None,' replied Crick, not believing a word.

The ties to Royal and War ran far deeper than Prime. War had the sword that was used to wield against the Primers for far too many generations by The Royal's. The peace between their peoples were now as old as some of their closest stars; it did not break that bond. Raz knew something that Crick didn't. War always knew something that Prime didn't.

Raz motioned for Crick to follow him to the platform that would bring them to the underground processing facility.

Crick watched Raz's artificial lower limbs carry him towards the platform. A loss he had suffered against the Roona beast. It had been foolish, all told, but the story of his victory against IGO's most ferocious predator had made him a legend and granted him the personal protection of the Queen herself. Crick could not touch Raz, not now, not ever.

He began his descent as the elevator sped swiftly down underground. When it finally came to a rest, he stepped off the platform and moved smoothly down the dimly lit corridor lined with rock on either side. At the end of the passageway lay a giant circular door that towered far above his head. Two guards stood at either side. They approached the interface and Raz formed a long tentacle, waving it in the air. Beams of light spread over his body and the release mechanisms unhooked. The giant door made a rumbled as it rolled back. The ground beneath shook with the weight of the mighty entrance.

As it rolled away, he was greeted with the true might of IGO War—the future of the IGO. Crick moved through the entrance and scanned the surrounding area. Long walkways stretched out in all directions. The giant cavern was a city in of itself. Hundreds of thousands of structures embedded into the rock face like nests of the Zirum wasp on IGO prime. There was as many as stars in the night sky it seemed. He began to walk through the heart of the processing centre. He moved to the side of the walkway and looked down. The view from below was almost a mirror image. There were millions of them, still not enough, but almost. He could feel the static in the air from the power generators. The surface of his skin felt like it was being charged. He relished in the sensation as he moved forward towards the depositing centre where the docked ships were now unloading their catches.

He branched off the main walkway into a wide-open area, which was a bustle of activity. The other members of the warring tribes stopped to great him by flashing the blue stripes along their backs in unison, he reciprocated as he looked up at the various transparent tubes. Inside, the black cocoons holding the harvested beings floated downwards, branching off to different locations throughout the cavern based on their genetic profile.

'Are they here?' said Crick to Raz.

'Momentarily,' said Raz, as he looked up at the transparent tube.

'I wish to examine them.'

'Yes, Protector,' Raz agreed, as he turned and relayed the instruction to Tek.

They stood in silence, watching as the black cocoons flowed steadily down the transport tubes.

'They are here,' Tek said, as he waved a long tentacle in the air bringing up a floating interface which halted the descent of one of the black cocoons. He looked to a row of foot soldiers and told them to surround the gooey looking mass. They did as instructed, aiming their weapons directly at it. Crick began to approach it.

'I would not get too close Protector,' Raz called.

Crick reverberated a strong high-pitched squeaking sound informing Raz, in no uncertain terms, that he would not be told what to do by anyone.

Raz lowered his head in submission. Crick continued over to the cocoon, he turned to the soldiers.

'Step back,' he instructed.

They immediately obeyed. He turned to Tek.

'Release it,' said Crick.

'As you wish,' replied Tek with a shrug.

Tek moved to a control panel and removed a device. He moved it over the cocoon before replacing it on the control surface where it seamlessly sunk back inside like liquid. He turned and looked at the cocoon as it slowly began unravelling as if held together by millions of little fibres all loosening their grip at once. The fibres fell neatly on the ground on all sides, revealing the incarcerated being inside.

Crick watched as the bipedal thing rolled onto the ground. It remained there, unmoving, and unconscious. The IGO watched, waiting for the oxygen levels to be sufficient to recuperate the odd-looking creature. Crick took a small step towards it as it began to move. It opened its primitive eyes located at the front of its cranial structure and moved them upwards to Crick. He noted the creature's heart rate. It began shivering as its body temperature adjusted to what was probably lethal to its species given enough exposure. White veils of carbon dioxide began billowing out of its feeding and communication orifice as it slowly became aware of its surroundings. Crick waited for the creature to react. He only had to wait a short while as it suddenly recoiled, emitting a high-pitched noise and crawling backwards on its bipedal walking appendages.

Its small visual aids grew wide as its darted its look around its alien environment. It began shaking vigorously as the IGO looked on with both curiosity and amusement at the odd way the small-framed thing scurried about. It began emitting more noise as it rubbed its higher appendages, apparently now aware of how cold its body temperature was getting. It pushed itself back against one of the control panels and crossed its appendages, turning its head around looking in all directions. Crick took another step closer as the being crouched into what looked like a defensive position.

'Holding clamp,' Crick said to Tek, not taking his attention off the being.

'Of course,' said Tek.

A long coiling arm descended from above and with a snap of its claw, quickly clamped its grip around the mid-section of the being, lifting it off the ground into mid-air. It emitted another screeching sound, obviously in pain. Crick stepped closer and watched as the red fluid that sustained these types of life forms began flowing from its mid-section. The high-pitched sounds became fainter. The small optical receivers now trained firmly on him.

'Remove the garments,' Crick said to Tek, who obeyed.

A sharp pair of smaller claws emerged from the holding clamps and swiftly began slicing through the outer coverings of the alien thing until all that was left was its bare skin, which was now shivering uncontrollably. Crick looked at the weak skeletal structure as all sounds from the creature had subdued to a whim-perish cry. He approached the being and extended a tentacle. Placing it next to its cranial structure, infusing it with his essence so that he could communicate with it.

'You understand?'

The biped pointed his vision holes towards him. It moved its head up and down.

'What are you?'

'Victor... Victor Pollard,' said the thing, 'don't kill me.'

'That is what you are called? What are you?'

The Victor thing looked at him, wincing in pain.

'Where is Amita?' said the Victor thing.

'Is that your planet?'

The Victor thing riled as the clamp on his back dug in through his flesh.

'What are you?'

'You think you can just exist?'

'What?' replied the Victor

'Little things, creeping ever closer,' said Crick.

The Victor didn't respond

'Where are you from?'

Victor remained silent.

'Where?' Crick repeated, infusing the things brain with an acidic substance that would begin dissolving its tissue momentarily.

The Victor thing emitted a howling sound and began writhing about. Crick turned to Tek who increased the strength of the gripping claws. Victor screamed but still ignored their questions.

'Extract him,' Crick said to Tek, releasing his bond with it.

Tek turned back to the control panel.

Crick looked closer into the light sensing holes at the front of the being. Thin lines of water began streaming from them and they had turned a reddish hue. It was beginning to shake. The metal on the grappling arm began to split and reform, part of it still holding firmly around the mid-section of the Victor and the other section altering its shape, splitting into layers of twisting finger like protrusions which gently wrapped themselves around the top of Victor's head.

He screamed one final time, as the top of his cranium was sliced cleanly open. The perfectly cauterized wound running a circle around his skull just above his eyebrows. His brain, now exposed from the surface of his head was held in place as the tendrils dug their way around the outer edges of soft tissue, burrowing beneath the back of his skull. He began to make a strange gurgling noise as his eyes rolled backwards and the muscles in his body became limp. With a smooth jerking motion, the gripping mechanism lifted upwards, separating the being's brain and spinal column from the rest of its body, which fell to the ground, lifeless. The grappling mechanism then held the bloodied cognitive centre and all its nerve endings in mid-air as it swung it over to a containment tank where it was plunged into the nutrient fluid.

Crick moved over to the control panel, stepping around the remains of the now hollowed out thing, which was now being picked up and removed by another grappler. He accessed the interface and began scanning though the imagery stored within the chemical recesses of the main processing organ. As the memory centres of this thing began flashing across the image processors, he wondered what it was feeling, if it was feeling anything at all. It was still very much alive, floating within its own experiences, unable to communicate or probably even recognize what had just happened to it. It was a minor curiosity. He saw these beings on home world, saw others like him, saw fields and water and buildings and space faring ships. He turned to Raz.

'I want to know everything,' he said to him

Raz nodded.

'Should I continue the harvest with the rest or extract?' said Raz.

'Continue the Harvest, time grows short.'

20

'Nothing?' Tam said, looking over at Chuck.

Chuck shook his head.

She looked at the long-range scans. 'No anomalies, no ships, no sign of anything, what the hell? Did she just spontaneously combust?' Chuck said.

'That is highly unlikely,' Urhan said from behind him.

Chuck sighed and flashed him a look of annoyance.

'The internal scans of the medical bay left a fractal space time effect,' Urhan said, looking up at one of the computer screens behind Tam.

'Meaning?' Tam replied.

'I am not entirely sure at this time,' Urhan replied.

'Who the hell is that girl?' Chuck said.

Tam shook her head. It had been thirty minutes since she'd vanished from the med bay without a trace. Tam turned her chair around to face Urhan.

'How did those readings appear on her bio scan?' she said.

Urhan didn't answer right away, he continued to look at the readouts on his screen.

'Urhan,' Tam pressed.

He gazed down at her.

'I do not know Tamara,' he replied, 'it should not be possible, human DNA would be broken down within nanoseconds of coming into direct contact with any part of the molecule.'

'So now what?' Chuck said.

'I don't...' Tam started.

'Med bay to Captain,' came Augustine's voice over the comm system

'Go,' Tam said, clicking the respond control.

'You better get down here Tam, she's back,' said Augustine.

Tam leaped out of her seat.

'Chuck stay here, Urhan you're with me,' she ordered as she made a dash for the door.

Med Bay

Tam entered through the sliding door of sickbay to see Augustine standing next to a bio bed and, sure enough, there was Ona in the flesh, laying on her side. She was shivering. She approached Augustine. Ona was taking short shallow breaths. She was still wearing the same clothes, her hair looked like it had ice crystals at the tips and her lips were blue. She had a look in her eye as she met Tam's gaze. An odd look of deflated resignation. It was a look of defeat, powerlessness.

'She has severe hyperthermia,' Augustine said, as one of the nurses adjusted the heat blanket so that it came up over Ona's ears and over her head.

Tam turned to Urhan who was watching the bio readouts on the screen above the bed.

'Tell me what happened,' Tam said to Augustine.

'I was over there,' Augustine pointed to a locker, 'just putting away some instruments when there was this cracking sound, followed by a blast of air and then she popped into existence. Wherever she was, it was cold, very cold, another minute and she'd be dead.'

'Can she talk?' Tam said, looking down and feeling a strange sympathy towards the girl.

There was something in those eyes.

'Not right now, I need another hour to stabilize her,' Augustine said, turning to Urhan, 'what do you make of it?'

Urhan glanced at her. 'May I see the bio scans you took upon her arrival Doctor?'

'Of course,' she turned to one of the nurses, 'I'll be back. Notify me of any change immediately.'

The nurse nodded.

'Come on,' she said, indicating for them both to follow her into her office.

Tam leaned over to Ona and placed her hand on the bio bed.

'You're gonna be okay,' she whispered.

Ona met her eyes.

The trio went into Augustine's office and she brought up the data on the wall screen.

Urhan stepped towards it, his head moving gently from side to side as he read the data.

'Well, there it is,' Augustine said.

'Urhan?' Tam said.

'This isn't possible,' Urhan said.

'What is it?' Tam said, stepping closer to him.

'Doctor, may I access your computer? I would like to take a closer look at this,' he ignored Tam.

Augustine put her arm out gesturing him to go ahead. 'Please,' she said.

Urhan began tapping lightly on the control panel, bringing up a visual rendering of the microscopic cellar data on Ona's body.

'I had not thought this possible,' Urhan said, looking at an array of what looked like clusters of DNAs on the screen.

Tam sighed in frustration, wanting to know what the hell was going on.

'There,' Urhan said, pointing one of his long grey fingers at a pinpoint of blue light.

'There what?' Tam asked.

'Tamara, this girl,' Urhan turned to her, 'has an STC molecule inside her body.'

Tam's eyes widened, 'She what?' she looked back up at the screen.

'There's no doubt about it.'

'That's not possible,' Tam said, bewildered, 'we'd all be dead.'

'Yes, ordinarily, I would tend to agree, however, it is there, and it is contained,' Urhan said.

'How?' Augustine asked.

'I must report this to the home world,' Urhan said.

'Are you out of your mind?' Augustine glared at him.

'Doctor would you excuse us?' Tam said, looking at a shocked Augustine.

She nodded and left the pair alone.

'Are you out of your mind?' Tam tried to hide the annoyance in her voice.

'Tamara, we are in great danger,' Urhan said.

'Yes, I know that Urhan, half the galaxy is now hot on our tails and you want to give away our position?'

'Tamara, integration with a biologic and an STC molecule could have profound consequences for the universe, we must think above ourselves.'

'What the hell are you talking about? She's a human being, who needs our help, I'm not turning her over to anyone until I find out what's going on. You are NOT to contact anyone, do you understand?' Tam said, injecting anger into her voice.

She came to the realization that it was a bi product of her frustration over Urhan getting her into all this shit in the first place.

'Tamara, the molecule was never intended for fusion with human tissue, the risk is…'

'Yes, the risk is the end of the universe, I know Urhan, you've given me this exact speech a thousand times now. Believe me, I know it off by heart,' Tam said, folding her arms.

'My responsibility goes far beyond that of which you can understand Tamara.'

Tam sighed, turning her back on Urhan and leaned against Augustine's desk. 'Urhan, how is it possible that a human has an STC molecule floating around in their body?'

'She must be taken to LAL home world where we can examine her.'

'No way,' Tam said.

'Your behaviour is puzzling to me Tam, you are the Captain of a rescue ship, are you not? You cannot help her while we remain, as you say, at large. The equipment on board this ship is limited in its capacity to perform the diagnostic of the human that is required. Why would you not allow her to be in the best possible environment for the maximum chance for her survival?'

Tam noticed Urhan's tilted head and knew that he was genuinely puzzled by her actions.

'Because there's more to this, Urhan. I want to know where she's been, I want to know what sort of experiments were being done to her and want to know if there are any more,' Tam insisted.

'That is not your purview Tamara,' Urhan said.

'My what?'

'You are deviating from your function.'

'We do that now and again.'

'May I make an observation?'

'Do I have a choice?'

'I believe you are letting your ill feelings towards your Uncle cloud your judgement in this matter,' Urhan told her.

Tam felt agitation creep into her stomach. 'What have you learned from us from your observations?'

'A great deal.'

'What have you learned about loyalty?'

'That you consider it to be a highly valuable trait.'

'Just as you are loyal to the guardianship of the molecule and to the protection of the fabric of the galaxy, we are to each other,' Tam reminded him.

'The presence of this girl, and what has been done to her seem to go against that principal,' Urhan said, 'not to mention Captain Deangelo's response to your escape.'

Tam was stumped by the comment, though she wouldn't admit it.

'Urhan you are either with us or against us,' Tam paused, 'it's that simple.'

Urhan looked away before turning his large eyes back to Tam. 'I will do what I can to get you the answers that you require, she would be better contained if she were to be placed in my quarters. The shielding around it should be sufficient, although not guaranteed to contain a breach long enough for you to evacuate the ship.'

'Okay, then let's do that,' Tam agreed, hoping that his loyalty was true.

'Where are you going to take her?'

'Thiral.'

21

The Lassen

Captain Deangelo sat in the centre seat on the bridge, his mind was too distracted that he hadn't heard Lefebvre asking him a question. It had been three days and still nothing and now they were waiting for 'The Tank' himself to come aboard. Something Deangelo could have done without.

He turned to her, 'What?'

She gave him an odd look.

'The Orion will be within visual range in four minutes,' she said.

'Thank you, Lieutenant,' he said.

She gave him another look. One he didn't like. One which showed she had something on her mind and didn't want to say it out loud in front of the whole crew.

'Not now,' he said, lowering his voice so that the rest of the bridge couldn't hear it.

Tamara Cartwright was no fool, he'd known that the minute he'd laid eyes on her in the bar affectionately known as, Mulligan's Irish Pub, on Arana. The first official off-world Irish bar and a favourite among ESDA crew and colonists alike. The quaint timber interiors carved from the surrounding alien trees had given the inside of the structure an old-fashioned homely feel. He'd caught her eye as she'd walked in a few days before the Lassen had been due to depart on a survey mission to a star a couple of light years away. He had been sitting with Lefebvre at a small table and was about to finish up when she'd entered. A ray of light from the setting sun had hit the side of her cheek in such a way it was if her eyes were actually sparkling. She was with a large guy with a beard, enough to put any man off from approaching her but after he overheard someone say it was her first officer, he sent her over a drink.

She'd smiled at him, thanking him for it and downed it in one go. He'd found her funny, intelligent and beautiful. He'd sensed there were cracks insider her, a rebellious streak held together with practice and polish. She tore through his own shields and they had just clicked.

And for one whole week, he'd been happy. She'd snuck out in the middle of the night, no word, no goodbye, nothing, normally it would have been the other way around. She'd gotten to him and he hated her for it. Or rather that's what he told himself. His rather unusual fumbling of letting her get away seemed to suggest otherwise. Something that hadn't gone unnoticed.

They had given her a rescue ship because she was smart, quick thinking and was serious on risks that needed to be taken. He wondered how many hearts she'd gone through in her life. His own included.

'The Orion, coming up on the port bow,' Lefebvre interrupted his thoughts, 'the Admiral wishes for you to meet him at the airlock.'

Deangelo took a breath. Whatever this was all about wasn't good. There was a very real chance 'The Tank' was here to personally rip the rank insignia off his shoulders and eject him out the nearest airlock.

He looked at Lefebvre and smiled, 'You have the con,'

~ ~ ~

Deangelo stood outside the airlock, his hands laced neatly behind his back as he waited for the pressure indicators to equalize. The airlock door swung back. Edge was standing next to someone Deangelo didn't know. He looked like security detail by the size of him, but he wore Lieutenant stripes on his shoulder so Deangelo reckoned it was an attaché from Earth.

He saluted Edge, who returned the gesture.

'Admiral welcome aboard,' Deangelo said.

Edge and Norr exchanged a look. They moved their gazes in unison back towards Deangelo.

'Take me to the bridge,' Edge instructed.

'Of course,' Deangelo said without hesitation.

He turned his back to the paid and led them through the ship to the nearest elevator. The trio entered and doors sealed shut behind them.

'How was your trip Admiral?'

Edge didn't answer. Deangelo's wrist comm chirped. He raised it.

'Go ahead,' he said, feeling a sense of discomfort at the odd behavior on display.

Either Edge was too furious to speak in public of there was something else amiss.

'Captain, it's Lefebvre, the Orion is requesting permission to disembark,' she said.

Deangelo looked to Edge.

'Stand by,' Deangelo said, 'you're staying aboard sir?'

Edge glared at him, turning to Norr briefly.

'We are Captain,' he said.

Something was very wrong.

'Permission granted,' Deangelo said, 'the Admiral and I are on our way to the bridge.'

Deangelo was about to ask Edge something when Norr hit the controls of the lift. It jerked to a halt. Norr and Edge turned to face Deangelo, whose instinct was telling him that this was beyond a simple dressing down. He was in danger here. Edge glared into his eyes.

'We need to begin,' Edge said.

'I'm sorry sir, I don't understand,' Deangelo said.

'You are about to,' Edge replied.

Edge's mouth opened wide and something began coming out of it. It looked like metallic spiders' legs. Deangelo reached for the comm system but it was too late. Whatever was inside Edge's mouth, had leapt out of hit onto Deangelo's face.

He felt a sharp pain in the back of his neck and the world fell away.

22

The Massey Shaw
Urhan's Quarters

Ona stared at the long thin alien. Eoin had shown her pictures of these things, but she'd never seen one this close. She was sitting in the corner of the room, her arms wrapped tightly around her bent knees, regarding Urhan as he spun the hologram around with his hand, a representation of his home world. She was lost, again, surrounded by strangers. He looked down at her. She looked curiously at his striking green almond eyes. They were beautiful.

'That is where I am from, can you see?'

Ona nodded.

'Have you seen this planet before?'

Ona shook her head. Urhan turned his gaze back to the planet and pushed out from the image. Several moons materialized into the floating field of view.

'These are our moons,' Urhan said, pointing to one of them, 'this one is called G'narn.'

He zoomed in on the rocky world. Ona tiny pinpoints of light that filled it.

'That's where my life began,' said Urhan, 'underground near the moons core,' he glanced down at her. 'Do you remember where your life began?'

Ona looked past him as if trying to reconcile the question, 'Earth,' she said.

'Yes, I believe that to be true,' Urhan said, 'what do you remember from that time?'

'Time?'

'Yes.'

Ona regarded him but stayed silent.

'I found that trust plays a large part in humans when it comes to revealing things about themselves. You do not trust me. Would that be correct?'

Ona tilted her head and bit her lip.

'That is perfectly understandable,' Urhan said, 'considering what has been done to you.'

'What?'

'You do not know?'

Ona didn't answer as Urhan deactivated the floating visuals.

'It would seem that my attempts on making you feel comfortable have failed, and for that you must accept my apology, Ona. Let me start from the very beginning and perhaps we can find another way for you to trust me,' Urhan said.

He moved gracefully over to a wall panel that slid open, revealing something in a packet. The exterior of the material seemed to dissolve in his hand as he opened his mouth wide, revealing sharp triangular teeth, and released the gelatin like substance into his mouth.

'I would offer to let you try it, but it would kill you instantly.' He paused, 'I am afraid,' he said.

Ona smiled.

'What is amusing?'

Ona shook her head, 'Oh, you were being serious.'

'Yes.'

'Never mind,' said Ona, 'do you like living with us? With humans I mean?'

'That is a very interesting question,' Urhan said, 'it has several answers.'

'How so?'

'Well, it is my duty to be amongst them.'

'Your duty?'

'Tell me Ona, what do you know about the STC molecule?'

She shrugged. 'I have never heard of it.'

'Never?'

'Never.'

'That is most curious,' said Urhan.

'What is it?'

Urhan moved closer to her. She flinched.

'I mean you no harm, Ona,' he said, moving sideways and tapping a panel on the side wall, which then flipped down to reveal an array of glass tubes, each filled with different coloured liquids.

He took two of the tubes, one filled with a blue liquid, the other crystal clear, and placed them in a little holder. He then took out a dish and added a small amount of both liquids before replacing the containers. Ona looked at the two mixtures as they repelled each other as if they were two molten positive and negatively charged magnets. They swirled around each other in beautiful synchronicity. Ona began to smell something both soothing and strangely intoxicating. Her muscles relaxed. A blissful sense of calm descended all around her. A fog began lifting from her mind as she no longer felt the drag of the exhaustion from the last several days. She felt rejuvenated, strong, and fresh.

'This may help you,' Urhan said, 'the healing fluids bring clarity and rest when they are needed the most.'

'What's happening?' she asked, feeling the effects as she began to relax.

'Give it some time, the effects can be quite pronounced, but you should begin to feel at one with yourself shortly,' Urhan said.

Urhan seemed to be glowing, his skin becoming iridescent. The world fell away, only Urhan remained, in a pure white space that seemed to bend and flex all around her. The emptiness was replaced with something Ona had seen in her dreams. She found herself standing in a room full of strange equipment, flashing lights and lots of people rushing about. She felt different, smaller somehow. She looked down at her hands. They were tiny. The pleats on her little white dress gently swaying under little legs. She looked around a familiar place, people were shouting, a red pulsing light overhead casting a sense of emergency into the environment. She felt fear. She looked at the strange alien, whose name was Urhan.

'Where's daddy?' she asked it.

It did not answer.

In her left arm, a soft brown bear, his name was 'Tigger'. One of his eyes was missing but she didn't care. She wouldn't let anyone pry him from her fingers long enough for it to be replaced. He'd been her companion through the long periods of time when her father had been working, which seemed to be every waking moment. She heard someone shout a name.

'We're losing it David!' came a scream.

David

That was her father's name. She was standing in front of a large metal pipe that stretched out as far as her eye could see. It was glowing a strange blue and making a hum that seemed to intensify with every passing moment. She wasn't supposed to be there. He had told her to stay put in another room behind a large window, but she'd snuck in, bored and tired. She wanted to talk to her Daddy. She'd been there for hours and the grownups had been so busy they hadn't noticed her slip through the large metal door. The men and women rushing about all wore white trousers and shirts. She heard a voice, a familiar voice, shouting at her from somewhere across the huge hanger.

'Ona run!' it shouted.

She heard a large bang. She looked up at the gargantuan pipe in front of her and saw it split apart. A blinding blue light exploded from within. The outer shell cracked open like an egg.

'Ona!' she heard a voice say, as she was engulfed in fire and pain. She screamed in agony. She felt her heart stop, unable to breath as her muscles froze. She saw a blinding light and felt as though her skin was melting off her bones as the scene dissolved away to the strange white place, the only thing now in front of her was Urhan. The pain was gone.

'You remember this?' Urhan said quietly.

'That was me,' she told Urhan.

'It would seem so.'

'What happened to my father?' she asked him, feeling a tingle at the base of her spine, 'oh no, it's happening.'

Urhan reached out his long arm and gently took her hand as she felt a cold wave spread through her. The strange white space vanished; her mind began to clear as she felt herself falling.

A split second later, she felt her body land on something soft. Dizziness followed. The world around her came back into focus. She felt warm sand under her fingers and the sounds of lapping waves nearby. Cold blue light blanketed the surrounding beach she was now laying on. She looked up and saw three large moons overhead, a black sky lit up with a billion stars. She saw Urhan, laying on his side, also looking up at the night's sky.

'I'm sorry.'

'Well,' he said, as they both gazed out across the moonlit ocean that lay before them, 'how interesting.'

23

Tam's Quarters

Tam sat back against the window and admired the blending colours in the distance as they spread across the universe. She crossed her legs and took a sip of the warm tea she'd just poured herself before activating the wall panel.

She took a breath, 'begin recording.'

The computer chirped; a blinking light let her know it was ready.

'Hi mama,' she said, 'sorry I haven't been in touch in a while. I've been a little busy.'

She took another sip.

'I'm in a little trouble here to be honest,' she said, 'I was in jail for a bit, so that's new.'

She smiled.

'I don't think this is exactly what you had planned for me. There's no easy way to say this but I'm pretty much a fugitive.' She raised her glass, 'so, cheers to that ay?'

The blank screen stared back at her.

'I guess I inherited your stubborn self-righteousness.'

She paused.

'Sorry, that wasn't fair, I didn't mean that. What I meant was that I inherited your pursuit of the truth, no matter what. I'm just not as good at it as you are.'

She swirled the liquid around in the glass.

'I don't think I'm strong enough for this,' she said, 'truth be told, I'm tired. Tired of saving strangers.'

She rubbed the bridge of her nose and ran her finger over the screen, bringing up a star chart littered with little red dots placed over it. With another flick of her finger she bought the stars, in holographic form, off the screen and began swirling them in the air with her finger.

'It's endless,' she whispered, 'an atom of a needle in a haystack the size of the universe.'

'And now they want to kill me for it.'

She flicked the floating hologram back towards the screen where it disappeared. She lowered her eyes.

'This is all your fault, you know that, right? What sort of person ejects their nine-year-old into space?'

'What the hell were you thinking?' she sighed, 'you and I need to have a serious conversation about parenting when I find you.'

'End recording,' she said, 'encrypt Cartwright 66313 lock'

'Locked,' the computer confirmed.

She got up, zipped up her jumpsuit and caught her reflection in the mirror.

'Well, you look like shit,' she said.

'Thank you, Captain,' she responded to herself and moved outside into the corridor.

Urhan's Quarters.

Tam pressed the button to Urhan's quarters and waited. Silence greeted her. She was about to leave when she had one of those feelings in the pit of her stomach. She entered her override code and opened the door, stepping inside and saw that it was empty. She looked around before pressing the comm panel on the wall.

'Captain to Urhan,' she said.

There was no response. She changed the channel to a ship wide announcement.

'Urhan contact the Captain,' she waited for a few moments before calling up to the flight deck.

'Chuck, you got eyes on Urhan or Ona?' she said.

'One-second,' said Chuck.

'Tam, I'm not getting a reading on him up here, according to this, he's not on board,' Chuck said.

'Stop engines!'

'Got it,' Chuck said, as Tam watched the star field returned back to normal through the windows, 'Ona isn't here either, Chuck. I need to know how long they've been off the ship.'

'According to sensors, twenty-three minutes,' Chuck said, 'where the hell did he go?'

Shit

'I don't know Chuck. How long will it take to get back to the coordinates at the moment they left?'

'Without Urhan we can't activate…'

'I know that,' Tam growled.

'We've travelled three quarters of a light year Tam, on engines alone you're looking at….'

'Years,' Tam interrupted again rubbing her temples.

There was a long moment of silence on the other end of the comms as she thought what the hell to do next. A cold blast of air answered her question as Urhan, and Ona burst into existence. They hovered for a split second in mid before landing on the floor.

'Tam, Urhan's beacon just popping back on the system, he's in his quarters,' Chuck said.

'I see him Chuck, stand by,' Tam said, deactivating the comm system and rushing over to Ona.

She leaned down and looped her arms under hers, lifting her slowly to her feet.

'Are you okay?'

Tam glanced over at Urhan, 'You okay?'

'I am fine, Tam, that was an extremely interesting experience,' he said, getting to his feet confidently.

She looked back to Ona, who was shivering.

'Hang on let me get the doc,' she said.

Ona shook her head, 'Please don't, no doctors, it will pass.'

'You're freezing,' Tam said.

'It will pass,' Ona said.

Tam felt Ona's bear arms as the warmth in her body seemed to return, even the colour in her face was turning from a pale shade of blue to a warmer pink.

'I just need to rest,' she said.

Tam noticed a salty smell coming from Ona's hair and it seemed to be laced with fine granules of sand. Ona shuffled her way backwards until her back was resting against the wall. Tam looked over at Urhan

'What happened?' Tam said.

'I believe that we have just been transported to and from another planet, without the use of an STC drive,' Urhan said.

'What?' Tam gasped, her mouth agape.

'The molecule inside this human had been perfectly fused with her body and is capable of forming a contained bubble of warped space around her,' Urhan said.

'That's not possible,' Tam said, looking back at Ona.

'Again, I will need to do far more analysis on the phenomenon,' said Urhan.

'Where did you go?'

'Of that I cannot be certain,' Urhan said, 'a planet with breathable atmosphere, it was a clear night, but I did not recognize any of the star constellations, I plan on inputting them into my central data base for reference.'

'You're going to input star constellations from memory?'

'I am,' Urhan said.

'Urhan, you need to tell me what the hell is going on,' Tam demanded, folding her arms across herself.

'I performed what is called a memory dive on Ona. During that time, the STC jump was triggered by part, or perhaps by whole, an emotional response. I made physical contact with her during the memory dive and was seemingly transported with her,' Urhan said.

Tam looked over at Ona and smiled at her, trying to make her feel a little more at ease.

'That's incredible,' she whispered, 'how did you get back?'

'I don't know, I always make it back,' Ona said simply.

Tam turned back to Urhan

'Will you excuse us, Urhan? I would like to speak to Ona alone. Just so you know I had to drop us out of the STC Wave. Can you reinstate it on the flight deck please?' She said, 'stop by the med bay on your way and have the doc do a quick scan.'

'Of course,' Urhan said, turning and leaving them to it.

Tam moved over to Ona and made her way down, sitting beside her, the pair now leaning against the wall.

'I don't need a scan.'

'No, I figured you didn't,' Tam said, glancing around Urhan's quarters, 'weird room isn't it?'

'A little,' replied Ona, wrapping her arms around her chest.

'Are you cold?' Tam said.

'Not really.'

'Okay,' Tam said, wondering what she's going to say next. 'So...'

Ona looked up at her with large eyes filled with confusion, resignation, and exhaustion. Tam noticed the dark circles laying neatly beneath.

'You like Pizza?'

'I don't know.'

'You never had pizza?'

Ona shook her head.

'Well, that's just unacceptable,' Tam said, getting to her feet, 'come with me.'

Tam's Quarters

The door swished shut as Tam led Ona into her quarters.

'Sorry about the mess,' Tam said, 'I haven't had time to clean up, I've been busy in jail.'

Ona stayed put at the entrance while Tam cleared clothes and other bits from the surface of her bed, table areas and throwing them into the corner of the room.

'Come in, don't be scared, I won't poison you,' Tam said pulling out a chair and pointing to it, 'sit.'

Ona slowly made her way over to the chair and sat, she looked around.

'Sorry, Jacob keeps telling me to get a potted plant or something, but it wouldn't last a day. I'm better at keeping other people alive, not my own things.'

Ona looked to the framed image on the side of the bedside. Tam caught her glance and went over to it, picked it up and handed it over to her.

'That's me, aged five, and they are my parents,' she said, pointing to them without noticing herself drifting away, hearing soft screams in the distance.

'Where are they now?' Ona said, softly.

Tam paused, 'I don't know.'

Ona glanced at her, 'Did they die?'

'I don't know,' Tam admitted.

'I don't understand.'

'Let's eat first, I never tell depressing stories on an empty stomach,' Tam said, heading to the food dispenser, 'you're gonna love this, trust me, I programmed in the recipe myself.'

Ona took one more look at the picture before placing it gently back on the side table. Tam brought out some glasses as she synthesized their meal and presented it on a large round wooden plat on the table.

Ona's eyes lit up, 'That smells so good.'

'That's a firewood American Hot,' Tam replied, slicing through the steamy dough with a pizza cutter.

Tam smiled as she saw Ona look around for cutlery, 'Watch,' she took a slice and folded it over like a taco and placed it into her mouth. She blew out gently and waved her hand against her lips.

'It's hot,' she mouthed, 'careful.'

Ona smiled, taking a slice, and doing the same. Tam watched as she closed her eyes, her muscles relaxing as the enjoyment began to sink nicely into her body.

'Mmmm...' Ona said, following up with a muffled food filled 'that's delicious.'

Tam smiled her, 'Heaven, is how it's best described.'

They ate in silence, Ona wolfing down every last slice. Tam offered her the last slice because she was too full to keep eating and sensed that Ona might be hungrier than she led on. Once they finished eating, Tam poured them some fresh Tea called 'Arat' found only on Arana. It was caffeinated enough to keep her alert, but had a sweet taste to it, unlike elderberry. Ona pursed her lips as she drank it and looked inside the container.

'You don't have to drink it if you don't like it,' Tam said.

'No, no… it's different, I like it,' Ona replied leaning back and smiling, 'how long have you been here?'

'On the Massey?' Tam replied, 'she's been all mine for the last six or so years.'

'What does the name mean?' asked Ona

'Well,' Tam said, taking a sip of her drink, 'she's named after a civilian sailing a boat in the early twentieth Century. During what used to be called Earths second world war, thousands of soldiers became trapped on the beaches of Dunkirk, France. With the enemy closing in they were running out of time. Hundreds of civilian boats from England sailed across the channel to rescue them. The Massey Shaw was one them. Turns out the designer of her had a prevailing romanticism of history and besides, I kind of like it.'

'So do I,' Ona lowered her eyes, 'he did something strange to me.'

'Who did?'

'Urhan, he showed me things,' Ona said, 'I saw my father. There was some sort of accident. I don't know what I am supposed to do,' she said, 'I've spent my whole life in an illusion. I don't know what's real. I have nobody left.'

Tam could feel her eyes starting to water, 'Okay,' she stood up and reached for the picture of her parents, 'let's do this.' She handed the photo to Ona.

'I lost my parents,' she said, 'not long after this was taken actually. My father was the Captain of an ESDA cruiser sent to take some readings on a nebula in a remote sector of the galaxy by ESDA command, which, I just found out, is bullshit by the way, but we'll get back to that,' she took another sip of her tea and looked out the window.

'My mother was head of astrobiology. She was trying to find a cure for the pandemic that was sweeping our colony on Proxima. A few days into the assignment they encountered an alien vessel. It's one of those days that's been chiselled into the soft tissue of my brain and there's nothing I can do to get rid of it,' she took another sip of her tea and looked at Ona, who's full attention was on her now.

'You have to remember that I was very young, but what I do know, was that in the middle of the night I woke up to the ship wide alert, my mother bundling me up and the two of us headed straight for the nearest escape pod,' Tam felt her throat tighten.

'The ship was shaking, people were rushing all over the place, my mother had my hand gripped so tightly around hers, I remember thinking she might break my wrist. There was a strange smell in the hallways. To this day, I don't think I've ever smelt anything like it. It's hard to explain but it was so vivid. I remember hearing screams from somewhere deep within the ship. Strange sounds, as if something were crawling through the walls,' she looked at Ona who was hanging on every word.

'Anyway, we moved quickly, and my mother put me inside an escape pod and told me she'd be right back, that she was going to find my father. She told me not to worry, gave me the tightest hug she'd ever given me and then sealed the door. I don't really remember what happened next. For years, I believed that I accidentally pressed the launch protocols from inside the pod but as it was later explained to me, that would have been impossible,' Tam said.

'She did it?' Ona whispered, her eyes wide.

Tam nodded, 'I eventually found out after I was rescued, I spent weeks on board, nearly died when the systems began to fail, but after they analysed the flight data; it was then confirmed that it was my mother's access codes that had launched the pod.'

'She must have had a reason,' Ona said.

'Yes, she did,' Tam replied, 'she was trying to save my life.'

'What happened to them?'

Tam hesitated before getting up from the table and activating a large screen on the side of the wall. She brought up the star map on the screen.

'Somewhere around here,' she said, circling her finger around the entire galaxy. 'Over the last twenty years we've lost a dozen or so to something we can't get a reading on.'

Ona rose from her chair and moved to the screen.

'What did it look like?'

'Something big,' Tam said, 'bigger than the LAL battle cruisers, bigger even that the Ongral transports.'

'The what?'

'They really never told you anything?'

'No,' Ona's voice was soft.

'You know of the Lal, right?'

'Urhan was the first one I had ever seen in person but yes I was told stories.'

'There are three main space faring races that we've encountered and have relations with if you could call it that. The Ongrals are one of them. They don't think very highly of either humans or the LAL. There're a few thousand years ahead of us and they keep pretty much to themselves, which I'm okay with. The others are the Kriset, they're the furthest away from Earth. A friendly race but hard to communicate with, they speak at hundreds of times the speed of humans, so discourse is a little tricky. You should see their home world, nearly five times that of Earth and just spectacular, again a non-aggressive species, quite the opposite actually. I'll give you a data disk for you to look at, so you can get up to speed.'

'How did you meet them?'

'How do we do anything? The LAL, of course' Tam said, 'do you know about the virus?'

Ona shook her head.

'Ah, well that's where it all started for us,' Tam said, 'a blessing and a curse. Towards the end of the twenty-first century, an alien virus nearly wiped us all off the face of the Earth. It was the LAL who saved us. We'd been to the outer planets of our solar system at that stage but were hundreds of years from being faster than light travel, then the Lal came and saved our beacon.'

'I don't understand,' Ona said.

'They had a vaccine. They knew what it was and chose us for survival. Don't ask me why. They gave us the technology to warp space-time and eventually to start colonizing other worlds. But it all came with a price,' Tam said smiling at Ona, 'and it looks like you're the result of that.'

Ona stared at her, waiting for her to continue.

'The STC molecule,' Tam said, 'they control it which is why Urhan is on this ship in the first place. Every ESDA vessel has a member of the LAL race on board, the STC guardians, they're the ones who have sole access to the STC drive and the only ones permitted to activate and maintain it.'

'What happens if they die or get sick?' Ona said.

'They don't get sick,' Tam said, 'but if something were to happen that means they won't be to access it, then we're on our own.'

Ona turned away, 'I was in a lab,' she paused, 'that's what they were doing.'

'Who?'

'Urhan,' Ona said, 'he showed me what happened to me, I think my father was trying to make it, but something went wrong.'

'You have one inside you.'

'There's something else Tam,' Ona kept her eyes on her, 'sometimes I hear voices,'

'Voices?'

'Voices, that haven't spoken yet,' Ona said, 'voices from the future.'

Tam didn't know what to say but nodded for her to continue.

'I haven't heard anything since I left the space station, which is strange, but I hear things before they happen. I can change it, but I don't know how to explain it.'

'What do these voices say?'

'They say whatever they are about to say, they do whatever they are about to do,' Ona replied, 'unless I stop them.'

'Stop them?' Tam asked.

'One small drop in a pond can make a ripple that goes around the world,' Ona said, 'that's what Eoin used to say. He's the one who taught me to stop whenever I heard them, to stop me from making small changes that could alter the future of the universe.'

Tam looked at her curiously, 'I wish I understood,'

'You will.'

Tam decided to leave the topic, 'Where is your mother?'

'I don't know. I have memories of her, but they never told me where she went after I woke up,' Ona replied, looking up at the screen.

Tam stayed silent, following her eyes.

'Looks like we're both on our own,' Tam said.

'Looks like it,' Ona said, looking at her. 'Do you think they are still alive somewhere?'

'I don't know anymore,' Tam admitted.

'You didn't leave them behind.'

'Yes, I did,' Tam reached over and turned off the screen.

They sat in silence for a few moments.

Tam glanced at Ona, 'Sorry, I didn't mean to be abrupt.'

'Where are you taking me?'

'The truth is Ona, you kinda picked the wrong ship to get rescued by, I'm in a little bit of trouble here.'

Ona waited for her to continue.

'We're both being hunted by the looks of it, have you ever heard of a man by the name of Biron Desaltas?'

Ona shook her head.

'Well, Eoin Tatum seemed to think that he was the man who could protect you and the truth is you're not safe on board this ship,' Tam said.

'I don't know who that is.'

'Are you sure?'

'Yes,' Ona said, beginning to look distressed, 'you can't leave me with a stranger.'

Tam felt something instinctive kick inside her. A protective wall went up around them both, a wall she'd make sure was completely impenetrable.

'Doctor Tatum said that he was someone with whom he trusted,' Tam reassured her.

Ona gritted her teeth and looked away.

'I mean think about it, you only just met me, what makes you think you can trust me?' Tam said.

Ona's eyes widened.

'I mean, you can,' Tam said, laughing 'obviously, you're the first person I've ever shared a meal within my quarters, my favourite meal at that, it was a rhetorical question.'

Tam felt a twinge of regret having said it and reminded herself to be more careful. She was slightly relieved when Ona smiled.

'I know I can,' she said, 'I'm not sure why yet.'

'Well, that's a relief,' Tam said.

They both smiled.

'They want to use me,' Ona said.

Tam didn't know how to answer that.

'They want to be able to control me or cut me open and find out how I'm able to travel to other places.'

'That would be my guess,' Tam agreed, feeling sorry for her.

'They'll find me,' Ona's voice was shaky.

'No, they won't.'

'Yes, they will, you don't know them, they know everything,' Ona looked sadly over Tam's shoulder. 'What is that?' she asked, pointing.

Tam followed her finger to where her Arion unit was recharging. She turned back and smiled at her.

'That,' she said, raising her tone trying to lift the mood, 'is Arion.'

'What's Arion?' Ona asked, the shakiness in her voice evaporated.

Tam rose from her seat and detached Arion from its unit, bringing it back over to the table.

'Artificial Reactionary Intelligence of Nurice,' she said, 'A.R.I.O.N.'

She sat down and put it on the table.

'What's Nurice?' said Ona.

'Nurice is the planet where this technology is manufactured,' said Tam. 'Don't be scared, it won't hurt you.' She turned to Arion, 'Arion, activate.'

Arion's legs shot out from under its belly causing Ona to jump with fright. Tam raised her hands.

'It's okay,' she said, smiling.

Arion raised up on its legs and pointed its tiny little eyes towards Ona, tilting slightly to the side, like a dog would, before turning back to Tam.

'Arion, this is Ona,' Tam introduced them.

Arion turned back to Ona and regarded her before slightly bending its two front legs and leaning forward, as if bowing. Ona leaned down to get a closer look, smiling at the little device.

'What is it?' Ona asked in amazement.

'Well, it's lots of things really, it hooks up to your ear and interfaces directly into your mind, it also has a bit of an attitude which I'm working on, but usually he's well behaved,' said Tam.

Arion turned to her, tilting its eyes.

'I'm only joking Arion. Don't go getting all offended,' she said, looking up at Ona.

'Watch,' Tam said, 'Arion attach.'

Arion immediately scrambled up Tams arm and up to her shoulder, crossing over to her neck and climbing up, settling in place behind her ear, wrapping one of its legs just inside her ear canal.

'Whoa!' Ona sounded genuinely impressed, 'does it hurt?'

'Not at all,' Tam said, 'want to try?'

Ona looked at her nervously.

'Okay?'

'Arion, initiate new interface with Ona Mendel,' she ordered.

Arion immediately detached and began scurrying across the table towards Ona. On seeing it approach, she froze.

'I promise, he's actually really friendly,' Tam reassured her.

Arion paused in front of Ona's hand, which was resting, palm down, on the table. It turned its little eyes upwards to her. She seemed to relax, nodding down to the small device. It then gently climbed up onto her hand, up her arm and shoulder before resting by her right ear. Ona kept her eyes on Tam the whole time. She started to smile.

'Yes, I can,' Ona said, 'it's very nice to meet you, too.'

Tam was sure she started to see her blush.

'That's very kind of you,' Ona said.

'Arion, stop flirting with Ona please,' said Tam.

Ona began to giggle and that was nice to see. Her body seemed to relax with the internal dialogue going on.

'Okay, Arion – that's enough. Detach,' Tam ordered.

'Yes, I look forward to that,' said Ona, before the Arion unit detached from her ear and scurried down to the table.

'Deactivate,' Tam said.

He complied immediately by curling its legs under its underside, its little lights for eyes turning dark.

'Well, that's Arion. What did he say?'

'He said I was very pretty,' said Ona smiling, 'he has a nice voice, is he real?'

Tam looked down at the device. 'The silver-tongued devil,' she said smiling, 'actually he is sort of, it's the consciousness of an elderly volunteer who donates their mind to join with an AI when they die.'

'You mean that was actually a person?'

'He was indeed. Normally they have specialized knowledge, they are former scientists, doctors, even engineers who figure being an AI is better than being dead. Can't say I'd fancy doing it myself, normally they have a large ego.'

'What was his name?'

'That's something they give up when being transferred, it's so that there's no real attachment and also its way of letting go of their old self and becoming something new, so we never know their real names or who they were,' Tam said.

'Do they still know?'

'I don't know,' Tam replied with a small shrug, 'I've never bothered asking, nor would I out of respect. It's a line we never cross and something they think breaks the respect of their chosen way of life. Think of them like monks who've vowed silence on their past lives and when you're paired with an Arion unit you have to respect that.'

Ona looked down at the unit, 'such a small thing to house a human mind.'

'Don't be fooled by its size, these things can pack a punch if they need to.'

'How so?'

'Maybe someday you'll find out, trust me on that though.'

Tam took a deep breath and looked out again at the distortion effects outside the window, not sure of what direction to turn in. The comm system bleeped and for once she welcomed the distraction.

'Cartwright,' she said.

'Captain we're twenty minutes from Thiral,' Chuck informed.

'On my way,' she clicked it off and glanced back at Ona, 'I suppose it doesn't really matter where we put you on this ship, does it? You will suddenly pop out of existence. So, there's not much we can do about it?'

'No, there isn't.'

'Well, then come up and see the flight deck.'

24

IGO WAR

Amita opened her eyes to blackness, unable to move. The strange whale sounds and clicks, coming now from all around her. She heard a crack as light suddenly flooded in. She shut her eyes against the pain. She was suddenly able to move again, her limbs falling free by her side. She felt something cold around her wrists. As her eyes adjusted to the light, she saw metal clamps. She squinted again, the blurry nightmare all around her coming into focus. She saw faces. Some were human. Crew members she'd recognized, held aloft with clamps around their midsections and necks. She saw other things too, not human—unfamiliar and strange creatures. She heard screams from somewhere off in the distance, voices that sounded human. She looked around for Victor as she tried to make sense of where she was through the boiling terror. All she knew for sure was that she's going to die here.

'Amita,' came the soft cry of a young female voice to her left.

She turned her head to see one of the young ensigns of the Taurus, she couldn't remember her name, it was Catherine something. She had light blond hair and was clamped by the neck by a swing arm. Beside her was a strange bipedal creature with blue skin and large yellow eyes.

'What's happening?' Catherine whimpered, tears flowing down her cheeks.

She was young, maybe twenty, fresh out of the academy and sent into deep space to die a horrible death. Amita didn't know how to respond, she was still trying to get a grip on her own terror, let alone try to fight off someone else's. Her father's voice emerged from the back of her mind.

Calmness, gentleness, silence, self-restraint, and purity: these are the disciplines of the mind.

A brief wave of calm settled her stomach as she tried to remember her father's teachings as a child. Panic served no purpose but to incapacitate a person when rationality and clear thoughts were needed the most. Even in this nightmare, she had to find clarity. She had to find some sort of peace. To focus. To push the body's natural release of cortisol and other stress hormones back to where they came from, at least for now. If she was going to die, she was going to die unafraid. She had chosen this. She lifted her head and took a breath, looking to Catherine.

'Be calm, everything is going to be fine, I am here with you,' she said.

'What are they going to do to us?' said Catherine, choking back tears, 'Where's the Captain?'

Amita tried looking around, it was like they were being hung up in an old-fashioned abattoir where animals used to be slaughtered before being consumed in the old world. She looked back at Catherine, the strange alien beside her was now pointing with what were probably eyes, in their direction and making squeaking noises.

'I can't see him,' Amita said, 'you need to try and be calm, focus, we're going to get through this, me and you.'

She saw movement below her and turned her head sharply. There was something definitely moving on a set of catwalks roughly fifty feet below. Dark things gliding about on sets of multiple legs. She couldn't focus on their features, they looked like spiders crawling around the floor of her bedroom when she was young. Somewhere off in the distance she heard those noises again. Strange haunting whale sounds, this time coming from all over the abattoir like a million haunting ghosts. She felt a slight vibration in her back as her body began to move ever so slowly to the right.

'What's happening?' shouted Catherine.

Amita didn't answer. She didn't know how. The conveyor belt was moving, she couldn't see where they were headed, but had a feeling that the lambs were being brought to the slaughter.

25

THE MASSEY

As the stars returned to normal through the forward-facing windows of the Massey flight deck, the bright blue curvature of the planet Thiral cast its vibrant hues across the faces of those looking on.

'Any sign of ESDA ships?' Tam sat in her designated seat.

'Scanning,' Chuck replied.

He took a breath, 'yeah we got one, docked on the far side of the planet, we can't stay in orbit too much longer or the jig is up.'

Tam aimed the bow of the ship towards the planet and engaged the thrusters at sixty percent.

'We're going down?'

'Yep,' Tam said, 'prep for atmospheric descent.'

'Got it,' said Chuck looking behind him to Ona, 'take a seat over there and strap in, this will get a little bumpy.'

Ona nodded and sat behind them. Chuck then clicked the comm system.

'Engine room, prep for atmo, clear the plasma vents and extend heat shielding,' he said.

'Understood,' Jacob confirmed.

The planet grew closer in the widow as Tam took the Massey down. She wanted to break the atmosphere as quickly as possible to avoid detection, so she was employing what she liked to call the Gannet. Like the sea diving birds of Earth, the aim was to dive through the atmosphere, only slowing enough so that the heat shield didn't burn away, then accelerating using the thrusters and dive bombing to the surface. It was a tricky and somewhat hair raising manoeuvre. She levelled the ship off and pitched up twenty degrees, allowing the planets gravity to turn the Massey into a meteor. She took a deep breath as the flight controls began to vibrate.

'Here we go,' She braced herself.

'Heat shield holding,' Chuck said, as the flight deck began to shake.

A low rumbling turned into a steady roar as the windows began to glow orange and crimson. Superheated atmosphere rushed past as the flight deck began heating up. Tam kept a careful eye on her angle of approach as a red light caught her attention from the corner of her eye.

'Shit,' Chuck said under his breath, 'one of the hull repair rivets just gave way, there's a micro fracture forming.'

Tam shook her head because she knew it wasn't good. She looked at her altitude, just another minute or so.

'Ignore it.'

'Oh, okay then,' Chuck replied, almost jovially.

She caught his glance and they both exchanged smirks, realizing that there were only really two options, they exploded, or they didn't. The Massey shook violently to one side, shoving everyone on the flight deck in their seats. Tam shot her eyes forward, grabbed the controls firmly and regained control.

'Watch your course Tamara,' Urhan gently reminded.

She gritted her teeth.

'Thank you Urhan,' she growled, 'sorry, that was my fault.'

Chuck looked back at Ona, 'all okay back there?'

Ona gave him a tepid smile, then a thumbs up.

'Hope you like rollercoasters,' he said, smiling back.

'What are they?'

'Well, you're on one.'

After a few tense minutes, the ship stopped shaking as the flaming glow from outside the windows was replaced with a bright blue sky. Tam squinted her eyes as they adjusted to the sunlight streaming into the flight deck.

'Okay, hold onto your lunches we're gonna hit the deck,' Tam said, pushing the nose of the Massey forward again.

As the nose pitched forward, she saw the horizon broken by a jagged mountain range. Snowy peaks cut across the horizon as Tam gazed at the breaking white crests of a vast ocean below. She was pushed back into her chair as she dived down towards its surface.

'Get me a hundred and two percent for two-seconds when I pull her out of this,' she told Chuck. 'Just a few more seconds Ona, close your eyes.'

The Massey continued to dive to the ocean now at terminal velocity, the familiar shake of the flight controls daring Tam to make a mistake. One wrong move at this speed and they were alien fish food. Her pulse quickened, they had to get low and fast.

'Eight hundred feet!' Chuck said.

'Almost!'

'Tam!'

'Not yet!' Tam said with grit.

The ocean was close now, she could see the break in the waves as they awaited their entrance to its cold depths below.

'Four hundred!' Chuck shouted.

'Okay that'll do,' Tam said opening the throttle to full power and pulling up as hard as she could.

The engines roared to life; the flight controls felt like anvils. The ocean, which looked close enough for her to touch, fell away. She must have been at fifty feet or so by the time the Massey levelled off across the surface of the sea. She pulled up a little more, keeping their altitude at around the one fifty mark as she felt the residual adrenaline course through her veins. She looked over at Chuck, whose face was ashen. She looked behind her to Ona, who still had her eyes open and smiled at her calmly. She was either incredibly brave or had more faith in Tam's flight skills that perhaps wasn't warranted. She turned back to Chuck who looked angry. For the first time it looked like she had actually managed to rattle him with one of her stunts.

'What?' he asked, the tone in his voice was brimmed with frustration.

'You all right?' she smiled.

'I'm fine,' he snapped.

'I'm sorry but we had to keep her below the two hundred feet ceiling, sensors and all that,' she said, 'didn't mean to scare you.'

'You didn't,' Chuck said, looking away and running some tasks on the computer.

'Right,' she whispered.

She eased off the throttle and allowed the ship to glide gracefully over the waves. The large orange Thiral sun cut across the approaching mountain tops, sending dramatic shafts of light across the rocky landscapes.

'According to this, we're supposed to go to this peak,' Chuck said, sounding calmer and pointing to the map rendering on his computer.

Tam reached down, activating Arion, who came to life, crawled up her arm and positioned himself on her ear.

'Ah, this is Thiral,' he said.

'It is indeed,' Tam replied, 'that was quick.'

'I've been here before,' said Arion.

'Oh?'

'Yes, in my previous incarnation,' Arion said.

'Another story you'll never tell me, huh?'

'That's correct.'

'I'll get it out of you someday.'

'Unfortunately, you will not.'

Tam smiled, 'okay, give me a heads-up display please and keep an eye on the comms traffic in the area, will you? Let me know if we've been spotted.'

'My pleasure,' said Arion, as virtual data read outs appeared in Tam's vision.

'Arion, log into the onboard computer and overlay the coordinates given by Eoin Tatum.'

'Of course, Tam.'

She watched the water speed by underneath as she felt a presence behind her. It was Ona. She looked back at her.

'You need to strap in,' she told her.

'Just a second,' Ona paused, her eyes glued to the window, 'I've never seen a real sky, or a real ocean.'

Tam followed her wide eyes and felt her wonder at the beautiful landscapes ahead that was blanketed in warm sunlight. Thiral was a particularly beautiful planet. The second to be colonized by humans after Arana.

'It's beautiful,' Ona's voice was soft, hypnotized to the view in front of her.

'Ona,' Tam ordered her with grace, 'I need you to strap in for me, you can take a long look around when we land okay?'

Ona glanced at her nodded gently.

'Coordinates acquired Tam, relaying to your HUD,' Arion said, as a small blue target appeared in the distance of her virtual display. She gently turned the Massey towards it.

'Go quiet,' Tam said to Chuck.

'Got it,' Chuck said, tapping his comms, 'engine room,'

'Go,' said Jacob.

'Silent running,' Chuck said.

'Understood,' Jacob said, 'engine room out.'

The lights in the flight deck dimmed slightly as Jacob began powering down the non-essential systems to reduce the emissions output of the ship. The engine dampers kicked in, reducing their heat signature as the ship began to engage its stealth tech. Going quiet was something that was necessary for a rescue ship for lots of reasons. One of them being the close proximity to sound sensitive environments, like planetary surface rescues off glaciers, or mountain tops where the vibrations of a ship the size of the Massey could cause avalanches or ice breaks. In this case, it also meant being able to become relatively impossible to detect. Like an arrow flung across the sky to an unsuspecting target. Or so she thought.

'We just got pinged,' Chuck suddenly said.

'From where?'

'Dead ahead, from those mountains.'

'Arion?'

The ship had been 'Pinged' from an old-fashioned radar pulse, common amongst the newer colonies as the technology was easy acquire with the components being untraceable as it didn't use LAL technology.

'Confirmed, Tam, we've been detected,' said Arion, 'I am triangulating the pulse now, it would appear to be coming from the same coordinates as were provided by Eoin Tatum.'

'Any activity?' she turned to Chuck.

'Nothing on the scanners, if they've got ship under the bedrock or in caves or something, I can't see them,' Chuck replied.

'I doubt that,' Tam said.

'Well, whoever it is isn't making any sudden movements, but they know we're here, so what move do you want to make, Cap?' he said.

She turned to Ona, who was staring out of the windows at the blue skies passing overhead.

'Cap?' Chuck repeated.

She turned towards the approaching rock face.

'Incoming transmission,' said Chuck.

'Let's hear it.'

There was a light bleeping noise as a male computerized voice flooded the comm system, unemotional and rhythmic.

'Approaching vessel, identify yourself or you will be fired upon,' Tam frowned and looked at Chuck. 'Weapons signatures?'

Chuck shook his head, 'I'm not reading any, then again if they've got missiles buried in that bedrock...' he shrugged.

The computerized voice came over the comms again.

'Approaching vessel, this is your final warning, identify yourself or you will be fired upon.'

Tam bit her lip and then hit the comm button.

'This is the ESDA rescue vessel Massey Shaw, on mission...' she paused 'Tatum package one,' she clicked off the comm system.

She looked at Chuck.

'Well, we just unzipped our fly,' Chuck said.

'I don't think that's the correct analogy,' Tam replied.

'Neither do I,' Arion agreed.

After a tense minute the computer voice replied.

'Land at the following coordinates, disarm any weapons and do not attempt to power up your STC drive without authorisation or you will be fired upon. I repeat, you will be fired upon.'

'Well, somebody is in a bad mood,' said Chuck.

Tam pulled away from the mountain and circled back on her course, doing a full loop, deciding to do a quick flyby of the area and get her bearings before landing, just in case.

After her scan of the area, she aimed the ship towards the designated coordinates and took them to it. As they reached the cliff face, she noticed what looked like a slice of bedrock, which seemed to have been carved away from the edge of the mountain. A large perfectly flat area more than big enough to allow The Massey to land.

'Struts,' Tam said, hovering the ship, turning it so that the bow was facing away from the rock face, a quick exit always on the cards.

'Struts down,' Chuck said.

A plume of dust and small grey rocks blasted past the window as the ship's thrusters angled downwards as they descended. With the lightest of touches, the Massey touched down on the solid rock. Tam idled the engines before deciding to shut them off completely. She gently rubbed the side of her face as she looked at her scanners, seeing if there was any movement around the ship. She turned to Urhan who had his arms neatly folded behind his back.

'Okay, prep the STC, we may need to get out of here fast,' Tam said.

'We cannot use a molecule while inside the atmosphere of a...'

'I know that Urhan, but I don't want to be caught with my pants around my ankles in orbit, so just make sure we've got one in the tube if this turns south, okay?'

'I understand Tamara,' said Urhan.

She turned to Ona and noticed something about her eyes. They looked like there were a thousand miles away.

'Ona, I want you to stay here with Chuck,' she said.

'And where are you going?' Chuck asked.

'To meet whoever is inside that mountain,' she said.

'You're not going in there by yourself, I'm going with you,' Chuck said.

'No, you're not. I need you here to take care of the Massey,' she said, getting out of the flight chair.

'Seriously? You're gonna make me rescue you again this week?' Chuck said, 'I nearly got my head blown off for that by the way.'

'Not funny,' Tam said, then looked at Ona.

'I'm gonna go in and see what this is all about.'

Ona's eyes were locked onto hers, she looked like she was trying to say something, Tam could see that her hands had started to shake slightly. She leaned forward and took one of them.

'What is it?'

Ona's eyes were wide. 'I should go with you.'

'No way, not until I know what's happening. I won't be long, trust me,' she said, 'try not to disappear again, okay?'

'It's not that,' Ona said.

'Then what?'

'I just,' Ona said, pausing and looking away, 'nothing.'

A moment of silence passed between.

'Okay I won't be long, Chuck open the outer hatch on deck two and extend the ramp,' she said.

Chuck was frowning at her.

'Arion, I'm holding you personally responsible for the Captain's safety,' Chuck said, 'keep an open comm link at all times, if anything happens it's shoot to kill.'

The Arion unit detached one of its limbs that was holding it in place around Tam's ear, bending its leg and giving Chuck was looked like a tiny salute.

'Are you armed?' Urhan asked.

'I don't need a gun, little Arion here is a far better shot than I am anyway,' she replied.

'I am not little,' said Arion.

'Figure of speech,' Tam tapped Arion, letting the others know she was talking to him and not them.

Tam took a breath.

'Okay then, standby protocol,' she said, tapping the comm system, 'engine room.'

'Go,' said Jacob.

'Fix the damn the hole in my ship,' Tam said.

'Okay, that wasn't my fault, I'm telling you. That ESDA sealant crap they gave us last year must have been a dud,' he said, 'I'm trashing the whole lot of it and creating a new compound as we speak, bloody amateurs.'

'Okay Jacob, and keep the thrusters warm,' she said.

'Got it, keep her hot and plug the hole,' he said, in a bad seductive voice.

'Jacob, I swear to god…' said Chuck.

'Okay, okay, tough crowd.'

'Cap out,' Tam smiled, shutting off the channel before he could set off Chuck.

'You really shouldn't let him get to you,' she said, slapping him on the shoulder.

'You couldn't have gotten someone with even a hint of professionalism?' Chuck's face was flushed.

'Ah you love him really,' she said moving to the rear door.

'Yeah, like a bad case of the shits,' said Chuck, making Tam laugh.

She looked at Ona, 'Be back soon' she activated the door and stepped out.

Ona knew differently, she had heard it. She couldn't change it, she wanted to, this time, but no matter how hard it was she kept her lips sealed.

26

THIRAL

Tam stepped off the lowered walkway and onto the polished flat stone below. She was hit instantly by the freezing cold air that whipped her face. It was minus fifteen at this altitude and she'd forgotten to activate the thermal regulator in her jumpsuit. She tapped the control panel on her wrist and instantly felt the warmth as the internal heating systems brought her body temperature back up. Whomever had carved out this landing area had done a hell of a job. The light white and grey striations of the rock face camouflaging it well from the air. She looked out over the calm blue ocean and saw small black winged figures silhouetted by light cloud cover. The birds, if you could call them that, on this planet were huge and easily seen at a distance, akin to pterodactyls from Earth's distant past. She moved towards the back of the ship where the rock face of the mountain appeared to be solid. There was no hatchway, no door, no entrance of any kind.

She walked steadily towards it, stopping short of what looked like a normal jagged rock face. She placed her hand against the surface and felt nothing out of the ordinary. She then took a step back and scouted around the surrounding area again. She couldn't escape the feeling of being watched. A light electronic sound chirped from inside the rock face as it suddenly dissolved away, revealing a metal walkway. She looked back at the ship once more before entering the now cleared entrance. The sound of the hard heels of her boots reverberated around the metallic walls as strips of lights along the floor illuminated in front of her. Suddenly, the sunlight that had been on her back was cut off. The entrance way had solidified again, locking her inside. She held her position, cut off. She looked back towards the end of the long corridor.

'What are we looking at here Arion?' she asked, as her display scanned the surrounding area.

'Two feet steel walls. No transmissions are getting out of here Tam. There's some sort of field generator blocking them. I'm showing solid wall twenty-two meters ahead. Would you like me to prep my weapons system?' Arion said, calmly.

'Not yet. I don't want to provoke whoever's up there into blowing my head off, I've had quite enough of that today,' Tam said.

'Very well,' said Arion.

'If you get a break in the field, send the Massey a ping and let them know I'm still alive,' Tam said.

'Of course, Tam,' Arion said.

Tam smiled, 'Thank you,' she took a breath and moved forward.

'STOP!' came a voice that reverberated around the walls.

Tam froze.

'Hold your position!'

It was definitely a male voice, but it sounded distorted. She saw a multitude of blue beams shoot out from unseen points around the hallway and run themselves all over her body.

'We're being scanned,' said Arion.

'Yes, Arion, I can see that,' Tam said.

'Well there's no need to be ru…'

'Deactivate your Arion device,' said the voice.

Tam tensed up, being out of communication was one thing, losing Arion's weapons was another. She thought about it for a second.

'No,' she said, surprised at her own defiance.

She waited for a few moments before a sliding door opened at the end of the corridor. A figure in silhouette stood at its entrance. Tam saw something catch the light in his right hand.

'Tam, he's armed,' Arion said.

'Stand by,' she said.

'So, you're her,' he said deeply.

The kind of voice that had authority and confidence weaved into its fabric.

She also noticed something else about it. She didn't find it threatening, there was a softness in there buried throughout the octaves.

'And who might you think I am?'

'Tamara Edge, all grown up.'

She didn't reply.

'Or is it Cartwright now?' he asked.

'Captain Tamara Cartwright,' she said.

'Ah, you kept her name, I can respect that,' said the voice.

Tam felt like she had been knocked off guard, struck from behind when she wasn't looking. She didn't like games and felt her body tense up.

'Come with me,' he said, turning and heading into the light.

She held her ground momentarily.

'Come on, unless you want to go back the way you came… but tell your Arion unit that if he even thinks about arming his weapons this will be his final incarnation,' he said.

'I'd like to see him try,' Arion said.

Tam followed the dark figure through the doorway. As her eyes gently adjusted to the bright light in its interior, she was met with a white room with a simple white desk at its centre. A tall straight-backed chair sat neatly in front of four view screens recessed into the wall. The man turned to her. He had dark skin and wore a simple though impeccably tailored and pressed suit. He was well built. He had dark eyes and a trimmed greying beard. She noticed a little silver pin on the lapel of his jacket. He smiled at her.

'You already know my name, but it would be impolite not to introduce myself,' he said, 'my name is Biron Desaltas. I knew your father.'

'It seems my father knew a lot of people.'

'He did,' said Biron, 'Ona is on your ship?'

'She's somewhere safe,' Tam said, taking her time to gauge the situation.

'Well, I'll give you this, you have quite the family history,' said Biron, turning and moving towards a small cabinet.

Tam glared at him.

'How about a drink?' There was something in his voice that sounded so familiar yet so distant. 'And no, we've never met,' he turned his head and smiled at her.

'I'm okay thank you,' Tam replied as he wiggled what looked like a bottle of red wine.

'Oh, come on, I don't get a lot of visitors, in fact you're the first person I've seen in the flesh in two years.'

Tam scanned his impeccable outfit.

'Yes, I know,' he said, catching her eyes on his clothes, 'it's how I keep sane.'

'I see,' she said.

There was a soothing nature to his voice, disarming. He pulled out two glasses and placed them on the table, pouring two and sliding one across the table.

'It's Thiran, one of the colonists makes it. You should see the size of the grapes on the southern continent,' he said, 'the size of basketballs.'

He gestured to a chair. 'Please,' he said, earnestly.

Tam took a step towards the glass and took it in her hand. She noted the fruity aroma, rich and inviting.

Screw it

He raised his glass. 'To Doctor Eoin Tatum,' he said, 'a good man, my friend.'

She noticed a crack in his voice. She raised the glass and took a sip, it was smooth, vibrant, possibly the best glasses of wine she'd ever had. She looked at the glass, swirling the liquid and looked at Biron.

'I know. It's something else, isn't it?' he said, 'now to business,' he leaned against the table. 'Eoin would not have sacrificed himself if he didn't think the cause was worthy. So, what could be more worthy than protecting the life of a young girl in the wrong place at the wrong time?'

Tam locked her eyes on his.

'We started it together. Well, actually Ona's father and I started it together, the experiments on replicating STC molecule. Before the accident,' he said finishing his glass and pouring himself another, then he paused.

'Is she stable?'

'Stable?' Tam asked, frowning.

'Is she still jumping?'

Tam looked away. Biron turned to his screen and tapped it. Tam saw her face, her official ESDA file begin scrolling down the screen.

'You're in a spot of bother,' Biron said, 'the LAL aren't happy that you blew up a star. Silly really, what when you consider how many there are in the universe but there you go. They're becoming a giant pain in the ass if you ask me. I can't say that I entirely disagree with your uncle's take on this whole LAL situation.'

He looks away from her and placed his glass on the table.

She frowned.

'Oh, don't worry. He doesn't know you're here; he doesn't even know I'm here. I slipped through the net when I realized what he wanted to do. Eoin died to protect two things. Ona and the knowledge of how the molecule was integrated successfully into a human host. Only one other person in the galaxy has that knowledge, and you're looking at him. So, here we are, the two most wanted creatures in the cosmos, sipping on fine wine. I know you want to think he's an evil man and far be it from me to ever interfere with family matters. I can assure you that he's simply got his ideas a little muddled,' he said.

'He wants to make her a weapon,' Tam said stiffly.

'Oh, it's more than that,' Biron lowered his face.

He began to chew the side of his lip.

'Captain Cartwright, there's a darkness out there,' he said, turning back to the screens and activating the one next to the one showing her file, 'a darkness you know all too well. A Darkness that I think your Uncle has just gone after.'

An image of the galaxy appeared.

'Eoin wasn't the only one following your career,' he didn't look at her, 'your rescue of the Clorinda was a daring move. I commend your efforts.'

He tapped the screen with the image of the galaxy on it as pinpoints of lights zoomed in to a set of coordinates.

'The truth is, I'm not sure Eoin sending her to me was such a bright idea, no disrespect intended,' he said, raising his head to the ceiling as if talking directly to Tatum's spirit.

He took a deep breath and turned back to Tam. 'What do you know of your parents and what happened to their ship? I know you were on board.'

Tam froze, 'What?'

'Your parents,' Biron said.

'Not as much as I'd like to,' she said.

'Ghosts perhaps?'

Tam felt the hairs on the back of her neck prick up. He turned again to the screen and tapped in some commands. The image zoomed in.

'This is where your fathers ship was last tracked,' Biron said, 'all those years ago.'

Tam took a step closer

Why is he telling me this? Who the hell is this guy? She thought.

She looked at the image and recognized the nebula cluster immediately.

'Yes, I know that,' she said dryly.

Biron faced her.

'Seven days ago, The ESDA cruiser Taurus was lost,' Biron said, oddly changing the subject.

'What?' her voice was caught.

'On board that ship was President Puri's daughter, needless to say he's desperate to get her back,' Biron said, 'one of the advantages to having such a close friendship with some of the smartest people in the universe is I get access to things I shouldn't.'

'What happened to the Taurus?'

'See for yourself,' Biron said, turning and activating another screen.

Tam watched as a distorted video played. The image was as crisp as when she had last seen it as a little girl. The dark shape had haunted her. It was real. Her hands began to shake. She almost dropped the glass, but she managed to place it down on the table. The slightly distorted video showed the ship. It was as clear as if she'd only seen it yesterday. The strange liquid poured out of his hull, spreading itself across the nothingness towards the camera before it warped and froze, before turning to black. She looked at Biron.

'Who are you?' she said.

'That darkness,' he said, 'the secret the LAL don't want us to know about, the reason they control us, arm us, allow us to evolve technologically at the rate that we have been doing, the reason they saved our species in the first place from that virus. They didn't do it so that we could join some grander vision of an evolved humanity. They were recruiting us.'

'What?' Tam said, confusion resurfaced her eyes.

'The darkness is coming,' Biron said, lowering his voice to where it sounded like he wasn't talking to anyone in the room except himself. 'The Ongrals know it, that's why they've shut themselves off, constructing a system wide Dyson sphere around their home worlds. They're doing it to protect themselves.'

'What are they?' Tam asked, pointing a shaky finger at the screen.

'Death,' Biron looked deeply into her eyes, a strange distant look as if he were trying to see inside her mind. He turned back to the screen.

'Your Uncle had a meeting with Premier Diren two days ago on Arana,' he said, 'following that meeting, he boarded a transport ship and intercepted with The Lassen. She has not been heard from since.' He tapped in a new set of coordinates and the screen pulled out to show an unexplored quadrant of the galaxy.

'What?' Tam said, stepping closer to the screen.

'You know the Captain well, do you not?' Biron said, raising an eyebrow to her.

Tam glared back.

'Like you, I had a keen interest in locating the source of those ghost ships and based on something I recovered from the LAL's own mother system, I found this.'

'Hang on,' Tam said, 'you broke into the LAL's home world computer? That isn't possible. All their computer systems are coded specifically to their DNA, you can't get in.'

'That's true, you need to not only have LAL access codes, you need to physically be one of them,' Biron said, 'unless you do something so egregious that you can never speak of it again.'

'I don't understand.'

'I sincerely hope it stays that way,' Biron says, 'anyway, the procedure nearly cost me my life, or to put it another way, will cost me my life. But it won't today.'

He smiled at her and pointed to the screen again.

'Seven hundred and twenty-two light years,' Biron said, 'it will require three STC jumps to get there and will take them eight days.'

She took a breath

What the hell is happening?

Biron folded his arms and waited. Tam turned and paced to the other end of the room. She paused and stared at the back wall.

'I know where your parents are,' Biron said.

Tam began to feel lightheaded. She turned back at him, her jaw now open, her blood running cold. She felt a surge of anger in her stomach. A crunching pain forming in her chest. She looked at the screens.

'My parents are dead,' she said, feeling a strange fury boil up in the back of her throat.

'Perhaps,' he replied, 'perhaps not.'

'Who the hell are you?'

'They'll find me, eventually. I've tapped too far into their security systems for them not to trace it. Ona is safer with you than she is with me, trust me,' Biron said, 'besides, you may have an opportunity here, that is to say if she can control it, which I am assuming she cannot?'

'Biron,' Tam took a breath, 'makes sense.'

His thoughts were scattered, she supposed it was the isolation. He put his glass down and rubbed his face.

'This star system,' he sounded frustrated, 'the crew of the Taurus, all those ships, the president's daughter, soon the crew of the Lassen and… your parents. ARE THERE!' he said shouting at the point of light.

'What is there?' Tam snapped.

Biron's face dropped, 'ghosts.'

Biron moved away from the table and opened a side panel on the wall. He entered a code and took out a data pad and handed it to Tam.

'What's this?'

Biron looked to her right ear, at the Arion device.

'I am the only person in the galaxy who has this, I stole it directly from the main ESDA computer core on the moon before I managed to disappear.'

'Okay?'

'Your father was wearing an Arion device when he was taken, as far as I can tell it was destroyed but before it was, his last request of the device was to implant a tracking node into the base of his skull, not for the faint hearted.'

Tam's heart began to race, 'That's not possible.'

'That's not entirely accurate,' Arion intervened.

'What?' Tam said, looking away from Biron

'Ask him yourself,' Biron said, pointing to her ear.

'There is a protocol within my secondary appendage which allows for a sub space transmitting device to be implanted should my host become incapacitated.'

'I didn't know that,' Tam said, 'why didn't I know that?'

'ESDA tech didn't want their hosts believing that technological retrieval may be a higher priority than that of the attached human,' Arion said.

'Sons of bitches,' Tam said, looking down at the pad.

'I can assure you Tam, it is something I would discuss with you before I ever attempted it and I would like to point out that I am, at all times, committed to keeping you safe,' said Arion, sounding almost guilty.

Tam looked up at Biron.

'You're telling me my father's Arion tracker is still active?' she said.

Biron held her gaze, 'Turn it on and find out for yourself.'

She looked at the inactive pad.

'Wait,' she said, her head spinning, 'Ona...'

'Isn't safe here. I detected your ship in orbit the minute you emerged into normal space. It was a nice try, trying to atmo dive in, but if my sensors tracked you, you bet your ass theirs did too, they're just waiting to track you here then we're both dead.'

Tam looked down at the data pad and activated it. It began making a signal, almost haunting beeping sound, roughly a half second apart but consistent. Her hands began to shake.

'You're the Captain of a rescue ship. Are you not?' Biron said.

'I am.'

'There's a young woman out there who needs your help, maybe in the process you can find what you've been looking for your whole life and more importantly, maybe Ona Mendel can help,' said Biron.

Tam didn't know what to say and she stared at Biron for a few seconds, 'what is she?'

'The next step in evolution? Mistake in science? Orphan? Take your pick. I'll do what I can to jam their scanners when your ship leaves orbit.'

'The next obvious question…' Tam began.

'Because if I wanted to bring you in, I'd shoot you right here and now,' Biron said, suddenly whipping out a gun, which Tam hadn't seen secured to the underside of the table.

He pointed it at her.

'I've got him,' Arion said, detaching one of his appendages from the side of her head and pointing it at Biron.

'Wait,' she said to both.

'He's quick,' Biron smiled.

They stood there, facing each other briefly before Biron lowered his weapon. 'That's why,' he said, placing the weapon on the table.

The sound of the bleeping signal coming from the data pad filled the room as loud as an orchestra. It was all she could hear.

'All right Biron,' Tam straightened her shoulders, 'you got me. Stand down Arion.'

Arion complied.

'I need to speak to my ship,' she said.

Biron tapped the computer, 'Go ahead.'

'Come in Massey,' she said.

'Go Cap!' Chuck said.

'Prep for launch.'

27

THE LASSEN

Deangelo screamed into the void, he was in the dark, memories of a past life screeched past his eyes and then was gone. He was in agony. It surrounded him, penetrated every pore, every inch of skin and bone. He felt like as if the innards of his skull were being torn out and replaced with something else. He felt as though his eyes were melting, the liquid remains leaking down his face. He felt as though his teeth were being pulled out one by one and that his tongue had been lit on fire.

From the darkness he saw strange figures, faces of his crew, distorted, and twisted into contorted dead like things that were crying out for help. He felt his body somewhere else, his mind disconnected as if his consciousness was being pulled to some unknown destination.

And so, the pain continued, then something else—a sensation he hadn't felt before. The pain faded away and he felt good, at peace, almost numb for a time. Then it was gone, replaced by sheer ecstasy and joy. The feeling intensified into euphoria. His mind cleared and came into focus until he became so hyper aware of the strange images being shown to him. Vibrant colours began to form in front of his eyes as the feeling of pure joy grew more and more pronounced. It was as if his veins were filled with the most potent form of opioid known to exist in the galaxy and for a time, he didn't care what had happened to his crew, or himself, all he wanted was to stay in this state for the rest of time. A state of bliss he would have given his life for. He remained in that state for what seemed like forever, as he felt something attach to the left-hand side of his head. He was sure that he'd heard something spinning at high speed, somewhere off into the darkness. He could feel something now, pressure against his temple, the breaking of the skin but still only that blissful paradise he was living in. He saw light, the darkness began to recess, and he was now in a strange place he'd never seen before. He didn't care where he was, all he wanted now was the feeling. There were faces he recognized, some with no bodies attached to them. Faces on heads attached to spinal cords and nothing else, their eyes open, blinking, AWAKE!

He knew he should feel something, but his mind would not allow it. He didn't care about the strange disembodied horror dangling all around him, he knew that he had found true meaning, true joy. He felt his head vibrate as the spinning thing penetrated deeper inside his skull. He welcomed it, he wanted more. Then the feeling stopped. Suddenly, as if all the blood had been drained from his veins all at once, his body went cold, the euphoria was gone, ripped away, and his mind was returned with brutal clarity into its natural state. The pain returned, this time with even more ferocity. He felt as though he were being boiled alive and with it returned his deathly, choking screams.

Tears streamed from his eyes as he begged for it to end. He couldn't live anymore, not like this. Through blurry vision and agony, he saw Lefebvre, or something that looked like her. He screamed out to her, but she didn't seem to hear.

He saw Admiral Edge's face, glaring at him through a fog.

Or was it something that only looked like him?

They were connected now. Fused into one, he understood now. A clarity of purpose and function overlaid itself onto what was once were memories, experiences, and personality.

Somewhere, under the layers of consciousness, what was left of Deangelo's own self, vanished forever.

28

THEA

The Massey hung low over the southern magnetic pole of Thiral's nearest moon, Thea. Tam took one last look at the scanners to make sure they weren't tracked before turning her seat around to face everyone else on the flight deck. She flicked a glance at Chuck.

'Keep an eye on that,' she said, pointing to the main scanners.

Chuck nodded, keeping his own flight seat facing forward in case anything happened. Urhan stood calmly, his long arms by his side. Tam gave one last glance at the STC chamber, which was now primed for another jump.

She gave Ona a reassuring smile, 'how are you doing?'

'I'm okay,' she replied, leaning forward and placing her elbows on her knees.

'Okay,' Tam said, rubbing her face. She then glanced at Ona, 'as you've probably guessed we didn't leave you on Thiral.'

'Yes, I noticed.'

'Okay,' Tam said, briefly made eye contact with both Chuck and Urhan, 'here's the deal. The Taurus was attacked by a Ghost vessel seven days ago. The whole crew gone, and among them was Amita Puri. She's the daughter of Earth's President, Puri.'

Chuck turned in his chair, 'holy shit.'

'We think that Admiral Edge has taken the Lassen to go find them,' Tam said looking at Urhan, his eyes suddenly wide, and his posture stiff.

Tam examined his movements closely, there was an odd sense that he was becoming agitated and for a moment she saw his eyes glance briefly at the loaded up STC chamber before turning back to her.

'Okay, so not be blunt but what's that got to do with us?' Chuck said, 'if Edge has bigger fish to fry then that's heat taken off you for now, no?'

All Tam had to do was give him a look and he already knew, 'you want to go after them, don't you?'

'Yeah,' she said, 'I do.'

'Where are the coordinates?' Urhan finally asked.

Tam turned in her chair and punched them into the navigation system. The screen locked onto a spacial grid, she looked back at Urhan, who was examining the screen intently.

'If they've already sent the Lassen, what do they need us for?' Chuck said.

Tam was still looking at Urhan, 'what is it?'

Urhan looked at the STC chamber again then back to Tam.

'I agree with Chuck,' Urhan said, 'I do not understand the rationale behind taking the ship into a potentially dangerous system, with little or no threat assessment data to draw up a comprehensive strategy.'

Tam sat back in her chair.

'Ordinarily, I would agree,' she said, 'what can you tell me about the star system?'

'I do not know what you mean,' Urhan said.

'I think you do.'

Urhan stood quietly, waiting for Tam to answer her own statement. But then a whisper cut the silence with a knife.

Tam turned to Ona, 'What did you just say?'

There was fear in Ona's eyes, looking at the star system configuration on the main screen. After a few more seconds she made eye contact with Tam, 'nothing, never mind.'

'Urhan,' Tam said, 'if you know what this place is, you need to tell me.'

Urhan suddenly reached over to the STC chamber and placed his hand on the control panel. Tam saw the blue energy field in the centre dim and heard the drive powering down.

'What are you doing?' she was startled. Then she reached out and grabbed Urhan's wrist.

He turned to her.

'Please release me,' he said calmly.

Tam glared at him but complied. Urhan took a step back and folded his arms behind. Tam looked down at the now deactivated STC chamber.

'Why did you do that?' she demanded.

'Are you out of your mind?' Chuck said.

'No, I am not,' Urhan said, 'but I cannot allow you to go there.'

'Go where?' said Tam, 'what is that place?'

'That sector of space is forbidden,' Urhan said.

'Forbidden by whom?'

'Humans are not permitted to enter that star system.'

'What?' Chuck said, 'The LAL have never made restrictions on where we can travel or how far.'

Urhan glanced away, 'I must speak to premier Diren about this.'

Tam looked to Chuck and saw the fury building in his eyes. It looked like he was about to jump out of his seat and clock the alien across the jaw. Aggression wouldn't work on Urhan, Tam knew that, it was the only reason. She tried to calm herself by placing a hand on Chuck's arm, shaking her head. He kept his place. She turned back to Urhan.

'Urhan, I know you're trying to protect us, but we have people in great danger,' Tam said.

'Those people are already dead.'

Tam's eyes widened, 'We don't know that!'

'I do.'

Tam glared at him; she curled her fingers into a fist.

'You can't go,' said a soft voice to her right.

Ona was looking up at her, her own eyes bright and filled with concern and honesty. Tam kept her eyes on her and softened her voice, 'why not Ona?'

'If you go to IGO,' she paused, 'you'll die,'

'Stop,' Urhan turned to Ona.

'Shut up Urhan!' snapped Tam.

'I'm the captain, I decide when the discussion is over, not you, is that clear?' she said, now unable to contain her boiling temper.

'Of course,' said Urhan, calmly.

Tam took a breath, composing herself before looking back at Ona and Urhan followed her gaze.

'What does that mean?' Tam asked softly.

'I'm not sure,' Ona said.

'What's IGO?' Tam said, turning to Urhan.

'It is too soon.'

'For what?'

'We are not ready. Humanity is not ready. Oan is correct, if you go to IGO, if WE go to IGO, we will all die,' he said, turning back to her, 'it is not conjecture nor is it theory, it is fact. This is for your own protection, not only yours but that of every species in range of that star system. Perhaps in a thousand years humanity will be ready, but not now. You will not find what you are looking for there, nor will you find anything or anyone alive, but aside from that, if they believe humans have found their home world,' he paused, 'they'll begin.'

'Begin what?' Tam said, a part of her didn't want to know but the truth of her parents simmered in her mind.

'The end of all things,' Urhan said.

There was an eerie coldness in that statement that cut through the flight deck like a winter storm. For the first time since she had known him, Tam thought she could sense fear coming from her other worldly friend. It was a sense that she took seriously. She tried to think of what to do next. She sat back in her chair and crossed her legs.

'Anything that sends the creeps up a Lal's back sends the creeps up mine,' Chuck said.

She glanced at Ona, twiddling her thumbs.

'What if we could get in and out without anyone or anything ever knowing we were there?' Tam looked at Urhan.

'Impossible,' said Urhan.

'Really? Up until a few days ago your people have always believed that it was impossible for anything organic to bond with the molecule.'

'That is true, however, this situation is different from a virtually unarmed spacecraft entering IGO territory,' said Urhan.

'Can someone please tell me what the hell is an IGO?' Chuck's voice was shaking with anger, his patience wearing thin.

'Urhan,' Tam said softly, 'I'm going, you know that I'm going.'

'How do you propose to do that?' Urhan said, folding his arms.

Tam grimaced.

'I'll take her,' Ona said looking up at him.

They all turned to look at her and smiled at each other.

'You cannot control it,' Urhan said.

'I'll learn to.'

'You'll be alone.'

'Unless you choose to help her,' Ona paused, 'yes, you're right, we're going to help.'

Tam sat back. 'Urhan, you're already in serious shit for breaking me out of prison, ever heard the expression in for a penny in for a pound?'

'I have not,' Urhan said.

Tam, Ona, and Chuck sat in silence, all staring at Urhan, who's eyes gently went from one to another before he finally spoke.

'Of all the ships I could have chosen,' he said lowering his tone, 'I must ask you please not to do this.'

'Urhan, I'm doing this,' Tam said, 'we need you.'

'What about the rest of the crew?' he said, 'do they? Are you doing it for them? Or are you doing it for you?'

Tam suddenly felt sick. He was right. Had she been so consumed by the thought of seeing their faces again that she was throwing her crew into a suicide mission? Was her judgement compromised? Was she even thinking about the Lassen, about Amita Puri? About anything other than either finding her mother alive or avenging her father's death? The feeling she most dreaded creeped inside her mind. Doubt.

'We're all here because we knew the risks,' Chuck interjected, 'that means all of us.'

'Please understand what it is you are dealing with, there are billions of you. You are uninteresting to them, simply bodies to use, they have not targeted your entire race. Yet,' he said, 'if they do, if they come, you will cease to exist as a species, I mean no personal insult to those you have lost.'

'Urhan,' Tam said, 'do you trust me?'

Urhan tilted his head, 'I do not understand,'

'It's a simple question, do you trust me?'

'We have no use for such things,' Urhan said, 'compliance is all there is.'

Tam glared at him.

'But within the human context, yes I do,' Urhan said.

She nodded, satisfied. 'Then let me do my damn job.'

Urhan's green eyes looked through the front window. He turned back, reached out a hand, and placed his fingers on the SCT chamber, reactivating it. The bright blue hues of the molecule came to life as the energy of the drive came back to full power. He looked at Tam, 'We will need a plan.'

Chuck smiled.

'That,' Tam said, taking a deep breath, 'is an understatement.'

29

IGO ROYAL

The King waited by the grand doors as the white stripe ran the length of his body, fluorescing. An unavoidable reaction to the high level of emotion running though his mind. He was finally given the honour of the sowing and with no doubt became the root of his excitement. As he waited for the entrance to open, he took his time to stare across the silver promenade that ran nearly all the way to the horizon. Above the planetary curve, the rings of IGO Royal were shedding their light across the star system for all to see. This was more than an honour, more than simple blood lines or luck. This was destiny. His only purpose was finally arriving. Lining the promenade, thousands of fellow Royals, their stripes glowing white, their uniform gazes willing him to complete the journey.

He'd waited for a thousand years for this day. He cast his look over the beauty of IGO Royal for one last time as a large horn sounded from above the main entrance hall. Then he to face the doors to the Queen's chamber. They split open as a second horn sounded. He stepped through the entrance and into the now darkened Queen's chamber. He had not seen her now for half a year.

The Queen's chamber was at the heart of the palace on IGO Royal and a sight to truly behold. Stretching from one end of the birthing ravine to the other was the Queen's bridge, always guarded by a battalion of her loyal guard. The doors to the Queen's chamber were sealed and the King moved towards the first set of guards. He turned his light receptors upwards and towards the carved rock above. Representations of the Kings had preceded him, and he saw himself as a large ceremonial covering cloth draped around the gargantuan sculpture made of diamond. He turned to the guard and waited for them to scan him. Two approached and without saying a word, pointed their vaporization weapons at his head, while a third circled his body and scanned his body down to the molecular level. He, of course, would never presume to take this ritual as a sign of disrespect, quite the contrary. At such a crucial time for their race, no risks could be taken.

The weapons would remain traced onto his body until the sowing had been completed. They finished their scans as the two members of the guard separated and bowed their heads in their first sign of reverence. Their weapons still trained on him. He acknowledged their sign of respect and proceeded past their checkpoint. He heard the soft electronic buzzing of the blast turrets mounted on their podium fixtures as they tracked his movements across the first boundaries of the bridge. The air in the Queen's chamber was musty, the humidity levels high, and the heat several degrees above what was considered normal. This was artificially created of course in order to make her more comfortable and to align with her own body heat during this month of physical transformation. In ages past, she would, of course have gone deep underground near the planets core while performing the sowing but had not been able to do that for a millennium.

The King moved gracefully, holding his body with stiff pride. The long diamond bridge refracting the light from the lamps, casting an array of colours across its surface. The long walk across the chasm of the Queen's chamber would take time, the distance itself a form of security. Every several hundred meters, another weapons turret locked onto him. The guards, behind him watched closely. For centuries, they had obeyed his every wish, his rule unquestioned. Today that had all changed. He was both the precious jewel and the threat. He continued his procession across the great chasm as he prepared himself for what was about to happen next. He stopped as his legs touched the platform on the far side and turned to look at the guards. They didn't move. He was now faced with a rock face that stretched upwards. He gazed up at the platform above his head, an outcropping barely visible as a small silver disk began to descend. He waited as it reached the ground level. He stepped onto it, waiting for the guards to follow. The disc ascended, slowly, towards the ledge above. The King looked out at the sowing fields below as he got his first real look at how many eggs there were. It was the first time he had ever witnessed such a thing. The secrecy known only to the royal guard, sworn to die to protect it. As he rose, he began to feel something that was unexpected for a such a high honour. He made sure not to give any sign to the guard that he was feeling it, or his journey would be ended far too prematurely. There was no doubt. It was fear. The silver disk began to slow as it reached the heights of the outcropped ledge, the King getting his first glance now at Zakia, his Queen and barer of all. He felt the heat from the stripes on his back as they flared, an inbuilt reaction to any perceived threat that gave the IGO an almost sixth sense to danger. His feeling of irreverence and sense of honour suddenly left his body as he looked upon his mate. He hesitated, looking at the guards, their weapons at the ready. No King before had ever been able to tell the story of what happened next but seeing Zakia now, her enormous distorted shape before him, bulbous, pulsating, as if in a trance, it was less ceremonial.

'Move,' said one of the guards, all sense of duty and respect lost completely from his voice.

The King, no longer the King, began to feel something cold decent upon him. He crept towards the large bulbous shape, slowly. The form, now five or six times her normal size began slowly moving towards him. The top of her body, leaned forwards as if looking at him. A sense of calm began radiating throughout him as if he were no longer in control. A sense of heat, of attraction towards the large form, towards his mate. The fear of what he had thought was a monstrous form only moments ago was gone, replaced with an uncontrollable urge to be a part of her. He could smell something, an intoxicating aroma which penetrated every inch of his skin. He moved closer to her as the beauty of her shape filled every one of his senses. He saw an opening in her body, a glorious place he knew he had to enter. He saw something inside the opening. Something glistening that shot out suddenly towards him, piercing his body. Was it a claw? He didn't care. He surrendered his body to her. He felt a jerking motion as he was pulled inside her. A warmth descended upon him as he now felt their bodies merge. He felt bliss. Then it was gone. The scent, the feeling, and everything he couldn't understand. His senses returned to him as if waking up from a dream. He now felt something else, suffocation and then the pain started. He could not move. He felt fire. His outer layer of skin began melting off his body. He was in darkness now. He began to emit a long stream of clicks from his vocal cords, but they too would not work. He felt them melt away. He begged the gods for it to be over as his mind suddenly realized what was happening. She was digesting him.

30

The Massey

Tam stood by the food dispenser in the messy hall and poured herself a cup of black coffee. Augustin was sitting at the table fiddling with a spoon. She'd asked to speak to Tam in private. It was late and she was tired. She needed an hour's rest before the briefing. The dispenser finished the drink and Tam held it to her nose, breathing in the aroma before letting the liquid burn her tongue slightly as she sipped. She turned to Augustine.

'Okay,' she said, 'let's have it.'

Augustine turned to her and smiled, shaking her head.

'I'm tired of being the devil on your shoulder,' she said, 'you've already made your mind up and I respect that.'

'Bullshit,' Tam said, leaning against the wall.

'Well, yeah, maybe it is a little,' Augustine said, 'you're not telling them everything are you?'

Tam stayed silent, she glanced down at her coffee. She reached inside her jumpsuit and removed the data pad that Biron had given to her and handed it to Augustine.

'What am I looking at?'

'The locator signal imprinted by my father's Arion unit when it was taken,' Tam explained.

Augustine's mouth opened, 'what?' She then sighed and glanced down at the data pad. Tam took another sip of her coffee and waited.

'Tam,' Augustine said.

'I know,' Tam said.

'You have to tell them,' Augustine said, 'they're your crew. I'm your crew for god sakes.'

'I know that.'

Augustine shook her head, 'Jesus,' Her face fell into her hands, 'Captain…'

'Don't,' Tam said.

'I can't allow you to take this ship into what looks like a suicide mission because of an obsession to find your parents,' Augustine sighed, pulling her face out of her hands.

'Listen to me,' Tam said moving towards the table, 'his beacon is still active!'

'You don't know why! God, this is crazy!'

'No, it isn't,' Tam said, 'if they're still alive, we can find them.'

Augustine glared at her. 'We've been through a lot, you and I, you've never lied to them. I should relieve you of duty just for that.'

'Silvia,' Tam said, 'I give you my word that I will not endanger this ship or anyone on board, if we don't find Amita, or anyone from the Taurus, I'll jump us away. This is our only clue to their location, it's a calculated risk, it's the only thing we have to go on. You can't argue that there isn't SOME logic in that?'

'There is logic,' Augustine said, 'but you're not doing it for her, you're doing this for you.'

'That's not fair.'

'Isn't it?' Augustine said, 'you have to let them go.'

'I have let them go.'

'You just lied to me again,' Augustine said.

Tam took a breath.

'Why can't I try both?' Tam said softly, 'what difference does it make? Maybe we find some of them, maybe we don't. For god sakes, we're being picked off one by one, families being torn apart, wolves feasting on the sheep of the galaxy and we do nothing. We… do… nothing. I want to know what these things are, don't you? Maybe my parents are dead, but I know that somewhere on Earth is a mother and father who are going out of their minds just to hold their daughter again. So, what if they're dead? I'll deal with it. But I'm sure as hell gonna try find them. You want to stop me? Certify me unfit for duty? Go ahead.'

Augustine lowered her gaze for just a moment before looking back up at Tam.

'You know I'm not going to do that,' she said softly, 'you know I want to find those people every bit as much as you do but listen to me. I know you. I know you'd rather die than let anything happen to this ship, or this crew but I also know there's something dark inside you that wants to take revenge for what happened to you. And if I think that side of you is taking over, if I think you've been compromised; I'll lock you out of your command codes and remove you as Captain. I've just as much a responsibility as you do to the people on board this ship. I can't have a Captain putting their lives at risk because of a personal vendetta.'

Tam smiled, 'I wouldn't have you on board if I thought otherwise Doctor.'

'I'm serious Tam,' Augustine said.

'I know you are,' she took a sip of her black coffee, 'I wouldn't want it any other way.'

31

URHAN'S QUARTERS

Ona watched Urhan as he removed something from a shelf. It was a small black object, flat and square, no bigger than her thumbnail.

'What's that?'

'This?' Urhan said, holding it up for her to see.

She nodded.

'This is part of a regulator I use within the STC chamber to control the reaction of the molecule with the ships engines,' he said.

'Okay? And what does that mean exactly?' she asked curiously.

'The molecule normally reacts exponentially when the energy is released into the surrounding space, meaning that it expands unless it is kept within a small field of reversing counter elements which prevents it from expanding too far and blowing the ship apart.'

'Okay, I understood the blowing the ship apart bit,' Ona said.

'It will become clear in a moment, just focus,' Urhan said.

'How come I haven't blown apart yet?'

'I do not know.'

'That's not exactly comforting,' Ona stared at the regulator.

'It is not intended to comfort,' Urhan said, 'may I ask you a question?'

'Of course.'

'You are afraid, are you not?'

'What?'

'You believe you are alone in the universe?'

Ona furrowed her brow, contemplating his question, 'I don't understand.'

Urhan took a step towards her. 'The human brain is one of the most intriguing we have encountered on our travels; did you know that?'

'No,' Ona replied, 'I did not.'

'It is, in fact, twelve percent larger than our own,' Urhan said.

Ona cast her eyes over Urhan's large head.

'Our cranial structure is thicker because our skulls are significantly denser, not because our brains are any larger than your own,' Urhan said, following her gaze.

'Sorry, I didn't mean to stare,' she said quickly, cheeks flushing.

'That is quite all right,' Urhan replied, 'there is a possibility that the human hypo-campus is naturally capable of harnessing and naturally compressing the molecule, once it has been integrated into your physique.'

'Okay?' Ona said.

'It is also why I believe that you are unwittingly activating it whenever you have an uncontrolled emotional response to external stimuli,' Urhan said.

'So, what's that gonna do?' she asked, looking at the flat square.

'With your permission, I would like to place this on your arm.'

'Will it hurt?'

'No.'

'Okay then,' Ona replied, rolling up the sleeve of her jumpsuit.

Urhan approached her and placed the small device on her upper right arm. Ona felt a slight tingle run up her shoulder. 'That felt weird.'

'The sensation will pass,' replied Urhan, 'tell me about what you feel when you travel?'

'It feels cold,' Ona replied, 'like ice, all over my body.'

'What else?'

'The cold is replaced by a warmth in the centre of my chest and then I feel dizzy.'

'What are you thinking about?'

'I don't know.'

'You must be thinking of something.'

Ona tried to focus. She thought back to her former home and saw Eoin sitting beside her next to the pond. She remembered all their conversations, her loneliness and suddenly felt strange. She heard something, a voice coming from all around her. It was a low, menacing, evil.

'What are you?' said the strange voice.

She looked to Urhan. He was regarding her curiously.

'Oh no,' she said.

'Answer me, or I will destroy you.'

She clamped her hands around her ears and closed her eyes.

'You are not like the others.'

'How many know of our existence?'

She looked up to Urhan, her eyes pleading, 'make it stop!'

'If you lie to me again creature, I will leave you in agony until you die.'

'The Queen will enjoy your nutrients.'

Ona screamed at the unwelcome intrusion in her mind. Something terrible was going to happen. Urhan reached for her. Before he could get to her, she felt a freezing cold wave come over her body. The world around her began to distort.

'Ona, think of Thiral, the planet right there,' Urhan said, pointing out his external window, 'think of it, think of Thiral, think of this place.'

Urhan turned the screen so she could see it. It was an area of flat land, green and lush with a snowy peaked mountain range in the background. In the foreground was a large monolithic rock.

'Go here Ona, Thiral,' Urhan encouraged her.

Urhan's voice diminished into a hum and the world around her flashed and disappeared. In an instant, Urhan's quarters was replaced by far stretching glacier. Ona's body lay in the frozen snow. The air stabbed at her throat as she closed her eyes against the blinding white sun overhead. She looked briskly all around her, seeing nothing but white. Her body began to shake, her fingers now numb as she took a step in no particular direction. She looked up at a washed out pale grey sky and wrapped her arms tightly around her chest. The silence around her was broken by the soft noise of something cracking in the distance. Her teeth began to chatter as she quickly rolled up her arm to see if the odd device was still attached. It was. She lowered her gaze and closed her eyes again.

'Come on!' she screamed into the ground as she tried to think straight.

Her lips were starting to freeze.

'You can do this, think Ona, think,' she said, through chattering teeth.

She tried to think about The Massey Shaw, tried to think about Urhan standing in his quarters. She opened her eyes as a blast of freezing cold air shot across her body, knocking her off her feet and onto the icy ground. She felt a sting of pain run up her arm.

'No,' she said, feeling an anger boil up inside her, 'ENOUGH!' she screamed into the air as the world around her swirled into nothing.

She felt as though she was floating somewhere, existing yet separated from everything. The world snapped back to her as she felt her body hit the ground once more. This time she looked up and saw Urhan standing over her. Her lips chattered as she curled herself into a ball on his floor.

'Hold on,' said Urhan, moving towards a container in the wall and producing a blanket.

Ona began to feel the warmth of it straight away.

'Urhan to med bay, please send someone to my quarters with an emergency med kit straight away,' he said.

'I'm on my way,' Augustine replied.

Ona looked up at Urhan and tried to smile through the mixture of numbness and pain.

'It did not work?'

Ona tried to get out the words but couldn't, she just shook her head vigorously.

32

THE MASSEY FLIGHT DECK

Tam sat back in her flight chair and looked at the images on the screen. It showed a long rage picture of the planetary system, the only image that Urhan had on file of the IGO star system. It looked rather unremarkable apart from one aspect, one of the planets, seen in the background drifting behind the large white star, Urhan had told them was a B class giant.

'What are you thinking?' Chuck asked.

Tam squinted at the image. 'Is that planet glowing?'

Chuck leaned into the screen.

'I don't know, it's grainy,' he said, 'I thought the LAL had kick ass imaging arrays. What the hell is this nonsense?'

Tam shook her head as the comm system bleeped.

'Flight deck,' she said.

'Captain, it's Augustine, I've just treated Ona again for mild hyperthermia, turns out that little experiment with Urhan didn't work out well.'

Tam sighed, 'is she all right?'

'Yes, for now, I suggest you have a word with Urhan about this. I don't think we have the facility on board to help her, Tam, she needs to be back on Earth where she can get the proper treatment for this.'

'I understand, Doctor,'

'Urhan wants to take her back to his quarters to try again and Ona seems determined to go with him, this isn't a good idea.'

'Can I speak to her?'

'One moment,' Augustine said.

Tam looked at Chuck who shrugged his shoulders, 'your call.'

'Hello?' Ona's voice filled the comm.

'Ona, are you all right?' Tam asked.

'Yes, I'm fine, I think we may be onto something here. I'd like to go with Urhan to keep trying.'

'Ona, I can't ask you to put yourself at risk for this mission, I think I might…'

'Tam, I want to help, I want to know what this is, you can't bring me back to Earth, you just can't. They'll stick me away in a cave and throw away the key. I won't go back,' she took a deep breath and continued, 'now if you will excuse me, Urhan and I have some work to do.'

Tam smiled, 'all right Ona, good luck,' she looked back at Chuck.

'She's got guts,' Chuck said.

'Doc you still there?' Tam asked.

'Yes, Tam,' she said.

'Is there anything you can do to protect her from extreme temperature changes when she doesn't end up where she'd supposed to?'

'Honestly, the only thing to do is give her atmo thermals, there's no drug to counteract environment.'

'Of course,' Tam shook her head, 'I should have thought of that, set her up with some and show her how to use them.'

'Will do.'

'That was stupid,' Tam said, 'I should have known that.'

'You can't possibly have known that,' Chuck said.

Tam shook her head and rolled her eyes.

'Tamara, with your permission I would like to go to Urhan's quarters, I think I may be of some assistance to the situation,' said Arion in Tam's ear.

'What are you going to do to help the situation?' Tam asked.

'What?' Chuck looked at her.

Tam pointed at her ear. Chuck nodded an 'Ah'

'I believe that I can help,' said Arion.

'Okay,' Tam replied looking at Chuck, 'back in a flash.'

Urhan's Quarters

Ona held Arion in her hand and looked up at Tam, 'don't look at me this was his idea.'

She looked back down at Arion. 'Okay then, come on up.'

Arion crawled up her arm and onto the right-hand side of her head, spreading its legs out to affix itself around her ear. Ona felt a quick charge of static, which made the hairs on the back of her neck stand.

'I'm terribly sorry,' came the soft voice in her mind, 'I neglected to dispel a small power surge, I hope I did not cause too much discomfort.'

'Not at all,' said Ona, smiling up at Tam.

'I'll leave you three to it, I have a lot of work to do on the flight deck,' she said, turning to Urhan, 'any problems, be sure to let me know immediately.'

Urhan nodded, 'of course.'

'If you wouldn't mind asking Urhan to attend to other tasks for a few minutes, I would like to try something with you and I would rather he not be here for it,' said Arion to Ona.

'Okay,' she said, looking up at Urhan as Tam turned and made her way out of his quarters, 'he says can you go be busy doing something else… he wants some privacy.'

Urhan tilted his head but nodded slowly and left into an adjoining room.

'Okay, now what?'

'Close your eyes please,' Arion said.

Ona did as she was told.

'And if you wouldn't mind sitting on the ground as I don't want you losing your balance, this may be slightly disorientating.'

Ona crouched down and sat on the ground with her legs crossed.

'Now, don't be scared, this may feel slightly strange. I must ask you before I do this,' said. Arion, 'can you keep a secret?'

Ona raised her eyebrows but kept her eyes shut. 'I've been keeping secrets my entire life.'

'In that case.'

Ona felt the external world fall away, as if she were falling asleep. She felt solid ground beneath her feet, opened her eyes and found herself standing in a large room filled with granite pillars, gold leaf encrusted archways, chandeliers hanging from a ceiling painted with the most vibrant motif of angles and kings in high relief. She was in a magnificent ballroom bathed in candlelight at the centre of the circular marble floor and saw a glowing ball of white light. A figure appeared from within its centre. It was an old man, in a dark tailored suit. Ona thought he looked just a little older than Eoin Tatum, maybe in his mid-eighties but healthy looking, with soft silver hair that framed a face from a handsome youth.

'Hello Ona,' said the old man.

'Hello?'

The old man looked at his hands, flipping them over. 'I haven't seen this form in a very long time. Strictly speaking, I'm not permitted to take any sort of human form again, but I thought it would make you more comfortable.'

'Who are you?'

'Arion,' said the old man.

Ona took a few steps towards him. 'This is what you look like?'

'Well, not exactly, it is what my human form used to look like, actually just a few years before the disease took over, but I wasn't very nice to look at before the upload, so this is as presentable as I could make myself,' he explained, 'no one has ever seen this form, Ona. This is the secret I wish you to keep.'

'That's amazing,' Ona said, 'don't you miss it?'

'Human form? Not really,' Arion said, brushing the sleeve of his suit jacket, 'although I'll admit that the feeling of a good suit is something any man would miss.'

'But now you're stuck in a small little robot,' Ona said, blushing, 'I'm sorry I didn't mean to be rude.'

'You weren't. Do not let my size fool you, I have ample space to move my mind around and by linking with others it allows me the supreme privilege of learning and knowing an someone else's entire history and personality, I can assure my existence is quite fulfilling,' Arion smiled.

'What was your name?'

'That, I'm afraid is something that I cannot say, it's the one thing we give up.'

'I promise I won't tell anyone.'

'That is the one secret that I cannot tell you.'

'I understand,' said Ona, 'so, now what?'

'Your mind is troubled,' said Arion, 'it is strange to be linked to it. I am feeling a strange presence, a power that is fighting against me.'

'A power?'

Arion closed his eyes, 'the molecule, I can feel it.'

Ona watched Arion's eyes as they flickered open, they were a light shade of blue, she could see them clearly now. He smiled at her and looked around the large ballroom he'd obviously created for them both.

'Your mind is sending false impressions to your bond.'

'What?'

'All you are, all you have become, the places you end up and...' he hesitated for a second, 'the other secret you're holding deep inside you. You can control it all.'

Ona kept her eyes focused intently on his soft gaze, he reminded her of a memory when she was young. A grandfather she'd only known for a short time. She remembered his kind eyes and huge hands that would devour hers up with warmth and kindness.

'I don't understand,' she said.

'You know, in all my time alive, do you know what I never learned to do?'

Ona shook her head.

'I never learned to dance,' Arion stared at her, 'would you do me the honour?'

Ona smiled and nodded, as Arion placed his right hand across his abdomen and bowed to her. 'I will, of course, try my hardest not to step on your feet.'

'It won't matter if you do, this is my imagination isn't it?'

'Your mind may not know that,' Arion extended out his hand.

Ona approached him and placed her hands in his.

'Now, correct me if I am wrong, but I believe that this is how it's done.'

'I'm not sure, nobody has ever taught me either,' she said, smiling.

'Excellent, the blind leading the blind.'

He began moving one foot towards her, she countered by moving hers back, he followed by turning her slowly and repeating until they began to sway nicely.

'Ah, I forgot,' said Arion.

From somewhere inside the ballroom, Ona began to hear soft music. They continued to dance slowly, Arion turned her, and guided her through the space.

'You're quite good at this you know,' he complimented.

They continued to dance for a time until the music eventually came to an end. Arion took a step back and bowed to her again. 'Thank you for that, I believe I may need more practice.'

Ona laughed.

'Tell me something,' he said to her, 'do you remember your family?'

Ona's smile slowly began to drop, 'not much.'

'Are you able to show me?' said Arion.

'I don't know,' Ona said, looking to the ground.

'Try,' Arion said.

Ona looked up, meeting his eyes before looking away and trying to imagine anything she could. The ballroom instantly vanished as the two were transported once again to the lab. Sirens blasted in the air as the chaotic scenes of the accident began to play out before them.

'Not again,' she said.

Arion looked to her. 'Do not focus on the memory,' he said, raising his voice so he could be heard over the commotion, 'detach yourself from it, you are not really here.'

Ona began to feel anxious, she tried to do as Arion requested but the moment felt like it would consume her. She heard a voice in the distance, her father's voice, as Arion raised his arm suddenly.

'Stop!' he shouted into the memory.

Everything froze. Ona's eyes were drawn to a fallen clipboard, now suspended in mid-air, the loose papers frozen in mid-flight. She looked to Arion.

'This is your only memory?' he said softly, his voice sounded like they were now in a small confined space.

'How are you doing this?' Ona asked, taking a step towards a frozen technician, and reaching out to touch him.

Her finger passed straight through his body.

'I am also a memory,' Arion said, 'I just happen to be a conscious one. When we merge with another, it allows us to control certain things. It becomes useful in emergency situations when a host becomes overwhelmed by their thoughts.'

Arion moved past the frozen lab technician. 'That voice,' he pointed to another man at the far side of the lab, 'your heart rate increased significantly when you heard it.'

Ona followed him through the frozen scene towards the source of the man's voice.

'It's my father,' she said softly.

They approached the frozen figure of a man with a long white coat and blue shirt, his arm outstretched and mouth open. He was tall and slender with light stubble and thick dark hair. He had a sallow complexion and his large brown eyes were wide open. He looked afraid. Ona approached him slowly. She tried to reach out to touch him but again, her hand passed straight through his body.

'Your Father?'

Ona nodded, not looking at him, 'I wasn't able to touch him.'

'I see,' Arion said.

'I shouldn't have been here, this was my fault,' her voice cracked.

'Nothing is anyone's fault,' Arion said softly, 'life unfolds as it should.'

Ona turned back to him, 'why did you bring me here?'

'I didn't,' Arion replied, 'you did. This is where you go when you are afraid. This is the last time you saw your father alive, is it not?'

Ona nodded as her eyes welled up. Arion approached her first looking to her and then to her father.

'Do not cry,' Arion said, 'these are the things that make us who we are, who we are destined to be, it was not your fault.' Arion approached Ona's father.

'He loved you,' he said, 'you can see it in his eyes, and sometimes that's enough.'

'I don't understand.'

'Parents cannot protect us forever. Look at his eyes, he would have given his life for yours, on this day or on any other.'

'He looks angry.'

'He is not angry Ona. That is regret. Regret that he is unable to give his life to save yours. All of this belongs to you now. The fragments of our past that shape our future. Those fragments can be controlled.'

'How?'

'Focus,' said Arion, 'control the memory, imagine running it forwards, running it backwards, freezing it, changing it.'

Ona took a deep breath and looked around the lab. She saw sparks frozen in mid-air coming from one of the machines to her right. She looked at the tiny points of light and tried to move them. Time moved forward slowly, the frozen papers from the clipboard floated through the air. She focused on the falling paper as time sped up to normal speed, the chaos resumed, she focused on the imagery again and the scene froze once more before moving backwards.

'Good,' Arion said, 'this is not who you are, it is who you once were. They are only images but until you master them, they will trigger the part of your mind which is also linked to the molecule.'

Ona ran the memory backwards and forwards, freezing it, speeding it up, slowing it down. She began to feel calm. The reality of it breaking, like looking at a photograph she could remove from its frame and place back. She began to feel detached from it.

'Now,' Arion said after a moment, 'take me to Thiral.'

Ona looked back at Arion and felt something else. Control. She saw the image that Urhan had shown her clearly now, as if she had known that destination her entire life. She closed her eyes and when she opened them, she was back in Urhan's quarters, she felt warm, stronger somehow. She saw Urhan. She smiled at him, raised her right hand, and clicked her fingers.

Moments later, Urhan's quarters was empty.

33

The Massey Flight Deck

'Did you see that?' said Chuck, pointing to the main sensors.

Tam had been running hull integrity checks and was standing at the rear of the flight deck. She was in the middle of checking the pressure seals on Jacobs repair. Her mind had wandered while running through the various system checks and hadn't heard him.

'Cap?' he said, turning in his chair.

She snapped back to him and turned, 'what?'

'There's something on the scope.'

Tam frowned, looking over his shoulder. They watched the sensor readings. 'It's a ship.'

Chuck looked at the darkness outside the window.

'Still too far out to get a definitive reading.'

A jump in the electromagnetic radiation made her freeze.

'Oh, oh,' Chuck agreed.

'Yeah,' Tam slid into the flight chair, 'try get me a visual.'

Chuck activated one of the heads-up view screens, linking the sensor data to the display. It flickered to life, showing a dark area space lit softly with a background star field. Tam brought up the main drive systems one by one.

'There,' Chuck said, softly.

They looked to the screen and watched as the star-field distorted and then disappeared.

'Is that what I think it is?' He squinted his eyes.

Tam watched the stars evaporate and be replaced by the glowing silver surface with smooth streamlined contours of a massive ship.

'That's a LAL battle cruiser,' she said.

'That's not ideal,' Chuck said.

'Have they detected us?'

'Well, it's on a direct intercept course. So, my educated guess would be yes,' he looked at her.

'Time to go,' she flicked on the comm system. 'Captain to Urhan, please report.'

There was no response. She looked at Chuck.

'Oh, not now,' she sighed, 'Urhan, this is the Captain do you read?'

She waited, watching the LAL battle cruiser approach slowly on the screen. She tapped the computer interface.

'Urhan here,' came the response, 'Tamara, Ona has just vanished.'

'Well that's just perfect,' she said, 'Locate crew member Ona Mendel,'

'Ona Mendel is not on board the ship,' came the response.

'Time for a discrete exit,' Chuck commented.

'Hang on, I'm gonna take us around the back of the moon,' she engaged the main thrusters and gripped the flight controls, 'let's see what they do.'

'Got it,' said Chuck.

Tam pushed the thrusters to thirty percent and dropped the nose of the Massey, reducing their orbit enough for the gravity of the moon to take hold. As soon as it did, she knocked the power back to idle and let the mass of the moon do the rest.

'Silent running,' she told Chuck.

Chuck nodded and began shutting down the main power systems. Tam flicked on the comm system again, this time to a ship wide hail.

'All hands, silent running, this is a code blue alert, this is not a drill,' she said, closing the channel and tapping the computer console again.

'Alert flight deck upon detection of crew member Ona Mendel,' she thought for a second, 'is Arion unit on board?'

'Negative,' the computers responded.

Tam took a breath and watched as the soft glow of the thin atmosphere of Thiral's moon grew ever closer in the window.

'Okay that's low enough,' she eased back on the controls.

The Massey drifted like a silent bullet across the ionosphere as Tam watched the sensor readings carefully

'Range?' she quietly said to Chuck.

'Fifty-thousand kilometres and closing, she's not changing course,' he said.

Tam watched the visual of the mighty ship. The LAL battle cruisers were formidable yet beautiful in design. She'd never seen the inside of one, but they were at least twice the size of the biggest ESDA cruiser and armed to the teeth with highly classified weaponry. She'd seen demonstrations of the technology while at the academy on a recorded visual and one of them blow an asteroid the size of a continent into microscopic dust. The ESDA had been screaming for the right to integrate it into their fleet, the LAL, predictably, had refused. While no LAL vessel had ever attacked an ESDA ship, the last few days had told her that she was now in uncharted waters. She could feel Chuck's tension and his muscles tighten.

'Relax,' she said softly.

'I am relaxed,' his eyes were magnetized to the view screen.

'Tell that to the vein on your forehead,' she chuckled.

'What can I say, a big brain needs a big vein,' he replied, 'she's still coming.'

Tam looked at the screen.

'She's altering course.'

Sure enough, the LAL ship was beginning to turn.

'That'll put her in orbit in six minutes,' Chuck said.

Tam bit her lip. She wondered how far she could get through the Thiral system on engines alone before they caught up to them. The answer came swiftly.

Not very far.

'We could try for Thiral and maybe get the Massey into one of the deep cave systems on the northern continent?' Chuck suggested.

Tam ran some numbers. 'They're faster, bigger and have serious weapons at their disposal.'

The ship-to-ship comm link chirped.

'Incoming transmission from the LAL battle cruiser,' Chuck said, 'looks like she's got us.'

'Not yet they don't,' Tam replied, 'let's hear it.'

Chuck opened the Channel.

'Massey Shaw, this is the LAL cruiser Crightal. You are ordered to shut off your engines and prepare to be boarded,' the stern voice rang through the transmission.

Tam looked at Chuck and pressed the comm button. 'Crightal, this is the Massey Shaw repeat your last.'

'Massey Shaw, stand down your engines and prepare to be boarded,' repeated the voice.

Tam pressed the response, 'Crightal, we're in the middle of a low orbit engine test, to shut down now could be dangerous given our altitude.'

'This is your final warning,' came the voice again.

Tam found herself chewing the inside of her mouth as she muted the transmission and glanced at Chuck.

'If we shoot the laser cutter across its bow then it might knock out those weapons,' he offered.

'We're not attacking a LAL cruiser, Chuck, they'll vaporize us.'

'Well, yeah there's that I suppose, still, rather go out fighting,' Chuck said.

'Nobody's going out anywhere.'

'Crew member Ona Mendel is now on board the Massey Shaw,' said the computer voice suddenly.

Tam pressed her comm button, 'Tam to Urhan.'

Silence filled the flight deck.

'Come on,' she said through gritted teeth.

More silence followed.

'They're still closing in and increasing speed. I'm getting weird energy readings,' Chuck said.

'Define weird energy readings,' Tam said.

'There's a radiation spike at the forward end of the ship, my guess, they're running hot. They might take a pot shot at us.'

Tam went to speak again but was interrupted.

'Flight deck this is Urhan.'

'Urhan, is Ona with you?'

'Yes, Tamara, she's here and safe.'

Tam and Chuck exchanged glances. Then said, 'we'll talk about it later, I need you up here now, we have to get the hell out of here, we've got a LAL warship bearing down on our asses.'

'I am on my way,' said Urhan.

'Chuck plot a course for the IGO star system and begin STC calibration.'

'We'll need to get at least eighty-thousand kilometres away from the moon,' he said.

'I know, we'll make a run for it as soon as Urhan gets here.'

'Well, this is going to be interesting.'

'Still sure you want to do this?' Tam looked at Chuck eyebrows raised, 'it's not too late to back out, I hand myself over to them and you get to have a normal life.'

Chuck didn't answer her, he simply folded his arms and smiled at her, giving her an expression that told her she was wasting time and to get on with it.

She slapped his arm, giving it a firm grip. He placed his hand on hers and then looked back at the navigation array and began plotting the coordinates, activating the STC tube, which rose from the centre console and opened. At that exact moment, the door to the flight deck slid open and Urhan entered with a glowing blue container.

'Are you all right?' Tam said.

'Yes, Captain, what is happening?' Urhan said, placing the container into the access hatch on the front of the molecule chamber.

'Is Ona all right?' Tam asked.

'She is fine, what LAL vessel is approaching?' Urhan glanced down at the view screen.

'The Crightal?' Chuck said, 'do you know it?'

Urhan glanced out the window, 'yes, Tam, it would be advisable for us to leave this vicinity, judging by the power increase they have charged their weapons array.'

'They wouldn't fire on a human ship, would they?' Chuck said angrily at Urhan.

'I believe given the grave circumstances that yes, they will,' Urhan said.

'Even with you on board?' Chuck said, surprised.

'Life may be sacred but death is not something that we fear.'

Chuck frowned, 'well, I don't know what any of that means, but it didn't make me feel any better.'

'Me either,' Tam said, 'Urhan load up a jump and let's get the hell out of here.'

'You will need to move the ship to a safe distance to …'

'I know Urhan,' she snapped.

There was an awkward silence.

'Very well,' Urhan said.

Tam gave him an apologetic glance, 'sorry.'

'No need to apologize,' Urhan loaded up the chamber and sealed it.

Tam watched the incoming visual of the battleship carefully. 'Okay, when she gets to within ten thousand kilometres we'll make our move,' she clicked the comms system, 'engine room.'

'Go,' Jacob replied.

'Jacob keep an eye on the reactor, will you? I'm going to be pushing the engines,' Tam ordered.

'Is that a LAL battle cruiser off our port bow?'

'Yes, Jacob we've all seen that.'

'Just checking, you never know. Engines are ready, Cap.'

'Thank you,' Tam switched the cannel to the internship frequency, 'all hands this is the Captain, prepare to jump, there may be some tight manoeuvring here so secure all stations and strap in if you can, Captain out.'

She looked at the STC chamber, Urhan had the molecule loaded and had his hand on the activation panel.

'And off we go,' Tam said softly to herself, as she throttled up the main engines and broke orbit.

The moons glistening horizon lowered gently downwards and out of view. Tam lifted the nose of the Massey upwards, pointing it towards the stars. She glanced slightly to the right, catching a glimpse of Thiral's largest ocean as it rotated past a thinly covered veil of cloud near its largest continent. She turned the ship a few degrees to starboard then gripped the throttle controls tightly and in one swift motion pushed them all the way forward, opening the fuel manifolds to full power. She felt the pressure in her chest increase as the steady force of acceleration hurtled her ship out of orbit and into the vast emptiness.

'She's on us,' Chuck said.

Tam looked at the view screen. The Massey was no match to the velocity and firepower of the other ship. She glanced at Urhan's hand, placed calmly on the STC chamber ready to inject it. A bright red glow shone past the forward windows. She shielded her eyes. The ship shook. Tam and Chuck looked at each other, both a little stunned at how powerful the beam appeared to be.

'Woah,' Chuck said.

'That was a warning shot,' Urhan calmly said behind them.

'Consider us warned.'

Tam gripped her flight controls and checked their relative bearing and distance from Thiral's moon, 'just another minute.'

'I doubt we have one,' Chuck muttered under his breath.

'I concur,' said Urhan.

Tam reached down and fired the aft port thruster at full power.

'What are you doing?' Urhan asked.

'You may want to hold onto something,' Chuck said.

Tam throttled up and began an evasive pattern she liked to call the corkscrew. She threw the Massey hard over and began a controlled looping flight path that would make even the most hardened fighter pilot lose his or her lunch. The gees increased as her middle ear cried havoc. It was basically like being sucked down a drainpipe, but it had the added benefit of being tricky to lock onto. She kept altering her course, ever so slightly as a second and third weapons shot streaked past the window. She increased the severity of her turns. The world began to blur. A haze descended on the control panel. She tried to turn to Urhan, recognizing that her body was about to black out.

She saw blue light somewhere to her right, the sound of something familiar, the stars began to disappear in front of her along with her consciousness.

34

Tam awoke feeling dazed and disorientated, with strange images in her mind from a dream she couldn't quite remember. Something about a cave with a pair of eyes staring at her in the dark. She saw the computer consoles of the flight deck, her mind now starting to clear. There was a bitter taste in her mouth and her jaw felt stiff. She leaned forwards. Her shoulders ached. She turned to her right to see Chuck passed out, slumped in his chair. She placed a hand on his shoulder.

'Chuck,' she moved his large shoulder, 'Chuck.'

She looked behind her to see Urhan rising to his feet before she glanced out at the familiar distortion that was generation by their STC jump. Urhan had done it, he'd gotten them into hyperspace.

'What the...' Chuck groaned, placing his hand on his head.

'You alive?' Tam coughed.

Chuck nodded, she looked back at Urhan. 'You okay?'

'I am,' Urhan said.

'Well, done.'

Urhan nodded.

'Bit of notice next time?' Chuck said.

'I'll do my best,' Tam flicked on her comms, 'engine room.'

'Go,' Jacob's voice vibrated through the comms.

'Everyone all right down there?'

'Does a diagnostic console covered in puke count?'

'Yes, it does,' she laughed.

'Then we're all fine thanks for asking,' he said, 'hey, is there any chance I can get a quick scan of Ona? I'd like to run a few energy absorption simulations down here.'

'I'll ask her,' she said, switching the frequency, 'med bay, flight.'

'Med bay here,' said Augustine, 'what the hell just happened Captain?'

'We ran into a slight issue with a pursuing LAL battle cruiser, is everyone okay down there?'

'I'm getting reports of some minor injuries, I need to go attend to, Captain,' Augustine sounded a little frustrated.

'Then I won't keep you, Doctor, let me know if I can do anything,' Tam said.

'Hmm,' Augustine replied closing the channel.

'She's not happy,' said Chuck, raising his eyebrows.

She connected the comm system to Urhan's quarters. 'Tam to Ona? Can you read me?'

'Ona here,' said a quiet voice.

'Are you all right?'

'I'm fine thank you, I was prepared, don't worry,' said Ona.

Tam was slightly confused by the comment and she furrowed her brow, 'okay, would you mind meeting me outside the flight deck?'

'Sure.'

~ ~ ~

'Are you sure you're up for this?' Tam asked Ona as they walked through the decks of the Massey towards the engine room.

'How long has Urhan been on board?'

'Three years,' replied Tam.

'Is he the first LAL that has been on this ship?' Ona asked, her tone uncertain.

'I've served personally with two,' Tam said, 'Urhan has been with us for longer than most guardian postings.'

'Why is that?'

'He requested an extension on his tour, I guess he likes me,' Tam chuckled, 'why do you ask?'

'Just curious,' she said, in a way that grabbed Tam's attention.

'Just curious?'

'He's just,' Ona said slowing her pace, 'different.'

'Well, yeah, he's an alien.'

Ona made eye contact and smiled.

'Yes, I know he's an alien,' she replied, 'he's just so guarded.'

'Meaning?' Tam's curiosity grew.

'It's probably nothing, it's just all a little strange to me.'

'You and me both,' Tam said, 'can I ask you something?'

'Sure.'

'Does it hurt? When you travel like that?'

'It's hard to explain,' Ona looked at her, 'it's like someone is pinching my skin, all over my body.'

'Sounds uncomfortable,' Tam said.

'It is.'

She stopped in the corridor suddenly and waited for a crew member to pass. Tam acknowledged him by giving him a friendly nod before folding her arms and facing Ona.

'Six months ago, I vanished when I was asleep,' Ona whispered, almost too low for Tam to hear, 'the place I ended up at was like a nightmare I couldn't wake up from. Molten rock everywhere, the sky was red, and my lungs were filled with something so toxic I started convulsing. It felt like I was on fire,' Ona stared at the ground, 'by the time I got back to the station I had burns all over my body and spent nearly a month in the medical bay. They had to regrow my alveoli apparently.'

'My god,' Tam said.

'So, that hurt,' Ona said.

'I bet,' Tam agreed, 'that must have been frightening.'

'Yes, it was. But after that, every time I left that place, I thought that it may be my last and I sort of accepted it.'

She paused, 'at the end I began to welcome it,' she gave Tam a look.

'And now?'

'Now?' Ona smiled, 'I think something has changed.'

Tam returned her smile, 'I hope so. It's a big universe but there's only one of us,' Tam stared into her eyes with sisterly love, 'come on.' She was right, something had changed.

They approached the engine room hatch and stepped through. Jacob was staring up at the STC fluid injection tanks and shouting to a crew member at the other end of the engine room.

'No!' he shouted, 'two degrees I said! TWO!'

'Sorry,' came the response from the young man behind a control console.

'Good!' he shouted, 'hold it there and for god sake don't let it get any hotter or your shore leave will involve me scraping your bones off the inside of the hull.'

He shook his head at the ground and then muttered, 'Jesus Christ.'

'Something wrong?' Tam said, making him jump.

'My god Cap, don't you know not to sneak up on an old man,' he said, holding his chest.

'Sorry,' she said, 'Jacob you've met Ona?'

'Hi there,' Jacob's eyes darted to Ona, 'I hear you can go faster than light?' he paused, 'cool.'

'Well, not exactly.'

'How's my ship?' Tam asked, observing the engine room.

'We had a slight heat regulation issue, but we've fixed it,' he said.

'What's a SLIGHT heat regulation problem?'

'It's probably better if you don't know about it,' Jacob said, waving his hand, 'I fixed it.'

'I see,' Tam said, folding her arms.

'Trust me, it's all fine,' he cleared his throat, 'so, Ona, there's no real polite way of asking this, so I'll just come out and say it. I'd love to get a scan of the inside of your body.'

He shrugged his shoulders in an apologetic way.

'Dr. Augustine already did that?' Tam chimed in.

'Not with an STC primer she didn't,' Jacob said.

'What's that?' Ona said.

'Honestly, it won't hurt a bit,' Jacob said, 'it basically reads the energy output and stability of the molecule, normally once injected into our drive systems, but since your body is a living drive system it might prove helpful to both of us if we can see what the little fella is up to right now. You know, for science.'

'You sure it won't hurt her?'

'Promise, will only take a second.'

'Ona' Tam said, 'that okay with you?'

She nodded.

'Cool, step into my office.' Jacob said.

Jacob and Ona went over to the diagnostic station as Tam walked towards the bright blue STC containment chamber. She stared into its sparkling centre. It was like looking at fluorescent plankton in an ocean swell. The gentle humming of the hybrid alien tech was one of the most soothing sounds on board the ship. She loved the engine room. The beating heart of the propulsion letting her senses know that the ship was hurtling through a vast galaxy. It gave her a true sense of the endless space outside. The engine room made her feel as if she were constantly in motion. Never really trapped, never really alone. She heard laughter behind her and saw

Ona giggling. Jacob was running the scanner over her back and telling her jokes to calm her down.

She turned back to face the glow of the engine and placed her hand on the transparent outer casing. She felt a tingling sensation on the tips of her fingers as she ran them over its surface. She thanked it in her mind and asked The Massey to be kind to her crew, to keep them safe and to get them all home alive. As she finished her request, she received a light burst of electrical energy down her arm.

She smiled at it and whispered

Thank you.

35

Flight Deck
49 Hours Later
On Approach to Star System IGO

There was silence on the flight deck as Tam checked her position. She turned to Chuck.

'Not too close,' she said, 'half a million clicks from the star system and we drop our power levels to take a peek.'

Chuck nodded.

'Urhan, get ready for STC in case this goes south,' she said.

Tam placed her hand on the drive control systems and deactivated the jump. She heard a sharp downward tone of energy as the engines returned the Massey Shaw into normal space. The distortion effect gave way as the flight crew looked on at the asteroid field. It was deathly quiet.

'Tam,' Ona's soft voice came from behind her.

'Yeah?' Tam whispered, not taking her eyes off the exterior view.

'There's something...' Ona was interrupted by a light bleep.

'Hold up,' Chuck said.

'What is it?' Tam glanced at him.

'That Arion beacon is coming from the fourth planet,' Chuck said, 'I've got something else.'

'What is it?'

'I've got another signal, ESDA,' Chuck said, 'confirming,' he said, 'it's the Lassen.'

'Where?' Tam's darted off into the view.

'Close,' Chuck said, 'looks like she's adrift just outside this asteroid ring,' he said, pointing to an enhanced image of the star system. 'Should we call her?'

'I would not attempt to do that,' Urhan interjected.

'Why not?'

'He's right,' Tam said, 'I don't want to risk detection,' she leaned in, 'can you get a life sign reading?'

'Not at this distance,' Chuck said, 'its power signatures are active, engines appear to be down, but attitude and thruster control don't seem to be working.'

She looked at Urhan, 'can they see us?'

Urhan leaned over to the screen.

'You can't go there,' Ona said, suddenly.

'Why?' Chuck turned to her.

She gave him a grave look, 'you just can't.'

'Ona,' Tam said, 'there could be people still alive.'

She turned her head slowly to meet Tam's gaze, 'there aren't.'

The comment seemed to cool the air on the flight deck.

'I would suggest that we attempt to do what we came here to do, Tamara and leave this place as quickly as possible,' Urhan said.

Tam looked at Chuck.

'Don't look at me. I'm not the one creeping everyone out with ominous warnings,' Chuck replied.

She looked at the signal from the Lassen again. 'Urhan how close can we get before we're detectable to their sensors?'

'I do not know,' Urhan said, 'in all likelihood, we may already be visible.'

'Well, we haven't been attacked yet, so that's something,' Chuck said.

'They may be observing us.'

'Arion'

'Yes, Tamara,' Arion said.

'Give me HUD,' she said.

'Of course,' he replied, linking to the computer and laying out the flight plan in her vision.

Tam gently increased the thrusters and turned the Massey. Tam kept her gaze firmly through the forward-facing windows as she scanned for anything out of the ordinary. She kept her mind focused. She felt like a gazelle wandered too close to a watering hole, predators in the long grass, silently creeping forwards with giant paws gently inching closer to her, unheard and unseen.

After cruising for thirty minutes, scanning and watching, they approached the asteroid belt. Huge chunks of rock drifted slowly past. She fired the bow thrusters, slowing her approach and activating the forward lighting array. High beams of white light cast their glow over the uneven and broken surfaces of the orbiting rocks as they gently passed by the forward windows.

'Lassen coming up on the port side in three minutes. Still no sign of any other vessels in the vicinity,' Chuck said.

Tam turned her head to try and get a visual on her. She brought the Massey to a full stop and waited as a particularly huge chunk of rock passed by the facing lights. She frowned and looked at Chuck.

'I'm not getting anything at all from subsurface scans, it's like the damn things aren't even there,' he said.

The shimmering hull of the Lassen drifted into view. Tam scanned its exterior for any signs of damage.

'It's got power,' she fired the port thrusters, bringing the Massey alongside.

'Looks that way,' Chuck said.

'Can we get a closer look at the third planet yet?' Tam asked.

Chuck shook his head, 'some weird interference from the asteroid field, we'll have to get past it.'

'Arion, plot me a safe course,' she said.

'Yes, Tam,' said Arion.

Tam examined the new course and looked over the Lassen one more time before hitting the aft thrusters and leaving her behind.

~ ~ ~

As the ship made its way through the giant rocks, weaving around the small spaces between them, the Lassen slowly raised the forward end of its main drive section, righting itself with its thrusters and began moving. The things on board watching the Massey Shaw as she manoeuvred through the floating rock. They watched the little ship closely. The things inside prepared.

36

Tam pulled back on the power and stopped the ship a thousand kilometres inside the inner boundary of the asteroid field. They were able to get more detailed scan of the system from here. She frowned at the readings, 'what is that?' she curiously glanced down at her sensors.

'Binary star?' Chuck answered.

'No, it's too small,' Tam focused in on the odd planet with glowing rings.

She paused looking at the image. 'Urhan, what am I looking at?'

Urhan gently lowered his head, turning his eyes to Tam for a brief second before looking back at the screen. 'That is IGO Royal.'

'The what now?' Chuck said.

'It is best we give that world a wide birth,' Urhan said.

Tam turned her gaze back to the glowing planet moving smoothly through the sky.

'Still no sign of any spacecraft,' Chuck said.

His voice sounded tense, it was mirrored by his stiff and alert posture. Tam locked on to the readings from the fourth planet as she tried to pinpoint the location of her father's Arion unit.

'What the hell is that?' Chuck asked, pointing at the navigation screen.

Tam shook her head looking back at the strange smooth sphere being shown on her screen. She looked back at Urhan, 'well?'

Urhan nodded, keeping his hand firmly on the surface of the STC cylinder. Tam saw one of his fingers twitch; as if he was ready to activate it at any second.

'That is IGO War,' Urhan said.

'That doesn't sound friendly,' Chuck said.

'I assure you that it is not,' Urhan said, 'Tamara, I suggest we do this quickly.'

'Everyone just take a breath,' Tam said gently, 'let's see if we can get a closer look at that signal.' She turned to Chuck, 'let's drop a football.'

Chuck nodded and moved to a console to his right, 'football prepped.'

The Football was an aptly named probe because of its shape. With its own inbuilt thrusters, cutting tools, self-guided navigation and host of other intelligent diagnostic and sensor arrays. It was able to boost signal strengths in hard to reach areas, assess and give first response analysis in terrain and environments the Massey was too big to reach.

'Keep the main systems running on diagnostic mode, keep her as quiet as you can, we need a signal boost,' Tam instructed.

Chuck made some adjustments to the football launching protocols, 'ready.'

'Pitch it,' said Tam.

Chuck pressed the launch command as Tam stared out the front of the ship. The oblong shaped craft only two meters in length shot out in front of the Massey, eventually disappearing into the darkness as its on-board thrusters fired it towards the strange looking planet.

'Time to intercept?' Tam said.

'Twenty-three minutes,' Chuck replied tensely.

'Okay, let's just hold here for now and see what it comes back with.'

Chuck nodded.

37

Tam held the thrusters steady at quarter power as she gently moved the ship forward.

'Probe data coming in,' Chuck said.

Urhan's hand was still firmly in place.

'Let's see it,' said Tam.

Chuck brought up the scans. The smooth almost metallic looking surface of the planet was unmistakably artificial.

'Readings?'

'There's definitely subsurface structures, but I don't see any access points,' Chuck said, turning his head towards her, 'it's constructed.'

Tam nodded, 'incredible.' she paused, 'Arion, are you detecting any transmissions coming to or from the planet?'

'No Tam.'

Tam rested her hand on the throttle and increased power.

'Can you lock on to the other Arion beacon?' she said.

'One moment,' said Arion, 'yes, Tam, I have it. Three kilometres below the surface at the following coordinates.'

A red marker point flashed on the planet near the northern most point on its current axis.

'So, how do we get in?' Chuck said quietly.

'We don't,' Tam said, turning to Ona.

Ona took a shaky breath, 'Okay, I'll try.'

'Are you absolutely sure Ona?'

'Yes,' Ona said, 'I'll zip in take a quick look and zip back.'

'Cap?' said Chuck.

Tam turned to see Chuck pointing at the screen showing the feed from the football. It showed static distortion.

'We just lost the football,' Chuck said.

'Cause?' Tam checked the feed manually.

'I don't know,' his voice uncertain, 'looks like the electrics just fried out.'

'Play back the last minute.'

Tam watched the last few seconds of the recording carefully before the transmission cut off. She saw a pulse of light strike the visual recordings, then static.

'I think we're rumbled,' Chuck said.

'Okay then let's not overstay our welcome here,' Tam said.

She turned to Ona, 'Arion, I'd like you to go with her,' Tam hesitated, 'will that be all right?'

Ona nodded.

'Arion, Ona won't be familiar with your defensive systems, so I'm authorizing you to defer to your own targeting structure should the need arise.'

'I understand Tam, I will do my upmost to protect her,' said Arion, 'see you shortly.'

With that, Arion removed himself from Tam's ear and crawled down her shoulder and arm, coming to a rest on the palm of her hand. She held him out to Ona, and he climbed up and attached himself to the side of her head.

'It's too quiet,' Tam heard Chuck say under his breath.

'Take it easy,' Tam said.

'Arion, activate your homing beacon,' she said.

She waited.

'He says its active,' Ona said.

Tam nodded and pointed at the screen.

'Okay,' she took a breath, 'the signal is here,' she pointed at a section of the planet.

'Three hundred meters below the surface,' she said, 'according to the readings from the football, there's an oxygen atmosphere but I'm not taking any chances'

Tam pointed to a locker at the rear of the flight deck, 'in there.'

Ona opened the compartment and took out the suit.

'This looks too big,' she said.

'Don't worry, put it on,' Tam said, 'it will adjust to your body shape.'

'Over my clothes?'

'No,' replied Tam smiling, 'there's a fitting area outside the first door on the right.'

Ona nodded leaving the flight deck and sealing the door behind her. Chuck glanced over at Tam.

'Don't lose that lock on her for a second,' she ordered.

'Don't you worry about that,' said Chuck, 'I won't.'

~ ~ ~

After a few minutes, Ona returned to the flight deck wearing the now fully fitted space suit. The material allowing full range of motion in every direction. Tam pointed to the control panel on Ona's right arm.

'Okay,' Tam said, 'Arion will interface with your suit and be able to activate and deactivate the helmet at will, he can also regulate the body temperature and monitor your vitals but you can still do all that manually with the control panel on your arm, see it?'

Ona nodded.

'Okay, Arion activate the faceplate,' Tam said.

A second later, a helmet appeared from behind Ona's neck. It snapped shut and formed a transparent seal around the front of her face, lighting it from internal lights inside the bottom front.

'Ready?' Tam asked softly.

Ona nodded and took a quick look at the readings on her arm.

'Okay hang on,' Tam said turning back to her flight controls.

She throttled back and checked her flight path again, scanning for any rogue asteroids or anything else ahead. She then turned back to Ona.

'Whenever you're ready,' Tam said.

Ona smiled at Urhan who was staring at her, 'back in a jiffy.'

'Yes, I am sure of it,' said Urhan.

Ona turned her gaze to the window her eyes growing distant. She took a breath and snapped her finger. There was a burst of air and she was gone. Tam looked over at Chuck wide eyes.

'Wow,' Chuck said, amazed.

'Wow indeed,' said Tam.

They would only have a few seconds to marvel at what had just happened before the flight deck exploded all around them.

38

Ona's feet touched solid ground. She felt lighter. The gravity in this place was different, definitely not as strong as Earth standard. She looked around and saw polished rock walls that glistened like and underground cave. They seemed to glow from within, lighting up a long pathway in either direction.

'Are you all right Ona? Your heart rate has increased significantly,' said Arion.

Arion was right. She was scared, there were no two ways about it.

'So would yours if you had one,' she whispered.

She quickly snapped her head around to see if she was alone. It seemed to look that way.

'It's too dark in here,' she whispered.

Arion stimulated Ona's retinas to allow more light in.

'Thank you, Arion,' she said.

'My counterparts signal appears to be coming from three hundred meters in this direction,' said Arion, forming a little direction indicator through the projection.

'Got it.'

'Proceed with caution.'

'I'll try,' Ona said, as she began moving steadily forwards.

This surface of the ground felt strange, as if she were walking on polished glass. She heard something off in the distance and stopped. She looked back at the long narrow pathway behind her. It seemed to stretch on for eternity. There were odd clicking noises coming from inside the rock, she was sure of it. It only lasted a few seconds.

'Did you hear that?' she whispered.

'I did,' Arion said, 'I am having a hard time localizing it.'

'Sounds like an animal,' Ona whispered again.

'I have no record on file that corresponds.'

'Whatever it was didn't sound friendly.'

'I would advise you to not let your mind run away with fear. When no fear has yet presented itself.'

'Tam said you had weapons?'

'That is correct,' Arion said, 'two forward facing projectiles attached to my lower limbs. It takes me several seconds to recharge once they have been used, so bear that in mind.'

'Won't you burn my face off if you shoot them beside my head?' Ona asked, worry brimmed in her voice.

'The pulses of energy are exponentially charged and do not reach their full strength until .002 of a second after firing them. Until that time they feel like a cold blast of air, I can assure you, you are quite safe,' said Arion.

'Good to know,' said Ona, 'how do I work them?'

'I think for now, it's best I operate my weapons systems. The targeting systems are not easy to adapt to.'

'Are you a good shot?'

'I am.'

'Okay then, I guess I'll have to trust you.'

'That would be greatly appreciated.'

Ona took a deep breath and moved on, the only sound she heard was the soft oxygen intake from the inside of her headpiece. After a few minutes of gingerly moving forward, she reached a wall.

'I'm reading it being solid,' said Arion.

She looked and saw that the ceiling was a good hundred or so meters above her. The wall wasn't made of rock but of metal.

'It's a door,' she said.

'It's composed of some sort of metal alloy that I am unfamiliar with.'

Ona looked around for an access panel but couldn't see one. 'Okay, now what?'

'Perhaps it would be advisable to return to the ship to look for a new set of coordinates.'

Another ghostly sound echoed down the corridor, which made the hairs on the back of her neck stand on end. She shot a glance behind her but still saw nothing.

'I don't like this,' said Arion.

'What's to like?' Ona whispered back as she looked again to the massive metal door.

She placed her hand on it and ran her fingers over the mirror like finish. 'Arion, can you tell how thick this is?'

'No,' said Arion, 'why?'

'Odds are it's not more than a few feet, right?'

'That's not something I can verify.'

'Based on its size, how thick do you think it is?'

Ona saw a beam of light in her field of vision. It looked like Arion was taking a scan of the structure. 'Ona there could be nothing behind this, there's no reason to believe this is not just a solid piece of polished ore from a meteorite or something. It could be a few meters; it could be a few miles.'

'I'm guessing it's not.'

'I'm not sure I like where this is going'

'It won't let me materialize into something solid,' Ona said.

'What won't?'

'The molecule, it won't,' she said, 'not if what I've heard is true, if I die now that would mean it won't happen.'

'What won't happen?'

'Hold on.'

'What are you going to…'

Arion was cut off when Ona took a breath and snapped her fingers.

39

THE MASSEY

Tam's eyes were burning. There was a fire in the aft compartment that Urhan was trying desperately to put out. She coughed as she grappled with the flight controls, turning the ship in an array of different directions in a desperate effort to evade what was pursuing them. Time seemed to be moving in slow motion. She heard Chuck shouting out the damage beside her. The comm systems had blown out so she couldn't reach the engine room or any other part of the ship, for that matter. Beams of red light streamed past the windows, each one closer than the next as their attackers adapted and homed in on her evasive pattern. She heard Chuck shout out the situation report as she twisted the ship is all sorts of directions trying to evade.

'Hull breach deck 8,'

'Hull breach deck 4,'

'Comms array destroyed,'

'Main power down to twenty percent,'

'Fire on deck 3,'

'Life support offline,'

'STC drive non-responsive,'

'Overload in main drive core, power at one twenty-three and rising, we gotta shut it down!' he shouted.

Tam decided that the risk of a breach versus the risk of being shot point blank with disrupters was pretty much the same at this point and if they were all about to die, she'd rather do it while flying her ship.

What the hell are they doing?

The ship had been empty, their scans had shown it. None of it made any sense.

'Cap?' Chuck said, injecting urgency.

Tam gritted her teeth and tried to think straight. She focused on the situation, not the reason. The Massey was dead, she knew that. She needed to find a way to save their lives before they blew up. She ran through everything she could. If she didn't shut the engines down in the next minute or so they were done, if she shut them down, they were done, if she ordered everyone to the escape pods, they'd be picked off one by one. More fire erupted across the top of the ship, Tam shoved the flight controls forward, they felt sluggish, resistant.

'We're losing thruster control,' said Chuck.

She turned to Urhan. 'Try once more,' she said softly to him.

Urhan nodded to her then placed his hand on the STC chamber and entered his activation sequence. Nothing happened.

'I am sorry Tamara,' he said, 'it's non-functional.'

She looked back at Chuck. The flight controls suddenly went limp as the sound of all the power on the flight deck faded away to nothing. Chuck looked to his computer as all the lights in the flight deck went black. It was a few seconds before Tam realized that she wasn't breathing. The taste of acrid smoke still lingered. The Massey tumbled gently through space.

'Main power offline,' said Chuck in the silence, 'we're dead in the water.'

Tam waited for the final shot. She looked to Chuck, her eyes wide. She wanted to say sorry but couldn't find the words. He smiled at her, letting her know that she didn't have to.

Seconds passed by, then minutes. The silence continued. The disrupter fire didn't follow. The temperature in the cabin began to fall. Cold wisps of air began to form as they exhaled. Chuck leaned up out of his chair to take a closer look out of the window.

'Where the hell are they?' he whispered.

Tam pushed herself forward and joined Chuck, peering out of the window. From the nothing, the hull of the Lassen suddenly appeared overhead as it slowly cruised within meters of the Massey before coming to a dead stop.

'Well, we're still here,' Chuck said quietly.

Tam glanced at the STC chamber and saw the blue light of the molecule shimmering under the outer casing. 'Urhan is there anything you can do?'

'Tamara the chamber will not activate, even the main housing and ignition tank in the engine room is non-responsive,' Urhan said.

'What do you think, Cap?' Chuck said.

Tam thought about Ona, wondering what was taking her so long.

'Cap!' Chuck said suddenly.

Tam followed his pointing finger at something outside the window. The stars behind were obscured by a huge dark shape. A shape that no human had lived to tell the tale of.

It was them. They'd finally come for her. She was nine years old again. The same ship, the very same ship now coming straight for her. She wanted it to come now. She wanted to vent all her fury at what those things had done to her family. It seemed different somehow. Unlike the monstrous thing she'd seen in her dreams which had eyes and a mouth and roared into the dark. This was more clinical looking, unfeeling. Just an alien ship. A ship she wanted to break apart with her bare hands. She caught Chuck's reflection in the glass and turned back to him.

She had failed them all. Ona would be lost somewhere, perhaps already dead, and they would soon be added to the ones who had vanished at their hands. She saw movement outside. She turned to see the Ghost ship open and begin pouring what looked like vast amounts of a liquid or gas into the void. It looked to have a life of its own. Unnatural movement and flow which denoted intelligent control. It was moving towards the Massey. She turned to Urhan.

'What do we do?' she asked, barely able to say the question.

Urhan shook his head, 'when all other options have been exhausted, then only one remains… we surrender.'

'What?' said Chuck, 'and how do we do that?'

'I believe that given our dire situation that eventuality has already been forced upon us.'

Tam looked to Chuck who reached inside the compartment and took out his firearm.

'Well, I'll be dammed if I don't go out with a fight,' he said.

Tam already knew that it wouldn't matter. She admired him and his dogged courage but didn't reciprocate the gesture.

'Put it away Chuck,' she said quietly.

'Cap?' he said.

Tam glanced back out the window, 'guns aren't going do anything.'

Chuck frowned but kept the weapon in his hand as he peered at the strange dark fluid that was approaching fast.

The floating liquid began to change shape as it reached the bow of the Massey and began flowing around it like lava around a rock. It touched the front windows, and everything went dark. She tried the comm system once more.

'Comms are down Tam,' Chuck said.

'Worth a try,' she muttered.

A strange buckling noise coming from behind the flight deck door made them turn their heads.

'You may still be able to launch the escape pods manually,' said Urhan calmly.

Tam didn't waste a second in responding. She leapt out of her chair and Chuck followed. She moved to the back of the flight deck and heard screaming coming from the other side. It was happening all over again, to her now and her crew. She looked at Chuck, the weapon still in his hand, and nodded to him. He raised the gun as she opened the flight door. The thing that was waiting for them on the other side wasted no time.

Darkness descended on all of them, enveloped them.

Moments later, the flight deck was empty.

40

Ona stood on the other side of the huge metal door after being successfully materialized. She let out a slow gentle breath. She tried to make sense of what she was now looking at. It was hard to comprehend. She was on suspended walkway over an endless gorge that stretched as far as the eye could see. There were things moving all over the place. Thousands of walkways and levels spanned the horizon interconnected with a system of raised conveyer belts. One of which was just off to her right. There were beings of all shapes and sizes dangling from these moving belts. She had never seen such creatures before. She crouched down to try and make herself as small as possible, as she looked up at the millions of things dangling from all over the place.

'What is this?'

'I have never seen anything like it, Ona,' said Arion, 'I think it would be wise for you to allow me to activate my weapons systems.'

Ona couldn't argue.

'Do it,' she said.

Ona felt Arion remove two of his legs. A light red dot appeared in the forefront of her vision and began scanning.

'What's that?' she asked, following the dot with her eyes.

'Targeting scanner,' Arion said.

'Right,' said Ona, 'now what?'

Arion didn't immediately answer.

'Arion?' she whispered, hearing strange mechanical noises off in the distance.

'Ona, I do not mean to alarm you,' Arion said.

'We're a bit past that point, don't you think?'

'Perhaps, in any case, I have lost my uplink to the Massey Shaw.'

Ona felt her blood freeze, 'what?'

'I can no longer contact The Massey,' Arion said.

'Maybe they're out of range?'

'My uplink has a range of a half-light year Ona, unless they have been forced to jump away, that should not be possible.'

'Maybe they're in trouble,' said Ona.

'There is one other possibility,' Arion said, 'they have been destroyed.'

Ona felt a surge of panic.

'Maybe, it's time to go,' Arion offered.

Ona tried to calm her mind to think, 'they can't be destroyed.'

'Why do you say that?'

'Because that's not how things happen,' Ona gathered her thoughts, 'maybe they had to shut down to avoid detection.'

'I don't understand.'

'I'll tell you later, let's see what we can see here. Tam is depending on us and then I'll jump back.'

'Okay, Ona,' Arion agreed.

'Can you find me a pathway to the signal?'

'One moment,' said Arion.

Ona saw a light beam scanning. She glanced around at the platform, which branched out to hundreds of walkways. She saw Arion light up a path and checked her surroundings again before moving forward. She cast her eyes up to the hanging creature's overhead.

'What are these things?'

While the suspended creatures all appeared to be from different races, they were all dressed the same. They had highly polished metallic exterior plates which appeared to be specifically tailored to match their varying body shapes.

Their armour plated chests had some sort of emblem or symbol emblazoned across them that glowed independently, pulsing gently like a slow heartbeat. Some of them had two arms, some had four, some had none. Some were definitely covered in some sort of flesh, some in scales. She saw grey skin colours, some blue, some dark green. Nothing that even remotely resembled that of a human.

'What are these things?' she whispered.

'I'm getting both biological and cybernetic readings,' replied Arion.

'How many are there?' she took in the scene around them.

'Within my current visual range and based upon distribution, I would estimate over fifty-million but without knowing the exact size of the structure, that figure could increase exponentially.'

'Are they all dead?'

There was a brief pause.

'Unknown,' Arion said, 'these bio signatures are most unusual.'

'Are these the Ghosts? Or the IGO?' Ona said.

'Unknown,' said Arion, 'Ona, I am detecting movement on the walkway up ahead.'

She froze, 'where?'

'Two kilometres, dead ahead and approaching slowly,' Arion said.

'Two kilometres?' she said, 'you can see that far?'

'I can,' said Arion.

'Okay,' Ona said.

She heard a light buzzing sound coming from somewhere off to her right. Followed by more clicking noises.

Ona sucked in a breath. She ran her thumb over her fingertips and tried to focus. She continued on. Another one of the conveyer belts above and to her right began moving. She spotted a group of similar looking creatures in a row, they had pale blue skin, closed eyes, and small holes in the sides of their large heads that looked like ears. They looked asleep.

After a few minutes of walking, the conveyer above her stopped moving.

'Stop,' said Arion.

She stopped and looked up. 'What am I looking for?'

'My counterpart, the signal is emanating to your right, and three meters below,' Arion said.

Ona moved over to the side of the walkway and peered over the railing. She saw another conveyer belt on the level below. Her mouth dropped open. She saw more hanging metal creatures, but these were different, much more familiar looking.

'They're human,' her voice soft.

She saw a little red dot home in on one of them. It was a male with dark hair. He looked like he was sleeping. His body was covered with the same chrome armour plating.

'What happened to them?'

Arion didn't answer.

'Arion?'

'I don't know,' he replied, 'but I think it's time for us to go.'

'We have to help them.'

'I'm not sure there's anything we can do, Ona.'

She looked around at the strange meat factory then back at the human male.

'Can you contact him?'

'I'm not sure that's a good idea, we could be detected.'

'I can't just go back without knowing what's happening here, Arion, you have to try. I can take us out of here if we're found,' she reassured him.

'I'll try,' said Arion.

Ona heard a light bleeping noise in her ear.

'Link up established.'

Ona stared over the railing, noticing that the person to the left and right of the male were also human. She moved her eyes along the line and saw more. There were rows and rows of human heads on giant mechanical bodies. She looked back at the male that Arion had locked onto. She suddenly felt the blood in her veins turn to ice as a pair of wide eyes opened and met hers. She composed herself and looked back over the railing, wondering if maybe her mind was playing tricks on her. A pair of wide human eyes glared back, the expression on the face was cold and apathetic.

'He's awake,' she whispered.

'Ona, I am getting some strange responses from the implant,' Arion said.

The eyes continued to watch her.

'I am uncertain as to his level of consciousness.'

'What does that mean?' Ona said, raising up a hand and waving gently at the face staring up at her.

The face showed no signs of response.

'Ona,' said Arion.

'Yes?'

'The signal has stopped transmitting.'

The ground shook. Ona heard two large thuds and spun around in time to see two of the armoured creatures hit the walkway in front of her. They towered over her, glaring at her with ferocious eyes. She saw something else behind them. A different creature, it was large, black, like oil, and moving in a smooth organic like way. It glided towards her with strange tentacle like legs.

'Run!'

Arion fired two shots from his weapons system, which bounced off the metallic beings' chests. He fired again, the pulses ricocheting off the creatures armoured chest. Ona raised her fingers and was about to snap them when one of the metal beasts extended a claw and grabbed her. She felt Arion dislodge from her head, followed by a sharp pain.

Then there was nothing.

41

Tam couldn't move. It was as if her whole body was sealed in a thick skin of plastic. This is how it had happened to the others, to the taken, to Amita, her own parents, everyone on board the Taurus, and to all those ships left adrift in space. This had been their fate. She wanted to scream but couldn't. She couldn't help the sheer terror of the enclosure from sweeping through her. She could feel the blood as it pumped like a freight train through her ears.

She began to feel dizzy, uncertain as to how much time had passed.

Had it been hours? Days?

She felt the walls of her reason break down and be replaced with being paralyzed.

She wasn't in physical pain, but she was in her worst possible nightmare. Suffocating in the smallest, darkest space. She begged for unconsciousness, even for death to make it stop. She saw a sudden crack in the darkness. White light flooded in, her cocoon opened and she fell.

She hit solid ground; her right shoulder took the impact. She waited on the cold surface. Everything was blurred. She took long, deep breaths as she tried to regain control. As her eyes began to adjust, her surroundings started to come into focus. She heard coughing to her right and turned her head to see Chuck. She then looked in all directions, seeing more of her crew, all in similar positions. The black fluid now gone, replaced by glistening walls that resembled mother of pearl, organically curving upwards into an endless spire. It was beautiful.

She looked back and saw Jacob and Augustine bunched together on their knees. She searched for Ona but couldn't see her.

'Cap?' she heard Chuck say. His voice echoed into the grand structure. It reminded her of a cathedral, the size of a small city.

She couldn't see any markings on the highly polished walls. Just beautifully ornate swirls of luminescent colour. She looked to Chuck, 'Are you all right?'

He nodded.

'Is everyone all right?' she said, looking to Augustine first, who was helping one of her nurses to her feet.

Augustine looked afraid but she nodded to Tam.

'We're okay,' she said.

Jacob approached her on her left. He nodded to her, 'well, that was different.'

'Hmm,' she responded, half ignoring him while trying to get a head count in her mind.

Chuck stood by her side and followed her lead, conducting his own head count to match hers when she was finished.

'Fifty-six,' Chuck said in a low tone

'Fifty-six,' Tam replied looking at him, 'we're missing one.'

'Where's Urhan?' Chuck said, coughing.

Tam looked around and couldn't see him, she felt a cold chill run down her back, she looked at Jacob who shook his head. She observed the scene, across the vast pearl floors as far as she could. She didn't see anything, or anyone.

'I don't see him,' Chuck said quietly.

Augustine approached them and stood next to the three senior officers, the rest of the crew stayed behind, knowing decisions would need to be made. Tam held herself high, her arms folded, making sure to project as much leadership into her outward appearance at least as to not alarm them. Chuck did the same.

'Suffice to say there's intelligence behind this,' said Augustine.

'No shit,' Jacob said.

Tam frowned at him, so did Augustine, he raised his hand in an apology

'That little ride we just took has me on edge, or more to the point it scared the living crap out of me, sorry,' he said, 'Where the hell are we?'

'A structure of some sort,' Chuck said, marvelling the gargantuan building.

'Okay… ignoring the fact that I'm an engineer and sort of had a grasp on that…' Jacob said, raising his arms and motioning towards the ceiling.

Chuck glared at him.

'Chuck, do you have your gun?' asked Tam.

Chuck checked his jumpsuit and shook his head. Tam's wrist computer was gone also. She looked to Augustine. 'Nothing,' she said.

Somewhere in the distance she heard something that sounded like a whale song. They froze.

'What the hell was that?' Jacob whispered.

'Stay calm,' Tam said, as the eerie sound came again, her nerves began to tingle.

There was something in here, somewhere, and something inside her was telling her to run. Fast.

'You know what?' Chuck asked.

Tam looked at him, 'I think we should start walking until we're presented with something new, at least it gives everyone a purpose.'

Tam nodded. She turned to the crew, 'Nice and slow, report anything out of the ordinary but keep tight, follow us.'

42

IGO WAR

Protector Crick directed his visuals to the little being suspended by the metal clamps.

'The feeder was correct,' said Raz, who was standing next to him.

Crick moved closer to the being.

'Lower it,' he said.

'As you wish,' said Raz, motioning to Tek to carry out the request.

The being began lowering to the ground level. Crick took another step towards it and extended a tendril.

'Protector, are you sure you should be…'

'Be silent Keeper.'

Crick reached up and touched the side of the life forms cranium. He then excreted a thin layer of his own bio-matter which was absorbed quickly by the thin flesh of the creature. He waited until his own essence had penetrated her skull and settled into the correct part of her brain where it began to bond. He instantly felt the connection and began sensing another awareness. The life forms ocular detectors opened almost immediately as its orifice emitted a high-pitched noise.

'Silence,' Crick said to it.

The creature fell silent. Its vision receptors were wide, it had a pigment in the centre of them, which Crick found interesting.

'Speak,' Crick demanded the creature.

It didn't respond. Crick stepped closer to the thing, which tried to recoil, but was held too tightly by the clamps.

'What... are... you?' Crick repeated

'What?' the creature asked.

'Good, you understand.'

'How?'

'Answer me or I will destroy you,' Crick said.

'I don't know what it is you ask,' said the creature.

'You are not like the others,' Crick said, 'you have it inside you.'

'The molecule?' replied the creature.

'Yes,' said Crick.

'It was an accident,' said the creature, its face now appearing wet from the secretions from its ocular organs.

'An accident? What is this?'

'I don't know why its inside me, let me go,' said the creature, 'I don't want to hurt anybody.'

'You will not,' said Crick.

'What did you do to them?'

'Who?'

'The others, like me,' said the creature.

Crick took another step forward. 'How many know we are here?'

'I do not understand,' said the creature.

'How many know of our existence?' Crick said.

'I do not know.'

'You are lying.'

'I am not.'

'How many?'

'I was alone, I came here because, the molecule brought me here.'

Crick sent a thought to the creature's mind, activated its pain centre. The creature wailed and writhed about. Then it slumped its head forward. Liquid streamed from its ocular organs.

'If you lie to me again creature, I will leave you in agony until you die,' said Crick

'Please don't,' it said softly.

'I have your small ship. I have all your ships. You came here looking for us, now you have found us, and now we will find you,' Crick turned to Raz. 'Have Royal been notified of their arrival?'

'IGO Royal are informed of all,' said Raz.

'I understand,' Crick said, 'I want to see these creatures before the Queen.'

'Yes, Protector,' he said.

Crick turned back to the creature.

'Don't hurt my friends,' said the creature.

'The Queen will enjoy their nutrients, you should be honoured.'

'Where are they?'

'Where you will soon be. But first I need to see inside you,' Crick stepped closer.

43

The silence in the grand structure was deafening. Tam moved steadily forwards. The design of the building seemed to repeat itself into infinity. Every juncture seemed to be the same as the last.

'We're nowhere fast here Cap,' Chuck said.

Tam agreed. It seemed endless, she wished Arion were here to give her some sort of mapping of the area.

'We keep moving,' she said firmly.

He nodded. Tam kept her eyes peeled and then noticed something odd. The interior seemed to be lit entirely from the strange glow coming from inside the glistening walls.

'Amazing tech,' Jacob said.

'Yes, it is,' she agreed.

'I feel a bit like a sheep.'

Tam looked at him.

'You know, a sheep, in a large paddock,' he said, 'waiting to have his balls cut off.'

'Jesus Jacob,' Chuck muttered.

'That's not what happens to sheep,' Augustine said.

'How the hell do you know?' Jacob responded.

'Because they need to reproduce, Jacob,' her tone serious.

'Maybe its cats I'm thinking of then' he teased.

'Jacob, I sometimes wonder how you're able to feed yourself,' Chuck said.

'Mechanical genius,' he said, bringing light to their current situation.

'I'm starting to understand why you're not married,' Augustine said.

'I'm married to my engines, they need all the love I can give them,' he said, lowering his head.

Tam saw sadness in his eyes, knowing full well that somewhere in that guarded humour was someone who'd once held a flame for her. Regardless of how long ago, or brief the encounter was. She dismissed the thought as quickly as it had entered her head. Now wasn't the time.

'We'll get The Massey back,' she told him.

Jacob smiled at her, 'If not, I'll avenge her.'

Chuck smiled then a sound from behind Tam made her turn. Her crew were all standing in a line. Shouting at her but there was no sound. Their hands were banging against an invisible barrier.

She rushed towards them, reached into the unseen barrier, and placed her hands against it. It was solid.

'Can you hear me?' she shouted.

One of them pointed to their ears and shook her head indicating that they couldn't. She glanced at Jacob who was running his hand across the invisible barrier.

'This wasn't here a minute ago,' he said.

They began looking past Tam, their eyes wide, fear and shock emerging. Her body froze as she looked at the creatures that had suddenly appeared a few meters in front of them. One of them was human. She knew the face all too well, the Tank, The Admiral—her Uncle.

She could feel the muscles in her jaw clamp shut as she watched. There were four things, black in colour, on each side of him. They had long conical bodies with smooth convex heads atop three tendril legs. There were no eyes that she could see, no faces, no discerning features of any kind. They looked like some sort of cuttlefish or octopus minus the extra limbs.

'Jesus,' she heard, Jacob say quietly

They were huge, at least twice that of a human. They stood there, only the occasional ripple under their smooth oily like skin.

There was something very wrong here. Something about the way Edge was looking at her.

'Admiral?' she said, taking a step towards him.

He didn't move. His eyes seemed vacant. The constant look of pressure, stress and intimidation seemed lost. She stopped a few meters from Edge and the aliens.

'Rubin?'

Edge took a step forwards, turning his eyes to Chuck and Jacob before back to Tam.

'Somethings off here Cap,' Chuck said.

Two of the creatures appeared to raise up their torsos slightly, increasing their height by another half meter or so. Edge took a step to his right and looked away, off into the distance as if he'd suddenly began daydreaming. Tam was in no doubt now that whatever was standing in front of her was not in control of his own body.

One of the beings adjusted their position and began moving towards them. They moved gracefully, like an octopus on the ocean floor.

What happened next, happened quickly. One of the creatures suddenly formed and extended a long tendril from its mid-section which shot out quickly past Tam, wrapped itself around Augustine's waste, lifting her off the ground and pulling her towards itself.

Augustine screamed and briefly reached out to try and take Tam's hand, but it had been too late. Tam tried to run towards her but in that instant her body hit another invisible wall that was placed between her and the now screaming Augustine, who was pressed against the bodies of one of the creatures.

'Silvia!' she shouted.

She watched helpless as Augustine, now with her feet dangling off the ground and being held firmly by a coiling black arm, glared at Tam, her eyes wide.

She looked at Edge, 'Rubin, wake the hell up! What are you doing?'

The creatures remained still, while Augustine dangled in the air.

'We have to do something,' Chuck said.

Tam ran her hands over her pockets looking for anything she could use as a weapon. She looked back up to Augustine's terrified eyes as she noticed another movement from the creature holding her. The black tendril around her waist had now moved to Augustine's neck and was slowly creeping its way up the side of her face. She screamed again, but only for a second as the muscles in her face suddenly relaxed, as if sedated. Her arms and legs went limp and her jaw slackened. Tam watched in horror, feeling completely useless.

The creature that was holding Augustine began approaching the barrier, stopping a meter or so away. Tam could see the texture of its skin now. It glistened with an almost mirror finish. She glanced back at Augustine and slammed her hand against the barrier.

'Silvia!' she shouted, to the ghost captivated with emptiness.

The creature turned Augustine's head with its tendril, her jaw still hanging open. Her strange lifeless eyes snapped to meet Tam's. Augustine began to speak.

'You understand?' said Augustine in a creepy monotone voice.

Tam gently placed her hands back on the barrier. 'Silvia?' her voice was soft, trying to hold back the tightness in her throat.

'Small things, you understand,' said Augustine.

Tam looked at the creature holding Augustine and realized that it wasn't her speaking to them. It was them, somehow. She looked to her uncle, 'I understand you.'

The creatures parted as the largest of the four crawled forward; stepping just in front of the one holding Augustine.

'I wanted to see you,' said Augustine, her soulless eyes still glaring at Tam.

'What am I speaking to?'

The largest of the creatures made a loud clicking noise, Tam looked directly at it.

'Crick,' said Augustine, injecting menace.

'Is that your name?' Tam asked, pressing for more information.

The creature clicked again.

'Where are the crew from the Lassen? The Taurus? Where are the rest of those like us?' Tam demanded.

'You found us,' said Augustine.

This time Tam looked at the creature, not her chief medical officer

'How did you do that?' said Augustine.

'We don't mean you any harm,' Tam wavered, 'we never have.'

The creature clicked.

'They did not tell us of your abilities,' said Augustine.

'Abilities?'

'It makes sense as to why they think so highly of you. They are afraid of you,' Augustine said.

'Who is?' Tam said, 'are you an IGO?'

The creature remained still, she looked at Augustine who was still staring at her like someone in a coma—frozen.

'They told you,' Augustine said.

'Who did?'

'Interesting choice.'

Tam was losing patience. Of all the things she didn't have affinity; it was interplanetary diplomacy.

'Okay enough of this bullshit,' She glared past Augustine, 'where the fuck are my people?'

She saw Chuck turn his head.

'There is no you,' said Edge, 'you are for us.'

Tam turned to see her Uncle's wide eyes meet hers. It wasn't him.

'You are such strange little things,' said Augustine, the pitch of her voice now sounding a little lower somehow, 'we don't need everything, only the things above.'

'What?' Tam said, confused.

The creature who called itself Crick turned its body. A flash of light ran across its front and it emitted a whale like noise. The other one holding Augustine raised her up. Tam leaned her face closer to the barrier.

'Inside the hard exterior is useful biology,' said Augustine, 'you have been granted the gift of something, there is no doubt, and yet you only see so small of things.'

Tam began to get nervous. She was in trouble. She had lost control of this, had plunged them all into an unknown kind of hell and it was her fault. She felt helpless and felt all control slip through her fingers.

'How you can live seeing only so little, it's such a waste,' said Augustine, not breaking eye contact with Tam, she hadn't seen her blink once.

The creature holding her formed another, thin tendril and brought it up to Augustine's face. It slid its glossy appendage across her cheek, until it covered her eyes. It then removed the tendril. Tam's jaw dropped in horror. Attached to the creatures slithering tendril were both of Augustine's eyes.

The optic nerves of both, sliding out from the now empty sockets before breaking off completely, leaving a trail of blood down both cheeks which dripped gently onto her uniform. The creature then allowed her severed green eyes to fall to the ground.

Tam felt lightheaded, she looked at Chuck, who's eyes were red, his jaw wide open but unable to speak. She looked back at Augustine's unmoving face.

'How can you call yourselves worthy with such fragile things,' said Augustine, who's now blood-soaked complexion made her look like something inhuman.

Tam had seen grotesque injuries on rescues before, had dealt with severed limbs, crushed and broken bodies but had never seen a life being taken away in front of her, someone she considered to be a close friend. She felt rage. She turned to Edge again. She wanted to kill these things, all of them.

'Rubin!' she screamed at him.

He didn't respond, so she turned back to Crick, 'you didn't have to do that.'

'You are not the same as the others.'

'What?'

'Why not?'

'What other?'

Crick moved a tendril up. A flicker of particles emerged from its tip. They floated up and formed an image. Tam's heart sank. It showed Ona, hanging from her wrists.

'No,' she whispered.

The image vanished.

'You are of no further use,' said Augustine.

The creature holding Augustine wrapped itself around her torso and in one smooth and ruthless motion, ripped her body in half. Everything seemed to move in slow motion as Tam watched her friend fall into two bloody clumps on the ground. She fell to her knees, she heard Jacob scream out, and Chuck was silent. She lowered her head, taking one last glance upwards to the creature, which was now moving away from them, leaving only Edge.

Silence descended.

44

Ona's shoulders ached, she felt alone, and the numbing terror made it difficult for her to concentrate. For the first time in her life, she wished she were back in her prison with Eoin Tatum, sitting by the lake and listening to one of his stories. Her brain felt like there were ants crawling all over it. Whatever the aliens had done to it, left a piercing pain. The alien's voice sounded so strange, not a male, not a female. It sounded like several different voices overlapping, like a heard of growling animals.

She was tired. She'd been watching them now, there were three of them moving to and from different computer stations. The two guards were standing at equal distance on each side of her staring at her with those cold human eyes. Everything below the neck was now a collection of chrome polished metal limbs. Those poor people had been transformed into machines. She wondered if they could really see her or whether they were already dead inside. For a moment, she wondered when they were going to do the same to her, but she knew different. The visions had told her different.

The aliens were now congregated around a console, making clicking noises. All Ona could do was wait, trapped. But something caught her eye on the ground, a light glint from behind a freestanding column, which made her eyes naturally flick to the source. She saw something small move, then a little leg, followed by the familiar little body that belonged to Arion. She held her breath and flicked her eyes back to the aliens then back to

Arion. She saw the tiny lights of his eyes look at her, he raised one of his legs and gave her a little wave before disappearing back behind the column.

She waited. There was stillness around her. The aliens continued to click at each other, she felt something on her leg but kept her eyes forward. It began to move upwards now, quickly. She heard light tapping of metal on metal as the thing on her leg moved over the restraint on her midsection. The movement stopped and she felt something else. The restraints on her arms and torso seemed to loosen, ever so slightly. She then felt movement on her shoulder and a second later, in one quick snapping motion, Arion attached to the side of her head. Half a second later she saw Arion's familiar heads up display. A weapons lock formed on all the aliens and machines in front of her. Arion fired twice, aiming at the biological aliens, striking them at the base of their necks. Ona's restraints cracked open suddenly and she dropped to the floor. She heard Arion, 'no time!'

She saw something in her mind. The inside of a ship she'd never seen before.

'Focus!' Arion said loudly now in her mind, 'GO HERE! NOW!'

Ona cleared her mind. She saw a large claw attached to a metal arm reach for her. She felt the power within her now, clear, accessible. She could do it, use it.

'GO!' shouted Arion.

The claw was now inches from her face. She saw the aliens getting up from the ground. She screamed at them, clicked her fingers and was gone.

45

A fraction of a second later, Ona materialized in the middle of a corridor.

'Where am I?' she whispered.

'You're on board the Lassen Ona,' said Arion, 'I apologize for taking so long but I found an unmanned computer terminal and was able to gain access to the alien's mainframe. I located the Lassen's orbital information. But you need to be very careful, we need to make our way to the astrometric lab on deck three.'

'Where is everyone?'

'I do not know,' Arion said, 'I suggest we move down the hallway to the crawlway.'

Ona began moving.

'What are those things?' Ona whispered, 'what did they do to me?'

'I can see that there is some sort or organic residue on your anterior cortex.'

'What?'

'Take this left and remove the grey panel on the right next to the first door,' said Arion.

Ona obeyed, looking up and down the deserted corridor. She moved around the corner and saw the panel, she unhooked it and looked into the crawlspace.

'Go inside, and move thirty meters to the ladder,' said Arion.

Ona obliged, crouched down, and made her way into the crawlspace. 'Arion, what's on my brain?'

'I am attempting to remove it, it won't hurt,' said Arion.

'They spoke to me,' she whispered.

'The IGO?'

'Yes.'

'What did they say?'

'They want the molecule, something about the Queen absorbing their nutrients,' Ona said.

A sudden noise made Ona stop, it sounded like metal on metal.

'What was that?'

'Scanning,' said Arion, 'you are okay Ona, I don't think they're on this deck.'

'You found a weakness in them?'

'It was an educated guess. I figured there was a link between the biological and technological implants at the exposed area near the base of their skulls.'

'You took a guess?'

'It was the best I could do given the situation.'

'Good job,' Ona said.

'It's still not going to be enough, there's something on board, if it's still there, which might help in that regard,' said Arion, 'Take the ladder two decks down,'

Ona took hold of the ladder and began the climb.

46

'It's not your fault,' said Chuck quietly in Tam's ear, soft enough so that Jacob couldn't hear him.

Tam was numb, she was standing, her arms folded, looking past Augustine's body to try and see any way out of this. Edge stood still like an automaton, glaring at them. She couldn't even look at him.

'How do you figure that?' she replied.

'She knew what she was signing up for, we all did,' Chuck said.

'You think she signed up for that?'

'Doesn't matter how it comes, you know that, when it comes… it comes,' Chuck said, 'focus on what we've got here.'

'What have we got here?'

'It's organic.'

She scoffed, 'Organic, technologically advanced, aggressive, no regard for our form of life.'

She looked to her uncle again. 'Rubin?' she said softly, 'talk to me Admiral.'

He didn't respond.

'What the hell did they do to him?' Jacob asked.

Tam shook her head, 'Jacob, what could generate a field like this?'

Jacob looked around him and shook his head, 'Cap, I don't even know where to start with this level of tech.'

Tam looked behind her to the rest of her crew. They looked dejected. She took a deep breath and straightened herself. Composed herself and remembered that she was in command. She turned back at Chuck and Jacob, the trio huddling in close.

The force field in front of them flickered with speckled light, then seemed to split open. It then reformed, creating a corridor of sorts leading ahead of them. Tam looked back at her crew, who were still held firmly behind the first field.

'Okay, is that an invitation?' Jacob asked.

'They're playing with us,' Chuck said, through gritted teeth.

Tam looked at Edge, who was staring at them.

'Follow the path,' he said suddenly.

Tam paused, wondering whether to comply. She looked at Chuck.

'It comes when it comes,' said Chuck softly.

'It's not coming today,' Tam said, 'not if I have anything to say about it.' She stared at Edge. 'What about my crew?'

'Move,' he said.

She looked back at her crew and made a gesture to them to hold their position. He then gave them a hand signal letting them know that she would be back.

The trio looked at Augustine's body.

'Come on,' Tam said, with stern determination as she led the way.

47

Ona entered the room and sealed the door behind her. Warm starlight cast its glow from a rectangular window. Computers lined the walls around a workstation in the centre. There was a glass dome in the middle with lights flashing over its surface.

'Bring me over to the table,' said Arion.

Ona moved over to the table and extended her hand. She laid it down on the surface.

'Back in a moment,' said Arion, detaching from her ear and moving down her arm towards the table.

He moved quickly around the dome before extending one of his legs and inserting it into an access port. The glass dome lit up. Light particles erupted from all around as a holographic image began to form. It showed the inside structure of the facility she'd just escaped.

She saw small bright blue spheres, row after row. The floating images began changing in rapid succession.

'What is all that?'

'Give me a moment please, the information downloaded has created an unpleasant electrical feedback in my main processing unit, I am attempting to clear it,' replied Arion.

'Unpleasant?'

'Yes, I am not really built to handle that much data, it can cause my core to overload and, well, I would rather it not happen.'

'Me, neither.'

'Thank you.'

'So, what are we looking at?'

'I was able to access the alien computer systems, I must admit that I am rather disturbed by what I have discovered,' Arion admitted.

'What happened to those people?'

'They aren't people anymore, Ona,' said Arion, 'they're something else.'

Ona waited.

'It would seem that this race is capturing species from all over the galaxy and transforming them into some sort of cybernetic hybrids.'

'That's horrifying,' said Ona.

'Yes Ona,' Arion said, 'now, move over to that screen, will you? I would like to access the onboard visuals.'

She moved over to it.

'Enter the following sequence,' Arion said, relaying the information across her eyes.

She did as she was told. The screen lit up to an internal image of the main bridge. Ona's eyes widened. There were two human hybrid robot things standing in the middle of the bridge and one normal looking human male.

'Who are they?' she said through her fingers.

'The unaltered male appears to be Captain Deangelo,' said Arion, 'his first officer Marielle Lefebvre and navigation officer Mark Johnson are either side of him. Or rather what is left of them.'

Ona moved her head in for a closer look. Their eyes had that same strange vacant look in them.

'The Massey is in orbit of the third planet. I cannot determine its condition at this range. We need to move this ship there.'

'How are we supposed to do that?'

'We have to get control of the bridge.'

Ona felt her stomach turn, she looked to the image of the monsters now inhabiting the control centre of the ship. She turned away from the screen and moved over to the window.

'I can't do this,' she whispered, looking out at the strange planet below.

'Yes, you can,' said Arion

'All I can do is jump to different places. I'm not a soldier Arion,' her head fell, her heart heavy.

'Stealth is a powerful ally,' Arion encouraged, 'that said so is firepower.'

'This is all too much.'

'I won't let anything happen to you, Ona.'

'What can you do? You saw what happened when you used your weapons on them, we got lucky,' she said, 'that's all.'

'Well, perhaps I can do something about that,' he said, 'I need you to leave this room and get to a munitions locker on this deck, there's something there which might prove useful.'

'Arion, what are you planning to do?'

'I think the crew of the Massey may still be alive on the third planet. I think we can rescue them and get out of here,' said Arion, 'now, open the doors, so that I can do a quick scan of the corridor.'

Ona moved to the entrance and did as he asked.

Arion made a quick scan. 'Okay it's clear,' he said, 'twelve meters down that hallway.'

She moved quickly and opened a darkened room whose automatic lights suddenly flickered to life. Lining the walls were a series of what Ona could only guess were weapons. They looked like the same rifles she'd seen on board the space station. The ones used to kill Eoin.

'Okay, over the far corner there, there a small hatch,' Arion said, pointing again to a wall container and Ona moved over to it.

'Okay, hold your arm out and let me onto it,' said Arion, detaching again from her ear.

He moved quickly to the access panel and used one of his legs to enter in a code. The hatch opened, revealing what looked like a mesh glove with the barrel of a plasma rife attached to it. Arion moved over to it, linking his leg to it for a second. A series of indicator lights came on before he detached and ran back up Ona's arm, he attached himself once more.

'Slip your hand into that, your right hand,' he directed.

Ona did as she was told. The glove felt cold to the touch but fit her perfectly.

'Okay, I'm linked up,' said Arion, 'all you have to do is point where my targeting scanners tell you to and I'll do the rest.'

'What is this?'

'A very big gun.'

48

IGO ROYAL

Tam felt like she had been walking for hours, but the narrow corridor that had been carved out of the structure was coming to an end. Ahead of them now, a series of archways, each hundreds of meters high. They continued onwards towards the opening.

Tam saw light up ahead. An opening appeared as two huge walls gracefully split apart. Edge turned to them and raised his arm.

'Move,' he said calmly.

Tam looked at Chuck who shrugged. She moved forward. The sunlight was blinding. The heat was intense as she looked out at a cityscape unlike anything she'd ever seen.

Several strange sounds coming from off in the distance caught her attention. It was like a chorus of whale sounds carrying their call in the wind. It was coming from all directions.

'What is that?' Jacob asked.

Tam shook her head as she tried to adjust to the blinding light, which seemed to come from all directions. She began seeing forms, dark, moving. Two large shadows approached from the light. Different in shape to the others. These were long, thin shapes that seemed to be approaching on two humanoid legs. The silhouetted forms grew closer, as Tam squinted to try make them out. They were definitely humanoid. She could make out slow moving of arms. They moved closer, the light still on their backs, until they were within just a few feet when the internal light of the grand structure began casting soft contrasting fill light, removing the shadow.

Tam's mouth felt suddenly dry. The figures approached the trio, stopping a few feet short of the barrier. They gazed down. Tam looked from one to the other.

'Urhan?' she said, the name taking all the air out of her lungs with one go.

'Hello Tamara,' he replied, 'permit me to introduce you to Premier Diren,' he said raising his right hand ever so slightly

Tam couldn't take her eyes off Urhan. The embers of a sickening rage stirred her chest. She flicked her eyes to Diren, who nodded his head slightly. Tam did not reciprocate. She'd never met Diren. That had always been above her pay grade. She looked back at Urhan before looking to Chuck, whose face had turned a pale shade of white.

'Please tell me you're a hostage,' Jacob said, breaking the silence.

Urhan turned to Jacob, 'that would be a falsehood.'

'Well...' Jacob said, looking at Tam before placing his hand on his hips, 'this is disappointing on so many levels.'

'That is understandable Jacob,' Urhan said.

'Urhan,' Tam said, through a clenched jaw, 'talk.'

'Perhaps it would be best if we take a walk,' said Diren, 'I trust that if released you will not attempt any violence. It would not be wise.'

Tam looked at Chuck, 'I am not a violent person.'

'Really,' Diren replied, 'your record would seem to suggest otherwise.'

'You have my word,' Tam said.

She looked to Urhan.

'The crew,' she said.

Urhan didn't answer. She looked to Diren.

'My crew are back there,' she said.

'Yes, I know Tamara,' said Diren, 'if you would follow me.'

Urhan gave her an odd look with those large green eyes.

'Please follow us,' Urhan said, holding out his left hand.

'Urhan what did you do?' she said to him, trying to unsuccessfully hide the betrayal, 'what did you do to my Uncle?'

He didn't respond.

Tam looked up to the sky to see a bright glowing ring of light slice across it from horizon to horizon. Incredible structures that made up this city reached out as far as the eye could see, with some breaking a thin layer of cloud cover. She saw rows of the dark aliens quietly moving almost in unison.

The two LAL turned making space between them so that the three humans could walk between. Tam placed a hand on Chuck's arm, his muscles were tense. She nodded to him to take is easy. He nodded back.

They began to walk past the archways and into the open space. Directly ahead, lay a building that resembled an inverted cone, its base curving inwards with its smooth outer edge reaching to the sky. They walked across an open flat concourse paved in what looked like polished diamond. She turned to Urhan.

'Where are we going?' she said quietly.

He didn't respond.

49

THE LASSEN

Ona moved steadily through the crawlspaces, making sure to make little noise as possible. She reached an ascending ladder and looked upwards before grabbing the rungs and starting up.

'How are you doing Ona? Try and take long slow breaths, your heart rate is going a little too fast for comfort,' said Arion.

'I'm scared out of my mind,' she whispered as she inhaled slowly, trying to calm her breathing.

'Understandable,' replied Arion, 'but remember that fear is entirely a construct, something that is controllable.'

'Any tips?' she said, as she placed one foot steadily over another.

'Control your breath and control your mind.'

Ona paused. 'Did you recognize that other Arion unit?' she said, 'the one attached to that man?'

There was a long pause.

'Arion?' she asked.

'Yes, I did,' he said.

'Who was it?'

'Arion units are specifically designated and bonded to each other and their hosts,' he said, 'the unit itself appeared to only be functioning as a beacon. The consciousness within has been lost.'

'And the man?'

'That was Tamara's father,' Arion confirmed.

Ona felt a knot grow in her stomach. 'What?' she said, 'are you sure?'

'Quite sure.'

'Oh God,' she whispered, 'that's why she came. Isn't it?'

'It is not the only reason, but it is a big one, yes,' Arion replied, 'I believe that she may have had hope.'

'What about her mother?'

'I did not see her.'

Ona glanced downward before beginning her climb again, this time picking up the pace. 'Then maybe we can make a difference.'

'Maybe we can.'

After a few more minutes of climbing, Arion directed her to another crawlspace, then he asked her to stop mid-way through it and open an access port. Behind it was a collection of power cables, diagnostic junctures, and a monitor.

'Okay, enter the following sequence on the panel Ona.'

Ona complied and the screen flickered to life. She saw the bridge again, the same three life forms, still standing, as if idling in the centre.

'We are directly underneath the main bridge.'

'Okay so what's the plan?'

'Well, first we need find a way to render those machines inoperative,' said Arion. 'an educated guess is that I may be able to render them inoperative with an EMP.'

'Meaning?'

'It requires a lot of energy and there is a possibility it may knock out my primary processor. I've never actually tried it,' said Arion, 'if it works, it will give you enough time to…'

He paused.

'Time to?'

'Well, blast them all to hell.'

She looked at the weapon she'd placed on her right hand. 'Arion, you saw how easily your weapons bounced off them, how do you know this is powerful enough?'

'Once we've hit them with an EM pulse, I am confident there will be enough disruption to whatever defensive systems they have, that this will work,' he said, 'a simple deduction will be to aim for the head, I am presuming they cannot function without their hybrid connection to the brain.'

She rubbed the bridge of her nose.

'Ona, this is a calculated risk.'

'And if it doesn't work?'

'Well, plan B in this situation is that you jump directly to the engine room and I interface with the core and detonate it,' said Arion, 'one less threat to worry about.'

She stayed quiet.

'Ona, with your permission I would like to give you something that may aid your focus.'

She frowned. 'I'm sorry?'

'I'm going to stimulate your adrenal gland.'

'You're gonna do what?'

'Trust me,' said Arion, 'you may need to rely on the extra strength and speed associated with what I am about to do. It is not permanent, and you will suffer no adverse reactions.'

Ona raised an eyebrow, 'You know what? Why not?'

'Thank you,' said Arion, 'now, are you ready? For my body to generate the EMP I will need to detach from you momentarily when we reach the bridge.'

'Hang on, how am I supposed to use this thing if you're not on me?' Ona raised her hand with the gun attached.

'Don't worry, I can program it to a firing sequence.'

Her hand trembled. 'I don't like this.'

'Trust me,' Arion said, 'and Ona, if anything happens to me, you jump away, as far away as you can get and don't come back, tell everyone what we've found here. Do you understand?'

'Yes.'

'Okay, remember, go for the head. I'll be guiding you the entire time,' said Arion, 'are you ready?'

Ona took a deep breath, she thought of Eoin Tatum, what he'd sacrificed to free her, how he'd entrusted her to the crew of the Massey. She thought of the voices and through whatever was about to happen, she knew, somehow, that this wasn't going to be the end. Not yet anyway. 'Let's do it,' she said, focusing her energy on the bridge of the ship.

'On the count of three,' Arion said, 'Three...'

Ona relaxed her shoulders and checked the weapon on her hand.

'Two...'

She took one final breath, cleared her mind, and felt a sudden rush of calm and focus flood through her veins. Everything seemed crisp, colours were heightened. She could almost taste the air; whatever Arion had just done to her mind washed away her fear in an instant. She was ready.

'One...'

She reached up her hand and clicked her finger.

The Lassen Bridge

Ona appeared at the rear of the bridge. Everything was still. She saw the two machines and Deangelo facing the view screen. She remained still for a few seconds, quickly flicking her eyes around and surveying for anyone else. Her breath was still, her lips firmly tightened, her teeth clenched. The first to turn was Captain Deangelo. There was a shiny metal plate attached to the side of his face and his eyes were cold. He was followed quickly by two others who glared at her with the same vacant eyes and empty expressions. They separated slowly and began moving towards her around the bridge in opposite directions. Two of the creatures reached up their arms, which seemed to alter their shape into snapping claw like appendages.

Time slowed as Ona held her position, flicking her head quickly from one to another. Arion's targeting scanners locked onto each one. She raised her arm and pointed her weapon at the thing coming up on her right. It was Lefebvre's head on a machine body.

She heard Arion's voice in her ear, sharp and confident. 'Not yet!'

Deangelo took a step towards her. She moved her arm quickly to lock onto him, as she did, she felt something pop on the right-hand side of her ear as Arion detached. He landed quickly on her shoulder. She felt heat as he leapt into the air. He activated a set of little thrusters on his underside and shot up. She watched as Deangelo's cold eyes immediately locked onto the small device, which had now started to spin. Lefebvre was almost on her now. She had nowhere to run to.

She heard a high-pitched noise followed by a quick flash of light. The machines stopped. Frozen in place, Lefebvre's left arm was within inches of Ona's face. Arion dropped onto the deck. Ona looked at Deangelo's eyes, which were now bloodshot red. She saw Arion leap into the air again, added by his little thrusters. With a second burst he changed his direction towards

Ona. He landed with force on her chest then crawled at speed back up to her ear and reattached himself. The whole manoeuvre couldn't have been more than a second or two. Her heads-up display returned.

'Take them out!' Arion ordered.

Ona ducked down and rolled towards the rear of the bridge away from Lefebvre's grasp. She kneeled and raised the weapon; her heart was now pounding in her ears, her mouth dry. The target locked onto Lefebvre's head and the weapon fired a bright blue beam of energy. Lefebvre's head exploded in a waterfall of red.

Ona felt the shock of it, the unexpected sight of it. She had no time to process the horror of it as she aimed at the second one. Arion fired again. The bridge became a crimson red. Blood spattered on Ona's face and clothing. She fought the terror of it, the horror as she stood and ran forward, she looked into Deangelo's eyes, pointed her weapon as Arion fired once more. For a fraction of a second, she thought she registered some sort of emotional response. She wasn't sure what it was, but it hit her hard.

Deangelo's head erupted.

The scene calmed. Ona's arm was still raised, pointing to the empty space where Deangelo's former self had been. She thought she heard Arion ask her something, but she couldn't hear anything. Her hand began to shake as the sounds of the bridge returned. The light bleeping of the consoles, now covered in blood, filled the almost serene scene. Terror seeped into her skin.

She heard Arion's voice return. 'It's over,' he said calmly, 'Ona, do you hear me? It's over. Breathe.'

Ona couldn't stop shaking.

'Breathe,' Arion said again.

She felt a warm sensation in her veins. She felt tears release and fall down her cheek. She lowered her hand and wiped them away. She looked down and saw blood on her hands. She started to furiously rub them together to try and get it off.

'Are you all right?'

'Give me a second,' Ona said, her voice broken and shaken.

She now felt a sudden flood of emotions, which threatened to overcome her. She fought it hard, trying to regain her composure.

'I didn't know that was going to happen,' she said softly.

'There was nothing you could do for them, Ona, you set them free,' said Arion.

She lowered her hands and took several deep breaths, looking again at the carnage around her. More tears fell. She continued to clear them away as a feeling of change spread through her, a sense that something had just broken inside her. Something that would never be fixed.

'What did I just do?'

'You did what you had to do. I'm sorry we've put you in this position. I really am,' he said, 'but we've got people out there we might still be able to save.'

Ona tried to block it all out. Like she'd been blocking out intrusive memories her whole life.

'I am going to interface once again with the ships systems and lock down the bridge, then I need to access navigation and get us, as fast as possible into range of the third planet,' said Arion

'Okay, you go do that.'

'Ona,' Arion spoke softly, 'it had to be done.'

'I killed them,' she said, realization filling her.

'I killed them,' said Arion, 'you just gave us a fighting chance for survival and for that I am eternally in your gratitude, they all will be. Now come on, we have work to do.'

50

IGO ROYAL

The gigantic doors Tam had been led through closed silently behind her. They had been led into another grand cathedral structure, this one even larger than the last. Its interior was in stark contrast, however. It appeared as though they were underground, within the confines of a cavern from a dream. She saw diamond like sculptures imbedded within dark glistening rock and a bridge that crossed an endless ravine. She likened it to being inside a geode.

'Please,' Urhan said, 'do not make any sudden movements, Tamara. Proceed forward.'

She turned to Edge, who was staring across the stone bridge.

Then she turned to Chuck and Jacob, leading them onto it. The air felt thicker here, small droplets of sweat formed on her forehead with the increased humidity. The gravity was different too, she felt lighter. But enough to make it noticeable. As they crossed the stone bridge, Tam tried to glance over the edge. She noticed something odd about the canyon floor. It was hard to make out but there were oddly uniform shapes, thousands of them all over the place. She moved steadily on, taking in as much of the strange environment. She saw movement every few meters from machines that were perched on rock pedestals. They looked distinctly like weapons of some sort. They tracked her as she walked.

They continued for several minutes before Tam spotted the landing point. A dark flat opening, all stone, which jutted out from the rock, face. She walked onto it and noticed another shift in her weight, this time the gravity had returned to a little over Earth standard. Urhan stopped and turned to face Diren. Both LAL stepping back, one on each side of the group. Edge moved beside Urhan and waited. Tam paused, noting that the area had two carved out raised platforms like an old Mayan sacrificial slab. She looked briefly behind her at two IGO who were standing there, blocking the entranceway back to the bridge. Her thoughts lingered back to her crew, wondering if they were still alive. She tried to keep her mind sharp. Something about the way Urhan had just looked at her caught her attention. She glanced at Diren.

'I understand,' Diren said.

'What do you understand?'

'What you must be feeling,' he said, 'helpless I would assume, confused, lost?'

Tam loosened her jaw and widened her eyes. A smile appeared on her face, which made Diren tilt his head.

'Premier Diren, we have never met, have we?'

'We have not,' he replied.

'It is never wise to presume what another is thinking, invariably, you are wrong.'

'And what are you thinking?'

'I'm thinking. You have about ten seconds to tell me what's going on before I break your damn neck.'

Diren faced Urhan, 'Would you like too? Before she arrives?'

A chill ran through Tam at that comment. She looked to Urhan.

'Tamara…'

'Captain,' she said, cutting him off.

Urhan's eyes flickered.

'Very well, Captain, I told you, you could not come here. I warned you, but you would not listen. You humans never do. You follow whatever path you wish and disregard consequences,' he said.

Tam lowered her gaze ever so slightly giving him an almost predatory look.

'You are on IGO Royal,' he said.

Her eyes flicked to Diren.

'Okay?' Jacob said, 'and that is?'

Urhan flashed him a cold stare. 'Somewhere no human has ever seen, nor will ever see again,' Urhan turned back to Tam.

'Get to the point,' Chuck snapped.

'Urhan,' Tam said softly, 'please just tell me everything.'

She saw Urhan briefly look to Diren then back at her, a little flicker in his eye, the same as a moment ago. She was sure there was something about it, which was off.

'The extra-terrestrial virus,' he replied, 'that almost wiped your species out of existence all those years ago.'

'What about it?' she replied, not sure she was ready for what was about to be revealed.

'It was a by-product,' he said.

'Of what?' Jacob inquired.

'A war,' Urhan said, 'one that extinguished most of the life from this galaxy and two others.'

'What?' Tam gasped.

'In human terms, a three-billion-year conflict of which the virus was all that was left. It was the last remnants of a weapon that ended everything.'

Tam glanced back at the aliens for a second, she felt a new dread enter her from somewhere, as if the weight of what Urhan was about to say would crush her. She waited.

'When they arrived at our galaxy, we had no allies. Humans were barely single cell organisms,' he said, 'the IGO were defeated, almost, by another race that sacrificed themselves by unleashing the virus to wipe out not only the IGO but all living things. They almost did.'

He paused for a second

'I'm lost, anyone else lost?' Jacob gave a quizzical look.

Tam shot him a glance to tell him to shut up.

'We are collectors,' Urhan said, 'to put it in terms that you will understand.'

'Collectors,' Tam said.

'Yes,' said Diren.

She turned to him.

'They call us feeders,' he said.

She waited for Urhan to explain.

'They allow us to survive, and in return, we seek and supply them with...' he paused, 'the means in which to rebuild their race.'

Tam's heart sank at what that meant. Chuck's head turned to Diren.

'Those things just killed my friend,' Tam said.

Urhan blinked. 'She was my friend also, Captain. The magnitude of what it is I am trying to convey may be hard to understand, but it goes beyond one life, or even that of a million lives,' he responded, 'when our species found Earth, it was, in essence becoming an uninhabitable wasteland. You were saved, given the technology and means to repopulate not only earth but a host of new worlds. What was taken in return, was a trade.'

A dark realisation began to emerge from Tam's mind.

'A trade,' she said softly.

'Yes, not only for your survival, but for ours, the Ongrals, the Kriset and many other races you have yet to encounter,' he said.

'What is wrong with Rubin?' she queried Urhan.

'Your relative has served us well up until his curiosity about the molecule overrode his judgement,' said Diren, 'he hid her from us.'

Tam looked at Edge's vacant eyes.

'Urhan,' she said, softly, 'what are they doing to us? Why kill Sylvia?'

'they need…'

Diren interrupted him, 'Tamara, where is Ona Mendel?'

The question threw Tam a little off balance and turned to him, 'why?'

Just as she did, out of thin air, another alien appeared. It looked very much like the Crick creature, but she couldn't be sure.

'She was on IGO War,' Diren said, 'and now she is gone.'

She escaped! Good for her.

'I don't know,' she answered, 'why do you want her?'

The large IGO that had just appeared climbed slowly off the platform. It approached Diren and stopped in front of him. It began making communication noises. Tam waited as Diren eventually turned to her, 'Tamara, where is Ona Mendel?'

Tam looked at the large IGO, 'I told you, I don't know.'

Diren looked to Urhan then back at Tam, 'You wished to know what is being done to your people?'

Tam was almost afraid to find out.

'Is that why you are really here? To rescue the president's daughter Amita. Am I correct?' Diren said.

Tam stayed silent. She moved her eyes to Urhan, then back to Diren. The large IGO took another step, this one a little past Diren, closer to Tam.

'Please step onto the platform,' Diren instructed.

Tam held her ground. Edge turned and stepped towards her.

They stepped onto a circular platform and stood as it began rising towards another level. What came into view as they approached the outcropping was jaw dropping. It was another one of the creatures. Though, this one, was four or five times the size of any of the others. It looked distorted, bulbous, and pulsating with heaving motions like a giant slug.

'What is that?' she looked at Urhan.

'That,' Diren said, 'is the Queen. She is the reason you are still alive. But that is about to change Captain, if you do not give us Ona. Not only will you and your crew be…' he paused, '…put to other uses, but your civilisation as you know will be deemed a mortal threat and wiped from its very existence. That is the choice that now falls on your shoulders. You, the person who almost ended your race prematurely when you destroyed a star.

Proving to the IGO that you were a threat above what we had classified your species.'

Diren took a step towards Tam.

Chuck took a protective step towards her.

'But that is not all is it?' Diren said looking at Urhan, 'you came for something else, for someone else?'

Tam felt her blood run cold.

Diren turned to Edge. 'It was his order,' he said, 'did you know that?'

'What?' Tam's voice went high pitched for a second.

'His order sent your father's ship to those coordinates.' Diren said, 'he knew what was waiting for them. He used them, as bait.'

Tam turned her eyes to Edge. Her Uncle was a sector commander and fifteen years older than her father. He'd been his commanding officer in the sector. She'd always knew that he was hiding something from her. She then saw a light reflection of something on the base of her uncle's neck. A disk-shaped object. She couldn't understand how she hadn't seen it before.

'He wouldn't do that,' Tam said, 'not without LAL interference.'

'Well, let's just say that he wasn't entirely aware of his actions. But it was he who sent your parents here. They are not deceased,' Diren said.

Tam snapped her head to Urhan, who, she hadn't noticed had stepped closer to Diren, moving behind the Queen IGO.

'I can take you to them' Diren offered.

She shook her head furiously. 'I don't know what you're talking about.'

'Of course, you do.'

The Queen made a sudden jerking movement. A tentacle appeared from her midsection which shot out past Tam. It grabbed Jacob.

'No!' Tam shouted, as she reached for it.

The Queen formed another tentacle, which hit her and Chuck, striking the pair and sending them off their feet. They hit the cold stone surface hard, the side of Tam's rib cage taking some of the impact. She turned to Jacob. The tentacle was curled tightly around his neck. His were vacant like Augustine's. They were staring over to her.

'You disturb me,' he said, in that same dead tone.

Tam got to her knees and slowly stood, still holding her side, and hoping that she hadn't just broken a rib.

'Just tell me what you are doing to us,' she shouted.

'Do you see my children?' the Queen asked.

Tam looked at Diren, Urhan was now standing right next to him. She looked around but saw no others.

'No,' she answered.

'Look,' said the Queen.

Jacob raised his arm and pointed in an arcing motion towards the cave system beneath the bridge. Tam moved towards the edge of the outcropping. She gazed over the edge, the light still making it hard to see but the shapes on the bottom, the uniform shapes. She looked back up, past the Queen to Urhan.

'They are eggs,' Urhan said.

Tam looked again at the glistening objects

'She is the progenitor of the entire race,' Urhan explained.

Tam looked at the Queen.

'You see now,' said the Queen.

Tam shook her head. 'No, I do not, why are you killing us?' she pleaded, her thoughts shifting to her parents

'We are not,' the Queen told her, 'little thing, you killed us.'

Tam frowned, looking at Urhan for answers.

'It was a bipedal species not unlike your own that nearly wiped them out,' he said.

'We have done nothing to you,' she said, shaking her head.

'Not yet,' the Queen spoke.

'Just let us go, we won't come back, I'll make sure of it,' she said, looking now at Jacob.

'Where is the hybrid?' he said coldly.

Tam paused, looking at Urhan.

'That's what it is,' she said, now looking only at Urhan, 'that's why you control it.'

Chuck glanced at her.

Urhan turned to Diren, 'It wasn't an accident, not a freak experiment gone wrong.'

The Queen released Jacob, who fell to the ground unconscious. She emitted a series of clicking noises towards the other one who looked like Crick. He turned back towards the transport device.

Tam needed more time to think, she felt as though her world was falling in on her

'You know where my parents are,' her voice was soft, fighting back the tears.

'Show her,' Diren said, turning to Urhan.

Urhan moved past Diren and stood next to Edge. Crick then waved a tentacle in the air. A series of symbols appeared as another form began materializing.

At first Tam couldn't make out what it was. It was a machine of some kind. Its large metallic body had three distinct legs jutting out from a powerful looking highly polished metallic torso leading up to what looked like…

Tam dropped to her knees. The air knocked cleanly out of her lungs as she was hit by an onslaught of emotion. She felt her eyes well. She couldn't blink, couldn't steal them away or close them. The machine stepped down from the platform, the sounds of servos attached to the unmistakable face that Tam had lost so long ago.

Her mother's face.

51

She felt completely broken, like shattered glass on ground. A pain she couldn't equate to anything she'd ever felt. She didn't know how to process it.

She wanted to die.

This mutilation was unfathomable. Her mother's face was pale, her eyes staring at her were not the ones she remembered. Like Jacob and Augustine, they were vacant, unrecognizing, unfeeling, inhuman. Her once long brown hair now was tangled, unkempt and burnt in places. She was a monster now. Tam was filled with a sadness she feared would drive her mad. She felt a hand on her shoulder from someone who now felt a million miles away.

'Tam,' a voice said quietly, Chuck's voice.

She couldn't respond. She couldn't take her eyes off what once was that warm blanket of safety and peace she'd relied on for so much. She felt her chest inhale, out of sheer necessity for oxygen to stop from passing out. The long desperate breath was followed by another.

'Captain!' Chuck's voice shouted into her ear so loudly that it cracked her out of oblivion just long enough for her to break eye contact and meet his.

'It's not her,' Chuck said, his eyes fierce.

She looked deep into them, tried to find strength in them, tried to syphon off his energy so she could go on. She continued to breathe, finding it easier now. She looked away back at the thing pretending to be her mother. She looked past it, to the Queen.

'What did you do?' she growled.

She heard Jacob's voice, a robotic voice, 'you are nothing,' said the Queen, 'little creatures stretching too far.'

Tam looked back up again at her mother's eyes. She stepped closer to her, or it. Chuck was right, it wasn't her. She could see no signs of recognition, not a glimmer of the sparkle her eyes used to carry.

She looked at Diren, 'All of them?'

'You could have flourished for a thousand more years,' he said, 'this army was not meant for you. It was meant for the Ongrals, they were the first to see. They chose to shut themselves off, to build their defences, to plan for invasion, before the merging of the molecule was discovered. No other race has been able to replicate a genetic merging with the molecule which, unfortunately, has just elevated your threat level to an unacceptable degree.'

Tam looked at the Queen.

'You're going to invade, wipe us out, turn us into this?' she demanded, pointing at the machine.

'Where is the hybrid?' the Queen demanded through Jacob.

Tam now felt nothing but anger, 'Where is my crew?'

'Tamara,' said Urhan.

She looked up.

'Now you know,' said Urhan, 'I wish to tell you, that my time aboard your ship, despite all you have lost, has informed me of things about the human race of which I find to be honourable.'

Diren turned his head to look at him and an upside-down smile formed on Tam's face.

'My responsibility was vast. My oath, unbreakable, and for that, perhaps I shall pay a price today,' he said, 'I tried to protect you from this, but I failed. I tried to carry out my duties to my people, and I failed. We have both failed on this day. Perhaps neither of us have a place in this, I ask for your forgiveness.'

He gave her that look again, and Tam looked at Chuck.

'And if you cannot give me that,' he said looking at Diren, 'I must ask one more thing of you.'

Urhan looked at Chuck, 'Save Jacob!' he injected force into his voice.

Urhan thrust his hands upwards towards Premier Diren's head, grasping it and twisting it with such effort that it spun completely around. Diren's lifeless body dropped to the ground in a twisted heap. He moved his long arm to the back of Edge's neck, snapping off the device that was attached it. Edge screamed out in pain as sparks reigned down behind him. He dropped to his knees.

'Tam!' Edge shouted over to her.

She met his eyes. Everything was happening so fast. He seemed confused, disorientated. In shock.

She saw Chuck move from beside her, making a mad dash towards the Queen.

'Chuck!' she shouted.

She saw the thing that had been her mother raise up one of its claw shaped arms towards him.

Tam began to move, instinct taking over. She saw Chuck diving for Jacob, contacting his shoulder against his mid-section, ripping him away from the Queen's grip. She saw Jacob's limp body and Chucks fall to the ground and slide, tumbling over one another. Her eyes widened as the pair kept going and going.

'No!' she shouted as Chuck, still holding onto Jacob tightly, disappeared over the edge. She had only a split second to decide what to do, where to go, how to help. She sprinted past her mother towards the edge. She slid on the ground and reached out. She saw Chuck hanging onto a rock with one hand, his other wrapped around Jacob's wrist. Their eyes met. His jaw was clenched as he wrestled with the dead weight. Tam reached over and took his wrist.

'Hold on!' she screamed, glancing back in time to see Urhan move quickly towards her mother, in time for him to take an energy blast to his shoulder.

She saw the Crick IGO suddenly vanish through the transporter thing, leaving the Queen. Then she caught sight of Edge. His eyes were red. He looked traumatized, distressed. He glared at her, then to the Queen, who was moving towards Tam.

'I'm sorry, Tam.'

Tam shook her head. She didn't understand. He turned away from her and let out a feral scream as he lunged at the huge form of the Queen. He impacted her hard, sending the monster off balance as a hail of weapons fired from the turrets on the stone bridge began bombarding them. Rock fell all around them. Tam looked back at Chuck who seemed to be pushed beyond his physical limits. His fingers were slipping on the rock. Tam focused all her energy on keeping her grip on them, from the corner of her eye, she saw the Queen and Edge tumble over the side and fall into the depths of the ravine. She heard her uncle's scream as he fell with her. It faded and faded, until it was gone.

'Chuck,' she said, 'you have to let him go.'

Chuck shook his head, 'No!' His words full of determination and grit.

'Chuck,' Tam said, feeling her heart crack, 'that's an order.'

52

A second passed by, then another, more than enough time for her machine mother to finish them off, but she didn't. Tam looked quickly to her right and saw a pair of legs standing next to Urhan. Her eyes quickly turned up to see Ona. She saw Arion on her shoulder for a moment before he leapt into mid-air, a flash of light followed. She turned back to Chuck.

She was a second away from losing them both when Ona appeared in mid-air, out of nowhere, inches away from Jacob.

She grabbed him around the waist, held tight and the pair vanished, leaving Chuck's arm free. He looked down, the sudden change in weight causing the hand he was holding onto to let go. Tam held his weight. He reached up and grabbed the outcropping. He looked at her, the look of surprise in his eye as Ona appeared again, wrapped around Chuck's waist. They vanished. Tam had no more time to think, she felt something on her shoulder, crawl onto her face and attach to her ear.

'Get up!' said Arion.

Tam rolled over, saw Urhan laying on his side, bleeding from the wound, a heads-up display formed in her field of vision.

'Get the weapon,' Arion said forcefully, indicating to the location of the palm disrupter Ona had been wearing, which was laying on the ground. She looked to the machine. Her mother's face frozen, bloodshot eyes darting around in crazed directions. She didn't think, she just moved. She scrambled over the weapon and put it on.

'What did you do?' she said, looking at her mother's face, the metallic weapon arm seemingly frozen in place.

'I engaged an EMP. It knocked out her systems, but I don't know for how long Tam,' said Arion.

The heads-up display flickered.

'My power systems have been overloaded and I do not think I will be able to create another one Tam. I have the ability to fire one shot,' he said.

'What?'

'Aim for the head,' Arion said softly.

Tam turned and looked at her mother, she stopped breathing.

'No,' she said softly.

'We don't have time,' Arion said, 'I am reading several life forms coming across the bridge.' Another shot from the turrets on the bridge sent another hail of rocks down on their position. Tam crouched down, covering her head.

Ona suddenly reappeared next to Urhan. The machine began to twitch, its weapon arm moving ever so slightly. Tam couldn't think straight. She looked to Ona briefly, who had her hand resting on Urhan. She then vanished with Urhan in tow. Reality seemed to break; nothing made any sense anymore. She looked back at her mother's eyes.

'Tam,' Arion said, 'aim.'

'No,' Tam said keeping her arm by her side.

Her mother's arm moved again. She saw a bright light, coming from across the long stone bridge.

'The life forms are approaching,' Arion said.

'We can save her,' Tam said looking to the light before looking back

'Tam,' Arion said, pausing.

Out of the corner of her eye another figure appeared, an old man. It wasn't quite real, his image, slightly distorted. A projection.

'Tam,' said the old man.

She took a step back, 'Arion?'

The old man nodded.

'I found him,' he said.

'Found who?' Tam said, her voice cracking.

'Your father,' said Arion.

Tam looked back at the abomination; her mouth opened.

'Is he?'

'Yes,' Arion said.

Her mouth went dry.

'Did you?' she said.

'No,' Arion said, 'but you have to let them go.'

Tam shook her head. 'We can save her,' she said softly, as the weapons fire continued to come.

The vision of the old man, Arion's true self, took a virtual step towards her.

'There's nothing left to save, Captain,' he looked at her with sincerity.

Tam looked at the monster now inhabiting her mother's body. She tried to see past the technology, into anything that may resemble her soul, but there was nothing.

'You told me you'd be right back,' she said, her voice cracking.

There was a flicker in the monsters' eyes. They seemed to soften somehow, as if there was some sort of recognition. Tam took a step. The monster raised its claw like arm and took aim.

Its face began to shake and seemed to be straining against it. Its mouth opened.

'Do…'

It paused.

'It..'

Tam felt her heart break in two. She raised her arm and aimed the weapon between her eyes. 'Goodbye mama,' she whispered, 'Arion…'

She took one last look.

'Fire,' she whispered, as the waterfall of tears fell.

Arion complied.

Tam closed her eyes, felt the soft touch of a hand beside her, felt a cold rush of air followed by a strange disembodied feeling.

53

The Lassen

Tam felt lightheaded. Her hand was shaking. She saw Chuck kneeling on the floor of the bridge, it was the Lassen's bridge. There were two headless machine bodies laid out on the ground. The carpet was stained in blood. She raised her arm instinctively, pointing at the nearest one. She saw what was left of Deangelo's body.

She tried to focus, tried to use what adrenaline she had left to assess the situation. Chuck and Ona were kneeling next to Jacob, who was making light groaning sounds. Tam looked at Urhan who was sitting up now, his hand covering his wound. She felt rage and pointed her weapon at him.

'Don't,' Arion warned.

Tam moved towards him, her teeth showing, 'Bastard!'

She was surprised at how fast and hard her anger had exploded.

'I will not fire,' said Arion, 'what are you doing, Tam?'

Urhan remained still.

'It was them!' she shouted, pressing the muzzle of the hand weapon against Urhan's forehead.

'It won't bring them back,' said Arion, 'Ona still has to locate the crew.'

Urhan gave her a serene look. Tam knew he wasn't afraid of death.

'You are within your right to take my life,' he said gently, 'I would not harbour ill will at your choice to do so.'

'Be calm, be rational, I know what you have just done but you have others to save now, the living, they are relying on you,' Arion pressed gently.

'Captain!' she heard Chuck shout, 'don't do it.'

Her face focused on Chuck who was now standing, 'without Urhan we don't go home.'

She turned back to Urhan, 'I trusted you!'

'As I do you,' Urhan said, 'I cannot explain to you now, my decision to turn against my people, regardless of when and how it happens, my life will be extinguished. I have killed the leader of our people. I can never return, all I can do now, is save your life and that of the crew.'

'Where are they?' she growled.

'Moved to IGO War for processing.'

'Where's Amita Puri? Is there anything left of her to save? Is there anything left of anyone to save?'

Urhan calmly answered, 'They have not harvested Amita Puri. She is being held in containment. Premier Diren requested she not be harmed, lest it brought Earth vessels to the IGO system before their time. However, I cannot guarantee that will remain the case. Protector Crick will no longer adhere to those guidelines.'

'Tam,' said Ona softly, 'we have to get out of here.'

Something in Ona's voice cut through the unbearable things she'd born witness too. Something so simple, it was a need for help. She knew that. Her mind could work with that, for now.

What was left?

'I am reading several ship converging on our location Tam, we must move quickly, I have interfaced with navigation and am plotting a course as we speak,' Arion said.

Tam looked at Ona, 'Can you get her and the crew?'

Ona nodded, 'with Urhan's help in locating her.'

'Another thing, Tam,' said Arion, 'I found the Massey.'

'Where is she?'

'In orbit of the fourth planet, still intact, there's damage to the outer structure but life support appears to be functional.'

'The STC drive?' she said, looking at Urhan.

He nodded to her, 'I would need to see its condition.'

'You're bleeding,' said Ona.

Urhan turned his head to her then back to Tam, 'With your permission, I would need access to the medical kit on the bridge, it is behind that panel, I may lose consciousness momentarily without it.'

Tam glared at him.

'Captain, there is something you do not know, something I need to speak to you privately about,' Urhan said, pausing for a moment, 'if you can at least spare my life until we are out of this star system.'

Tam sighed and looked at Chuck. 'Get the med kit.'

Chuck nodded and proceeded to get the equipment, he handed it to Urhan who then used it on his wounds. She heard a groan and saw Jacob open his eyes. She moved quickly over to him and placed her hand under his head.

'Jacob,' she said softly, 'can you hear me?'

'Ouch,' he moaned, as he brought his hand up to his head, meeting her eyes. He looked at the bodies lying on the bridge floor. His eyes widened and flickered back to Tam.

'Cap?' he said softly.

'Are you all right?'

'What happened?' he said sitting up, looking at the machines, 'where am I and what the hell is that?'

'What do you remember?' she asked.

Jacob looked at the blood-soaked carpets and glanced around.

'We were somewhere dark, that thing....' He trailed off, 'then nothing, well not nothing. My head feels like a hundred bottles of tequila went through it all at once.'

Tam turned to Ona, 'Get me the med kit.'

Ona complied, rushing over.

'I'm gonna give you a shot to help with the pain,' she gave him a cocktail of pain relief and a stimulant.

'Oh, thank god,' Jacob said removing his hand from his forehead, 'that's the stuff.'

His eyes brightened and his breathing seemed to relax.

'Can you stand?'

He nodded, looking around the bridge. 'Okay?' he mused, 'anyone care to explain?'

He looked at Urhan.

'What is he doing here?' he said.

'We don't have time,' Tam said, 'we're on the Lassen. I need you to look at the scans of the Massey and see if you can tell how badly she's been hurt.'

He turned back to her and nodded, 'I presume you can fill me on the way to wherever the hell we're going?'

Tam nodded, 'I will.'

Urhan stood and began walking towards her, Chuck blocked his path. 'Where do you think you're going?'

'It's all right,' Tam said, 'Chuck I've got this,'

Chuck nodded and let Urhan pass.

'The engine room,' he said.

'Arion,' Tam said, 'is there anyone else on board this ship, or any… thing?'

'My scans show that the ship was controlled by only these three, it seems the rest of the crew was taken to the planet.'

Tam's eyes looked to Ona. 'Thank you,' she paused, 'I forgot to say thank you.'

Ona gave her a strange look. A look that told her she still knew something she wasn't telling her.

You die there.

Ona gave her a smile.

'Cap, we're on course for the fourth planet,' Chuck said.

Tam turned to him. 'Arion is remotely linked to the Lassen's navigation,' she looked back at Jacob, who was tapping away at a computer console, 'we're going to make one more run at this, we get whoever we can and then,' she paused and turned to the view screen.

She then glanced around to Deangelo.

In her mind she heard the clink of a champagne glass from over a year ago. She saw the bartender place a small mat under it and point to the man who had sent her the drink. She saw him smile at her and something else. A charming nervous look in his eye, as if he wasn't quite the ladies' man, he was making himself out to be.

She saw them laugh as they walked down the promenade of the alien world their ships had docked at, his light touch on her hand as he kissed her under the two moons. She remembered the intensity and heat of their bodies between his sheets. A feeling of connection she could use to mask the pain. It had been one of the most passionate nights she'd ever experienced. She remembered waking up while the sun hadn't yet split the horizon. Had remembered that nothing lasts. Had remembered that no matter what, she'd end up back in the that pod, drifting alone through the galaxy. She'd slipped out that morning, not because she hadn't felt that closeness in her mind, but because the only connection she could process was the one she'd just been forced to destroy. It had taken everything from her. Her life, her loves, her hope. She felt rage.

'Jacob,' she said.

He looked back at her.

'How long would it take to initiate an overload of the Lassen's engine core?' she kicked the memories out of her head and swallowed down her regret of not getting the chance to know what could've been—if she had stayed.

She saw Chuck frown.

'Cap?' Jacob asked.

'How long?'

'For the engines to hit critical mass the main coolant has to be shut off. That needs a command level override, there's nobody left on board that can do that.'

'That is not entirely accurate,' Arion interrupted.

'Explain, Arion,' she said.

'You have command level access.'

'Not to the Lassen I don't.'

'I believe I can help in that regard,' said Arion, 'may I know what it is you are planning to do?'

Tam glanced at Chuck, giving him a look.

'You've got that look in your eye,' he said.

'What look?' Jacob urged.

'That I'm about to do something crazy' look!' said Chuck.

Tam turned to Jacob and clenched her hands into fists.

'Oh yeah,' Jacob said, 'that look.'

54

Tam didn't want to sit in the Captain's seat of the Lassen, apart from it being soaking in blood, it wasn't her ship and all she wanted was to be back on the flight deck of the Massey. Jacob had gone to engineering to check it out while Chuck and Ona were on the bridge, she'd given Arion to Ona who was helping guide her through some of the navigation and weapons systems. She was in Deangelo's ready room, the private office next to the bridge. There were two of the IGO ships on their tail at the moment. She was now leaning on Deangelo's desk, thinking of that moment where he'd brushed her hair behind her ear but allowed the memory to fade out like the ending scene of a motion picture. She crossed her arms and stared at Urhan who was standing just inside the sealed door.

'You have two minutes,' she said to him, 'if I don't come out of this room by that time, Chuck will come in guns blazing, so make your point and make it quick.'

'The Clorinda,' Urhan said.

Tam frowned, 'what about her?'

'There was a moment, during the rescue,' he paused for a second.

Tam tilted her head, her attention now firmly on Urhan.

'When I truly believed that we were not going to break away from the stars gravity,' he said, 'statistically speaking our survival was, what you humans like to call, a miracle.'

Tam stayed dead silent.

'At that moment, where the termination of my life was imminent, I…' he paused, taking a step towards her.

She slowly stood from the table.

'You what?' she said.

'I was about to save you,' Urhan said, 'and only you.'

'What?'

'There are those amongst my people who do not believe in what Diren, and his predecessors, have been doing to save our race,' he said, 'I am one of them.'

Tam felt a wave of sadness and anger spread through her, squeezing her chest.

'I just killed my mother,' Tam said, 'you were a little late in that turn, don't you think?'

'I needed to gain direct access to Diren. I also needed direct access to the Queen, that could not have been accomplished if I had told you sooner,' Urhan said, 'I hoped to get the two of them together, but I also failed in that respect, you may have lost your progenitors Captain, but by my calculations, it was worth the lives of your crew. Perhaps your entire race.'

Tam waited.

'As I was saying, Ona's bonding with the STC molecule was not an accident,' he said, 'albeit that is only a half truth, there is nothing unique about her physiology that has allowed her to bond and utilize its abilities. It is the reason that the molecule is kept so strictly under guard when around humans at all times,' he said.

Tam's eyes widened just a little.

'It was not an accident, because all humans are compatible,' Urhan said.

Tam's mouth gently opened.

'You,' Urhan said, 'Chuck, Jacob, your president, your commanders, your Captains, your colonists,' he paused, 'everyone, everywhere.'

Tam felt lightheaded.

'What?' she said through a gasp, 'you're telling me…'

'That humans could settle on any planet, go anywhere, anytime, to any galaxy, access any technology and be able to destroy, control or dominate any civilization. Yes. You are the biggest threat the entire universe faces.'

Tam's legs felt weak. 'Why keep us alive at all?'

'Only a few were allowed access to that sort of information, as a guardian, my position within the grand plan was a simple one,' said Urhan, 'protect the molecule.'

'Your propensity for violence, for revenge, and for domination is well documented,' said Urhan.

There was a bleep

'Captain to the bridge,' came Chuck's voice.

Tam made her way up to Urhan, he stood to one side. She stopped and looked up at him, boring a hole into his eyes.

'I'm not in the mood for a philosophical debate on the human spirit,' she said activating the door mechanism.

She turned back to him.

'But you got one thing right,' she said, 'and it's a dish best served cold.'

55

Tam looked at the view screen. Large dark shapes casted their shadows against the star's huge silhouetted pursuers.

'Two vessels,' Chuck said, 'I'm also showing movement on the surface of IGO War, more vessels emerging, they're going to have us boxed in pretty quick here. Call the ball Cap.'

'Arion, what's the status of the Massey?'

She could feel a new sense of purpose within her, she wondered whether it was rational, or if it was only driven by pure rage. She tried to find the logic, tried to find the justification she needed to plunge what was left of them into a suicide mission.

'No life signs,' replied Arion.

She turned to Ona, then to Chuck, before clicking on her comm system.

'Jacob, you alive down there?'

'It's a ghost town down here Captain, but the engine room in intact, all systems online,' he said.

'Arion can you get me access?'

'Already done,' he said.

She took a breath, 'Jacob, how long until we can reach critical mass on core?'

'Eight minutes,' said Jacob.

She looked at Ona, 'I need you to get Chuck, Jacob and Urhan to the Massey, then get back here.'

Ona nodded.

'Hang on a second,' Chuck said.

'Get the Massey ready for STC, keep the power levels low, life support, engines, navigation,' she said.

'What the hell are you going to do?' Chuck demanded.

'I'm counting on you to get me out of this, so keep your fingers nimble on the flight controls,' Tam said.

'Jacob, start the overload on my mark and stay in engineering, Ona will meet you there in a moment,' she said.

'Aye Captain,' he said.

Tam moved over to the navigation station and plotted a course. She looked at Chuck, who checked what she'd just done. He gave her a look. She smiled at him. 'Jacob, now.'

'Go get her,' Chuck said, smiling back as Ona approached him.

The pair vanished as the lights on the bridge turned red.

'ENGINE CORE OVERLOAD, EVACUATE!' came the computerized voice, 'ENGINE CORE OVERLOAD, EVACUATE!'

She turned to Urhan, 'I'm counting on you.'

Ona reappeared.

'Chuck and Jacob are on the Massey,' Ona said, looking at Urhan.

'I'll be waiting for you,' he said firmly.

'Be right back,' Ona said, taking Jacobs's hand and vanishing.

The klaxon continued to sound.

'Just you and me, old friend,' she said.

'Our odds are always favourable when that is the case,' Arion said.

'I wouldn't have it any other way,' she smiled, 'how much time do we have?'

'Seven minutes forty-two seconds.'

'Do Urhan's coordinates check out?'

'We're about to find out.'

Ona reappeared.

'Go,' she said.

Arion disengaged and quickly made his way over to Ona, attaching himself.

'I understand,' Ona said, reaching out her hand.

Tam took it. 'I'll need him back quickly,' she rose her hand with the weapon attached.

Ona nodded, 'You're gonna crash the ship into the planet? What happens when the core overloads?'

'We don't want to be around to find out,' Tam said smiling.

Ona nodded. Tam saw the fear in her eyes and gave her hand a gentle squeeze.

'Anything goes wrong you get the hell out, don't wait for me, do you understand?' Tam said.

Ona was silent.

'Do you?' Tam demanded forcefully.

Ona nodded. Tam took one last look at the remains of Oscar Deangelo, the only man who truly loved her and knew her. Seconds later, the bridge was empty. Only the sounds of the computer remained.

'ENGINE CORE OVERLOAD, EVACUATE.'

56

Tam felt a chill run through her as she tried to adjust quickly to her new surroundings. She didn't have much time to react as she felt Arion jump onto her arm and reattach to her head. Bright fluorescent light brightened from nearly every direction onto cold steel. An endless underground facility stretched out as far as the eye could see in all directions. It reminded her of the shipyards at Proxima, where many of the ESDA vessels were built inside giant orbiting rigs. She was standing on a connecting walkway between two main arteries of levels containing hanging things. She quickly recognized those things as similar machines to the ones that were on board the Lassen, and what her mother had become a part of. There were thousands of them, hundreds of thousands of them, level after level, row after row.

'We have to move,' said Arion.

She saw her heads-up display flicker to life as Arion showed her the way. He was right, they didn't have much time.

'How long?'

'Seven minutes,' Arion replied, 'thrusters on the Lassen are now at full power and have locked onto our coordinates.'

She looked at Ona, 'come on,' she pointed the way.

Her targeting scanner began focusing in on the various hanging machines. None seemed active. Or rather, none seemed to have noticed her arrival. They moved down the walkway and turned onto a main artery.

'Hold on,' said Arion, 'I've got movement.'

Tam motioned to Ona to stop, they both crouched down and waited. More seconds ticked by. Tam shook her head.

'There's no time for this,' she whispered, sweat trickling down her brow.

'It's okay, proceed forward thirty meters.'

They moved on until they came to a break in one of the rows of hanging monsters.

'To the right,' Arion instructed.

Tam turned, seeing another section with rows of glass sealed tubes. She moved quickly towards them. Their interiors hidden through frosted glass. She moved up to one of them and began wiping it with her forearm. It was empty. She looked to Ona, 'find her,' she said.

Ona began moving from one tube to the next. Tam tried another one. She found a face. A human face. It was a young man. He looked to be asleep.

'It's not her,' she said.

'There's more,' Ona said.

Tam looked to the row of tubes. 'How long?'

'Five minutes,' Arion said.

'There's too many,' Tam said.

'You can't save them all Tam, do what you came here to do,' said Arion.

'How long?' Tam asked again, feeling her muscles freeze up.

'Four minutes four-seconds,' said. Arion

'I found her!' said Ona.

And there she was, Amita Puri, sleeping away as if in the middle of a quiet night's sleep at home safe in her bed. Tam went into autopilot.

'How do I open this?' she said frantically.

'Force!' said Arion.

Tam stepped back and raised her hand weapon and fired a single shot at the base of the container. It erupted open in sparks and steam as Amita fell out onto the floor. Tam rushed over to her; she felt like ice. She heard movement, mechanical, the deck plating began to vibrate as from either side, machine soldiers dropped from their hanging mechanisms. She didn't have time to react as beams of heated energy blasted past her head. She looked up to see an IGO standing in the middle of the walkway, approaching slowly. It was Crick. She was sure of it.

'TAKE HER AND GO!' she screamed at Ona, raising her hand weapon, and firing wildly in every direction.

She saw a look in Ona's eyes, one of recognition. Was this the death she had spoken about? Her final look before she was consigned to oblivion?

Ona hesitated

'It's okay,' Tam said.

She saw Ona's eyes well up.

'Get out of here! That's an order!' she screamed.

Ona took Amita's cold hand and vanished. Tam ducked down and rolled towards the edge of the walkway. A hail of furious weaponry lit up the surrounding area. She ducked and rolled under cover.

'Two minutes,' Arion updated her.

Wave after wave of weapons came at her from all directions. She saw a railing at the end of the walkway. She turned back and began firing again in Crick's direction. There was no way out of this. She knew that now. Dove out of the cover and began to run. Fire and light came at her from all directions. She felt heat and pain strike her right arm. She pushed on. She reached the edge of the platform and held on as her body teetered over the edge. She looked out at the endless machines, which spread for kilometres. Beneath her, an endless drop into a precipice of metal and horror. The weapons fire continued as the sounds of approaching machines grew close. She looked over the edge. The weapons fire stopped. She turned back to see the machines holding their ground. She saw Crick move between them. He began making clicking noises as he drew near.

'You're not going to make me one of them!' she screamed.

She was done, she knew it, they wouldn't take her body, defile it, mutilate it, turn it into one of those things. She was tired.

'Thirty seconds,' Arion said.

She looked upwards, then back at Crick. She felt blood poruing down the side of her arm.

'I'm sorry my old friend,' she whispered, 'thank you.'

She tapped her communicator.

'Massey Shaw, this is the Captain, break orbit and get the hell out of here, that's an order!'

She then clicked off the comms not waiting for a response.

'I'm with you, Tam,' Arion said.

Tam smiled, 'Goodbye Mama,' she closed her eyes and rolled over the edge.

She fell in silence. She felt the rush of air as it passed her face. The world fell away. She fell forever. Her body turned, seeing now how far she'd gone. The ledge from which she'd rolled now distant, far above her. She felt a sense of calm as a blinding light erupted from far above and everything. She saw the hull of the Lassen split through the opening. Everywhere was instantly engulfed in a fireball. She saw red and blue and white encompass everything. She heard a sound so deafening she feared her head would cave in. She continued to fall and felt her skin burn like touching a branding iron all over her body.

She then felt something else—a hand, touching hers.

Then there was nothing.

57

EARTH

PRIVATE RESIDENCE OF THE PRESIDENT

President Aarav Puri placed the tea gently onto the small bamboo table next to his wife. She'd been asleep now for twenty minutes or so. He looked out as the sun set over their quiet residence, which looked out over the coral river. The soft sound of the leaves as they swayed gently against the backdrop of the autumn reds where at the very least, part of why he'd brought his distraught wife to this place. It was where they had met 36 years earlier and where he felt she would most feel at peace. The sound of the china cup, as slight as it was, was enough to wake her from her light sleep, something which had eluded both of them for weeks now. He placed his hand on hers and smiled at her.

'I am sorry,' he said, quietly.

'I do not wish to sleep,' she replied, turning, and placing her hand over his.

He sat beside her and poured himself a cup.

There they stared off into the distance. He tried to think what he would do now. He thought about joining his little girl if she had indeed ventured into that other place.

'Was it all worth it?' he suddenly heard his wife say.

It had been more than she'd said to him in several days.

'To create a life, to make it better for those who come next?' he answered, 'it is the nature of things. She knew this, she loved it and we loved her for it. So, I would have to answer yes.'

'I hope so,' said his beautiful wife.

He felt a particularly cool breeze which made him wrap the scarf he had on a little tighter around his neck when he felt a blast of cold air from behind him. He turned. His teacup releasing from his hand and landing on the decking. She was there, Amita. Smiling at them as if she'd just come home from school. She was standing next to a woman he had never seen before. He heard his wife scream in both joy and fear. Aarav felt like he was living in a dream as his terrified wife ran towards what he could only have assumed to be a ghost. A ghost whose eyes were full of tears. A ghost who embraced his wife, solid, real.

He couldn't think, he didn't care if this was a fantasy or whether or not it was indeed the spirit of his daughter. He ran to her. Felt the softness of her face against his as he embraced her. She was real. Somehow, she was real. He couldn't speak. He forced air into his lungs, past the tears, past the fear, past the elation. The moment continued. He heard his wife crying uncontrollably, weak at the knees as she asked one-word questions.

How? How? Why? How!

He turned to the woman with her who was looking almost as happy as they were. He asked her name, he asked her how this had happened, he asked her everything.

'My name is Tamara Cartwright,' the woman answered before something equally strange happened.

She smiled at him. A tear released from her eye. She then clicked her fingers and vanished into thin air.

~ ~ ~

THE END

Printed in Great Britain
by Amazon